FALLING STARS

STARS

A NOVEL...

ashlyne huff revelette

Clovercroft Publishing

Falling Stars

© 2015 by Ashlyne Huff Revelette

Published by Clovercroft Publishing, Franklin, Tennessee

Cover Image by Ashlyne Huff Revelette

Cover and Interior Layout Design by Suzanne Lawing

Edited by Tammy Kling

Copy Edit by Gail Fallen

Printed in the United States of America

978-1-940262-92-5

★ DEDICATION ★

To my love, Mase.

✳ PROLOGUE ✳

Tall Southern pines blurred as they whipped by the car windows. The white strips of paint looked as though they were connected mile after mile after mile, never coming up to take a breath. Raindrops spattered slow and steady on my windshield, slightly muffling the sound of the country radio station that blared through the speakers of my Nissan Pathfinder.

All of a sudden, seventy miles per hour seemed like the speed of a brisk walk. I hadn't even been driving for thirty minutes, but according to my Garmin GPS, I still had 429 miles left to go.

Is this really happening?

The air coming out of the vents felt like fire all of a sudden, stifling and sucking all the oxygen out of the front seat, making me wish I had an inhaler and hadn't scarfed down a Kit Kat before I left the house.

Wait, what am I doing?

I could feel my heartbeat thumping all the way to my fingertips, and I held the steering wheel so tightly, my knuckles turned white. Sweat trickled down the small of my back, the radio station's commercials seemed to get louder and louder, and the rain picked up speed, pelting my trusty silver SUV with a machine gun of water bullets.

Where did all the fun go? Just a few minutes ago, I was on cloud nine, confident and singing at the top of my lungs, daydreaming about my next steps, my big break. Just a few minutes ago, Nashville was only seven hours away, but now it seemed like time was moving at the pace of a snail—an injured one. Just a few minutes ago, this all looked like a fantastic, possible, achievable thing. But just like my rain-drenched car, all the confidence I had worked up in the past few months seemed to have washed away, revealing smudges of fear and regret underneath.

Even though I wanted to, I knew I couldn't call my parents yet. I'd promised them a call at the fourth of way mark, halfway, etc., so surely it would have be even more excessive to call thirty minutes in? They would think I was having second thoughts—that I made a mistake, and they would try to tell me it would be fine to turn around and come back home. And I could not let that happen, would not let that happen. I, Lilah Marie Carson, would not crumble under the pressure. I had some pride.

Pressing the screen on my Garmin, I cringed as the automated woman's voice spat out more bad news. "Continue four hundred twenty-eight miles and then take exit 209B for Demonbreun Street." There it was. All I had to show for my freak-out moment was a mile. One mile?

HONNNNNK, HOOOOOONNNKKK!

"OH MY GOODNESS!" I yelled as I swerved back into my lane, away from the car I nearly sideswiped. My thoughts were going to end up *killing* me if I didn't pull myself together. *Calm down, calm . . . down . . . shh*, I thought as I breathed in a way that could have been mistaken for Lamaze. The only upside to my breakdown was that I would have very little trouble giving birth—in the *very* distant future.

I had a very good reason for driving seven hours from Mobile, Alabama, to Nashville, Tennessee. A very, *very* good one. I simply had to.

1

(Three Months Ago)

"Hi, may I speak to Ms. Lilah Carson?"

"This is she," I answered in my "phone-tone" my mother taught me ages ago. I was in the middle of studying for my last English exam *ever*. Whoop, whoop!

"Oh, hi; we haven't met, but I know who you are, of course. My name is Deborah, and I am a coordinator in the sports department at the University of Mobile?"

"Yes, ma'am?"

"OK, I'll just cut right to the chase. We are in a bit of a pickle. I had someone slated to sing the anthem for tonight's game against Spring Hill College, but she has come down with the flu! Can you believe that?"

"That's awful," I answered, suddenly wishing I hadn't answered the call, and for the first time ever, wishing I had the flu, strep throat, a flesh-eating disease, *anything* to make me somehow unavailable.

"So, as you might guess, we need someone to fill in. The game's at seven. It'll be super quick, I promise. Plus, you're a pro. This is like second nature to you I'll bet, huh? Ha! So, please tell me you're in town . . . I forgot to ask you that."

I took a long, deep breath in, stalling. I couldn't lie, especially to an adult, and one in need; it went against everything I believed in. My dad was a *preacher* for goodness sake. But I did not want to sing. Ever again. Not at a college game, not at one of my own high school games. And maybe it was presumptuous, but should my wants take a backseat to her needs? I had every intention of turning her down. So what if I enrolled to go there next year? This would be the last time I would ever even utter the words "anthem" and "University of Mobile" in the same sentence. Ms. Deborah was nice, but kindness wouldn't be enough for me to break my promise. It was seven years strong. And one anthem wasn't worth it. Not for a second.

And besides, it would just be a regular ole game, right? How many people would even get there before the first pitch anyway? Surely, not *that* many. So it wouldn't hurt the game at all. Deborah probably had a recording of the band or ensemble for *this* type of predicament. Heck, even my high school did for our ill-attended hockey games. They could find someone else to sing the most difficult song on the planet. It was a beautiful tune, no doubt, but a challenge. And these days, vocal challenges were not on my to do list. And another thing: I wouldn't be caught dead on U of M's campus any sooner than the day of orientation. It was too soon. Too raw. Michael's dorm was on that campus. Nuff said.

"OK," I whispered, realizing a moment too late what I had said. My voice had totally just betrayed my brain. *Wait, what did I just say?*

"What did you say? Sorry, I missed it," Deborah asked as well.

"Umm," I stalled again. I was a master staller. "I said . . . yes."

"Oh, bless you, child. Praise the dear Lord. Thank you, thank you! Do you know where the field is?"

"No, ma'am."

"Oh, this is so wonderful! I'll give you directions. Thank you, thank you, Lilah!" Deb squawked.

"You're welcome," I whispered, still in shock.

As I hung up my cell phone, one extra thought floated around in my room. *What if Michael is there? Maybe that might not be so bad.*

Later that evening, around 6:15 p.m., I was cursing— well, not actually cursing—my decision, my weakness. But because I was also in full-blown Michael mode, I got out of the car anyway and started walking, my mind doing a couple flips. *He doesn't like baseball, but what if he's there? With another girl—the girl, the home-wrecker? Oh gosh, what if I mess up in front of them? Guess I should get used to it, though, if I'm going to go to school here.*

Deborah met me at the entrance to the field holding an old microphone and disposable earplugs.

"Unfortunately, we don't have a state of the art system like you're probably used to, but some of our singers say these ear plugs help block out the delay of the speakers. You're welcome to use 'em if you'd like!"

"Thanks," I said as I took the mic, its extra-long cord, and the spongy orange earplugs.

"All right, so the game starts in a half hour, but you'll sing at 6:55 p.m. Report back here at 6:45 p.m. Is that all right? Sorry we don't have a green room or anything fancy. Once we're done here, I would say scoot on back to your dorm, but you don't go here, do you?"

"No, ma'am, but I'll be a freshman this fall. I'm about to graduate from Cherry Hill."

"Oh my goodness, that's fabulous! This can be the first of many anthems for you, my dear! And, oh, my grandson goes to Cherry Hill! His name is Lenny, do you know him?"

I wanted to laugh and say "fat chance" to the many anthems part and "no" to the Lenny—poor guy—part, but I was way too nervous to think straight. Instead, I think it came out as a grimace.

I followed Deborah down the bleachers, and I felt a woosh of the old days. She looked nervous and giddy. What did *she* have to be nervous about? As we got to home plate, Deborah continued. "Let's go ahead and get this part done 'cause fans are startin' to get here! You'll stand right in between here and the pitcher's mound and face the crowd. After the prayer, look at me, and I'll signal you when it's time to sing. Do you want to rehearse real quick?"

I shook my head instantly. "Noooo, I'll be fine. But thanks."

"Such a pro-fess-ion-al!" Deborah beamed. She handed the mic to an uninterested college student who probably had plenty of other things to do other than this, and we walked back off the field. "I can't wait to tell all the ladies back at the office that you're singin'! They'll all be here just for you from now on! Baseball? What? We want the infamous Lily Black!" she joked.

I should have been flattered or something, but I wasn't. It had been a long time since people had shown up just for me, and I don't know if I was up for jumping right back into the deep end just yet. And just as I was about to ask if there was possibly another person that could fill in, that I changed my mind and did not want to sing in thirty minutes, Deborah asked the question.

"So, I've always wondered: do you ever forget the words?"

I nearly tripped up the bleachers. If it had been a horror film, the music would have changed right then. *Dun, dun, DUUUUUN!* You don't ask singers, no matter how experienced they are, if they are afraid they will forget the words to the national anthem before they sing it. You can ask them after, but not before. Cardinal rule! Because after the question is out, you can't take it back any more than you can un-ring a bell. It's out there, that fear, and all the singers can think of from that point on is *Do I even know the words?* and *What are the words?* or *Ooooh-saycanyouseebythedawnsearlylightwhatso . . . whatso . . . ohhh, no! I don't know the words!*

I was sure Deborah had no idea what she'd done, but she had done it, and on the one day that I needed to be focused. I cared less about my English exam! I had a reputation to protect here, and plus, I had waived my right to a sound check. Probably shouldn't have done that.

"Do you need anything else? Some Coke? Water?" Deborah asked.

Poor Deborah had no idea. Coke was the last thing singers needed. But that wasn't the point. Deborah was just being nice, I reminded myself, and it wasn't fair to project my fear or bad attitude on this woman no matter how freaked out I felt. I could practically hear my mom quoting Scripture in my head. "Water is fine. Do you have any that's room temperature?" It was a long shot, but I had to ask.

A few minutes later, Deborah returned with a bottle of Winn Dixie brand water in hand. "You're in luck, darlin'! All right, you have about eighteen minutes 'till you need to be back here. I'll meet you then?"

I took the water, thanked Deborah, and immediately hustled back to my car to practice hard and pray harder. When I got there, I was so relieved I hadn't broken down and called Michael. He didn't deserve it anyway, but more importantly, there was no time to spare.

A long time ago, I made a vow never to sing in public again. It was a big promise to make, but I hadn't wavered once since then—not in seven whole years. Even when my best friend begged and begged for me to sing with her every year for the talent show. (Much harder than it sounded.) And now, as a lame high school senior, I was about to sing in front of a crowd of my future peers. Call the stupid police. A hard song, loaded with patriotic honor, was not my idea of a comeback. Too many potential mishaps. But I had agreed, and minutes were passing. Luckily, I hadn't told a soul, not my family or any of my friends because the whole thing was a big mistake, and I wanted to be able to pretend it never happened once I finished singing the word "brave."

At 6:40 p.m., I said another quick prayer as I walked back toward the field. I had been completely wrong about the amount of people: it was packed. And of course it was!

The University of Mobile Rams were playing the Spring Hill College Badgers, their biggest rivals. I should have listened better. Or perhaps written everything down.

Oh, gosh, I groaned as I put on a fake smile and passed through the fans to make my way down to the field, my eyes peeled for scummy, cheating Michael Kimsky. Nothing. Deborah flagged me down with excitement, and I felt as if I was going to throw up. The words of the "Star Spangled Banner" on the inside of my sweaty hand were smudged by then, I was sure of it. There went plan B.

"Are you ready?" Deborah yelled over the noise of the crowd behind us.

I nodded once, careful not to show any fear, but also careful to keep my stomach from lurching forward.

"Let us bow our heads in prayer," a voice boomed from the speakers. To the fans it probably sounded normal, but to me, the voice sounded ominous.

Heavenly Father,

We pray for the safety of these athletes out here today, Lord. That they would play to Your glory and that You would protect them from injury. We pray all this in Your name. Amen.

I have to confess, I prayed a totally different prayer, one that had nothing to do with the players or their safety—sorry. A moment later, I heard the words that at one time in my life had made me buzz with excitement rather than this anxiety.

"And now, would you stand and face the flag as Mobile's very own superstar Lilah Carson sings our nation's anthem."

Here we go.

". . . Oh say does that Star-Spangled Banner yet wave . . . "o'er the land of the free and the home of the brave."

The crowd roared for what seemed like forever. And it was done. The seal was broken, and I remembered everything I'd tried for years to forget. The past came rushing back as I stood looking at all my adoring fans (until the first pitch), feeling right at home all over again. Just like old times.

It took me right back to the night I performed at the Country Music Awards. I was ten years old, kicking booty and taking names—well, I was learning names at least—and winning the Horizon Award for best new artist. That award show was my first standing O. Tim McGraw, my new tour mates the Dixie Chicks, Faith Hill, Brooks and Dunn, George Strait, Reba McEntire, Martina McBride, and every other country star in the audience stood up for me, even after the TV producer announced that they had gone off air to a commercial. They still clapped. I couldn't believe it.

It was the same feeling I had right now. Like heaven. And even though I was much wiser at age seventeen, I still wanted it just as badly. Maybe more.

2

I didn't set out to be a child star. There were no singing reality shows back then. And my parents probably
wouldn't have let me go anyway. Preacher's kid problems.
Fame wasn't one of those things we all sat around talking
about. At any rate, I was, what they call, "discovered."

My daddy first noticed my voice. I was singing into my
older sister Natalie's hairbrush to my "audience" of stuffed
animals and dolls. I had totally outgrown the dolls, but
they served a purpose. After that, it was only a matter of
time before I was singing in the choir, the youngest soloist
Cherry Hill Baptist had ever had in "big church." By then,
our so-called church secret was no longer a secret, and on
my choir director's insistence, I entered all the local talent shows. *A natural talent like yours should be showcased,*

she'd said. And at the time, my response was pretty simple: "OK, why not?" And then I went to ask my mom.

The first prize for one of the talent shows I won was to sing a song on the Pepsi Stage at Bayfest in downtown Mobile, Alabama. It was there, at Bayfest, where the entire city came to watch some of Nashville's biggest names— where Reba McEntire sang "Fancy," and every single person in the crowd sang along; where Tim McGraw wore his tighter-than-crap (sorry, Mama) jeans while he sang his very first number-one hit "I Like It, I Love It" to a lucky blushing thirty-something; where "Sweet Home Alabama" was an anthem—and it was there at Bayfest that I was truly discovered by Jake Slaughter, nicknamed the "Gold Miner," and a household name on Music Row in Nashville.

How he saw through my terrible attempt at "style," a faded blue-jean sundress with a bucket hat and pigtails— there were pictures on the mantle, so I could never forget—I would never know, but he did. He was, after all, the Gold Miner.

After that day, I had a whole new life, whirlwind style. Jake convinced Mama that he would take care of me (and he did), and in less than a year, I was one of the biggest stars in country music—and undoubtedly the youngest. As Lily Black (my stage name), I had access to clubs I couldn't go into, all the clothes I ever wanted (even though I had nowhere to wear them except for on stage), and I had money, even though my parents put it all in the bank. Seriously though, all jokes aside, it really was amazing until it all ended. They say the higher you go the further you fall. They're right. They also say what goes up must come down . . . and it did. It really did.

It was my twelfth birthday party, right after everything fell apart, and I was back home in Mobile. I'd never forget how my house was decorated in purple and white—my favorite colors—and how my whole grade at school showed up, even though I didn't think very many would. And I'd especially remember the part when I walked out to the pool area to my party: people everywhere, boys splashing with cannonballs and pool basketball and girls playing Marco Polo and doing toe-touches off the diving board. Amy and Lauren were in the deep end clinging to the ladder when I walked up.

"Hey, girls! Can I go next?"

(I specialized in toe-touches and pikes.)

"Umm, maybe later," Amy said, not even looking at me. "We're kind of in the middle of this round, ok?"

"Uh, OK," I answered, feeling my face turn as purple as my swimsuit. Lots of purple in my life.

When I turned around to go toward the food table, anywhere but there, I heard Lauren talking to the rest of the girls. "I thought famous people were supposed to be pretty," she snickered, and they all laughed. Another girl added, "Mark Conners was right. She is totally the Beast from the East."

I didn't know what else to do, so I ran into the house, knocking over pool bags and kicking flip-flops on my way. But I didn't care. Natalie and her boyfriend Judd followed me up the stairs. And of course, my save-the-day sister demanded to know what happened. In my weak moment, I caved and told her. The next thing I knew, Natalie had sprinted back down to "take care of it," leaving Judd and me in my room. Super awkward moment, since I was crying uncontrollably with snot hanging out of my nose. Not long after Natalie did her deal, the pool was empty. The streamers were dangling into the pool. The sandwiches were all eaten, the chips in little pieces on the patio. The cake was partly wet from one of the boys' cannonballs.

I just wanted to go to sleep, but my mom and dad basically forced me to do the whole sing "Happy Birthday" thing anyway. Mama said, "It's still our tradition. Plus, you have to make a wish!" She still did that.

What did I wish for? To disappear.

The day after the party was a low point. I wasn't the type of kid that stayed in my room for hours. I normally liked to stay up late with my parents and watch TV or something. So when I had gone in after my party the day before and hadn't come out yet, my mom knew something was really wrong. It wasn't going to pass in a day.

"I'm ugly, mom. And fat! And stupid. And no one likes me."

My mama looked heartbroken. I knew the feeling.

"Sweetie, you're none of those things. And I know they like you, deep down," she said, sighing. "Kids can be so cruel. They were awful to me when I was young, too. It usually means they are just jealous, though. And I'll bet they don't know how to go from seeing you on TV to all of a sudden sitting next to you in science class. It's just an adjustment for everybody."

"Can I add to this conversation?" Daddy asked as he entered the kitchen in his elephant-gray robe, burgundy house slippers, messed up hair, and ancient bifocals. Mama called him her "hunk"—I always liked that, even though it kind of grossed me out. My *dad*? Anyway, he carried his Bible and a yellow legal pad, which meant that he had been awake for hours (even if he looked like he just rolled out of bed after being electrocuted), already writing and re-writing his sermon for the following Sunday. He wrote in an old, worn leather chair with a reading lamp that almost hit the pages of the Bible, it hung so low. Daddy said he saw the chair at a garage sale when he and Mama had just gotten married, and the moment he saw it, he said he knew it would be where he would write sermons. That eventually led to its official name around the Carson household: the Lord's Chair.

"Of course, Cole," Mama said, getting up to grab another mug and the coffee pot.

"Can I have a cup?" I asked.

Mama looked at me funny, probably because I had never been a coffee drinker pre-Lily Black. But she still got me a cup and sat back down at the table.

"Li, I know it's hard right now. What your mother said is true," Daddy said. His bellowing preacher's voice was no act. Daddy was a Teddy bear of a man. He dwarfed little ole Mama, who stood at all of five feet one inch. She said he made her feel safe. I agreed. "The kids at school don't know how to deal with you being all the way in big Nashville and getting awards and being on the cover of magazines and then, all of a sudden, seeing you back in Mobile. They just need time to adjust, and so do you. And you need to forgive them, honey."

"WHY? WHY SHOULD I FORGIVE *THEM*? I'M NOT THE ONE CALLING THEM 'THE BEAST FROM THE EAST' OR SAYING THAT FAMOUS PEOPLE SHOULD BE PRETTY. I'M NOT THE ONE WHO PUT AN EGG IN THEIR SEATS IN HOMEROOM. I'M NOT

THE ONE WHO POURED SALT IN THEIR SWEET TEAS OR GOT UP AND LEFT THEM AT THE LUNCH TABLE WHEN THEY SAT DOWN. I DIDN'T DO ANYTHING, SO WHY SHOULD *I* HAVE TO FORGIVE *THEM*?"

I slammed my fist on the table so hard I felt like the house shook. It probably didn't, but I was twelve, and everything felt big. I knew for a fact how my parents felt, though. There was no mistaking their faces.

They were stunned. They knew I had been teased a little, but I guess they just thought it was silly and harmless. Inevitable adolescent stuff. They had no idea it had been happening ever since I started back at school halfway through the spring semester. That was probably my fault, but how could I tell them? It was so embarrassing!

"Why didn't you tell us this before we had your party, honey?" my mom said softly before my daddy erupted.

"Who did this?" he yelled. He very rarely showed any emotions other than cheer, comfort, and patience, so it kind of freaked me out.

I suddenly wished I hadn't spilled my guts and quickly pretended it wasn't such a big deal. It would be even worse if my dad *went* to my school and made a huge fuss. I would never have friends, then.

"I don't know who did it," I lied.

"Lilah Marie," Mama said with I-taught-you-better eyes. Her go-to response.

"Why does it matter if I just get my tutor back? Then I can just forget about the whole thing."

"That's not how we deal with problems, young lady," Daddy answered, his anger subsiding. "You can't just quit something just because it's hard."

Tweenage attitude filled the air. I was a quick learner of that. "Fine, since I'm clearly the one you should be mad at right now. Mark and Jason Conners did the stuff at school. They make my life a living hell. Amy and Lauren and their little group said the stuff about me being ugly. There, are you happy now?"

I folded my arms in defiance. On any other day, under any other circumstances, I would have been grounded on the spot for sassing, for using that kind of language in our house. But that day, there were bigger fish to fry.

Daddy shook his head. "Of course, we're not happy. I can't believe John Conners' boys would do that."

Mr. Conners was the head of athletics at Cherry Hill Academy and a deacon at Cherry Hill Baptist. Daddy knew John and how embarrassed he would be to know how his twin boys were behaving.

"Would you like your father to talk to Mr. Conners? I can talk to Amy and Lauren's moms," Mama offered.

"No! Please, no!" I begged while the tears dropped onto the kitchen table. It was like an instant monsoon. I shouldn't have had any more tears left after those two days.

"OK, OK; shh. We won't say anything," my mama assured me. "Let's just take it a day at a time. Tomorrow will be better."

We walked into the living room and tried to resume a normal day, but I remember wondering if my life was going to be like this forever. The total opposite of my life as Lily Black.

I had no idea that I was about to meet my new best friend.

It turned out that the only girl that *would* have talked to me at my twelfth birthday party wasn't even invited. JoBeth Miller had moved to West Mobile while I was off in Nashville, which explained how I could have missed her. But once I was asked to try out for cheerleading, I learned everything I needed to know about my future best friend. JoBeth Miller had become instantly popular at Cherry Hill, and if JoBeth handpicked you, you suddenly were liked by everyone in the whole grade. Even Amy and Lauren. Just like that. And, oh, "everyone" included boys.

In the three years I was off touring the world, it was as if I had completely skipped the whole chapter when boys stopped chasing girls on the playground. When they were annoying . . . and not as cute (well, in the I-want-you-to-want-me way, at least). JoBeth was a different story altogether. She'd been boy crazy since kindergarten, or so I was told.

It was no wonder why JoBeth became the overnight "it" girl. She had it all. She was cute, blonde, super talented, and had the cheerleader look, the look the boys liked. She had gotten all the right curves in all the right places at all the right times. Unlike me.

Adolescence wasn't one size fits all, and my personal experience only made it harder to shake off the mean-but-true words of Amy and Lauren. I grew boobs, but they were more like overly inflated balloons—growing rapidly and in danger of popping. Jobeth's were the perfect size, steadily growing at a safe speed. While JoBeth had been born with a perfect set of pearly whites, I had to wear a full set of metal, plus a spacer in the roof of my mouth to correct my cross-bite. JoBeth had naturally olive skin, but freckles sprouted all over my pale, pinky skin. And while

JoBeth's hair was always sleek, cropped, and so blonde it seemed white, I constantly wrestled with dry, frizzy brown locks that seemed to expand overnight. It didn't help that I had grown taller than almost all the boys by the time I reached fourteen. "Beast of the East" was mean, but sadly accurate.

Eventually, though, with JoBeth's help, I'd become one of the most popular girls at Cherry Hill. The Conners twins had even apologized to me one morning after church. No more eggs in my chair, no more salt in my sweet tea. In fact, I had been elected to be the freshman, junior, and senior representative for homecoming court. Of course it would have been even better if I'd been crowned queen, but JoBeth really deserved it.

Being friends with JoBeth had other perks, too. Boys. They actually noticed me. And, boy, did I notice back, longing all of a sudden for a first kiss, a slip of the tongue, a wandering hand underneath my school uniform blouse. I know, I know. Unbecoming of me, but I was young and stupid, OK? Plus, even if I had *wanted* to do all of that, I had to wait until I was sixteen. Cole Carson's rules. My sister Natalie had waited and had "done just fine" Daddy always said. But truth be told, I didn't think I could afford to waste time. If a boy liked me, he wouldn't wait until I was sixteen! He'd find someone else, someone like JoBeth. I wanted to obey my dad, I really did, but I was a teenager, and I was . . . hormonal.

I'd tried dating boys at my private school, but they just didn't do it for me, not after I met some boys from the public school. Public school boys had a sense of adventure that the boring private school boys didn't. They weren't afraid of getting into a little trouble, and more importantly, they didn't care that my daddy was a preacher. For the few that did, I swear it made them want me even more . . . and I kind of thrived on that thrill.

By the time I was a senior, my teeth were finally straight, my hair had found a pH balance (thank the Lord for the Chi straightener), and I had somewhat grown into my body. No more baby fat, no more weird bulging curves, and my boobs were finally proportionate to the rest of my body. I was "hot"—according to JB—all of a sudden, and to be perfectly honest, I hadn't really known how to handle all of the attention. Long gone were the days I wished I had an at-home tutor, let's just say that.

Wading in the deep end of memory lane, I nearly missed the sound of my cell phone ringing. That happened a lot.

"Hello?"

"Hey, Li."

It was JoBeth Miller, my savior.

"Hey! Where are you?"

"Uhhhh . . . wait, let me look. I'm on the road; I just don't know where I am."

Typical JoBeth. Never paying attention to her surroundings.

"Let me guess. You've been talking to . . . Logan?"

JoBeth hesitated at first, clearly about to dispute the obvious. But then she burst out laughing. "You got me. He misses me already, apparently."

"I knew he would! He snuck into our room every night on senior trip! I could hear you two. I'm afraid I'm gonna have to stay awake all night to make sure you don't grope me when we get to Nashville!"

"Oh, hush: we weren't that bad. Just once . . . or twice
. . . a night. It's not my fault he's needy. I just help him out,"
she giggled.

"Gross, JB. You almost got caught by Coach Wheeler!
We might have lost our walking privileges at graduation!"

"Lilah, you have got to loosen up! You're using words
like 'privilege.' It's done. We're fine. We walked. We can't
live in a tiny condo if you are afraid of a little physical fun.
You need to get over Michael, already!"

"I *am*! And I'm not afraid of that kind of fun!"

"Then why are you so obsessed with leaving Mobile the
day after graduation instead of enjoying your last summer
as a kid?"

"I'm not running. Plus, I don't want to be a kid anymore. I'm going to Nashville to get back what I lost, and
I'm ready to really focus. Michael Kimsky is the last thing
on my mind. Promise. Oh, and the real world doesn't get
summers."

"Well, I have no problem multi-tasking. And just a few
months ago, you were so excited about majoring in jour-
nalism at U of M, so don't even pretend that you've been
planning on this 'real world' bullcrap."

"I changed my mind, *sorry*! Do you not want to go
now?

"No! Are you freaking kidding me? We are moving to
Nashville!"

"Language, Jobs."

"Sorry, sorry. I'm just excited! Screw college!"

"Oh, don't bring up college." I instantly got a sick feeling, one I'd been getting a lot lately, ever since I told my
parents about my change of plans.

"Oh, gosh, what's wrong?"

"My parents still aren't exactly thrilled with this decision. It's a sore subject at my house. They think I should go to U of M, at least for a little while and then see how I feel about Nashville."

"What do you think? This is your life, ya know?"

"What do you think I think? But I still hate bein' on bad terms with them."

"You worry too much! It'll be fine! This is Cole and Sandy we're talkin' about. They'll come around. Probably already have! Plus, wouldn't it have been the same thing if we'd gone to college in Tennessee—just a few months early?"

"Ugh, I know, but I hate disappointing them."

"Then turn around."

"What?"

"Turn around if you're so concerned about your parents that you'll give up your dream."

I squeezed the steering wheel, still feeling guilty, but maybe a little more determined, too.

"Fine. You win."

"Thank you. Oh, and by the way, your parents weren't the only ones who bucked at this whole thing!"

"Really?"

"Yeah, but they eventually caved."

"Obviously!" I laughed. "Ok! New subject. I have a question. Two, actually."

"Shoot."

"Ok, first, do you know where you are yet?"

"I'm not far from Priester's, I know that much. I've seen some billboards."

"Wait, wait. You aren't even to *Priester's*? Exactly when

did you leave Mobile?"

"I had some last minute things to take care of." I could hear the mischief in her voice. She'd perfected it over the years.

"Logan."

"You got me. Yes, yes. OK, I'm a slut. I had a hard time leaving him! I mean, we're moving! And I'll sorta miss his cute butt."

"You don't even like him all that much, do you?"

JoBeth never had long-term boyfriends. Just a steady stream of hot and steamy flings.

JoBeth paused for a second, then giggled. "Well, no."

"Exactly! But I still don't want to picture Logan Price's behind."

"You asked."

"No, no; I did not ask. And again, new subject! My second question is actually serious."

"You're so easy to make queasy!" JoBeth sang.

"Hush! Focus please! Who do you think I should be? Lily or Lilah?"

"Hmm. That's hard," JoBeth teased.

"I'm serious! I've been racking my brain trying to fig-ure it out."

"I'm serious, too! Don't get your panties in a twist! Hmm . . . I don't know. I like Lilah because I know Lilah real well. But I remember watching the great Lily Black on the CMAs and stuff, too. But wait, what about me?"

"What do you mean?"

"What should my name be?"

"Umm . . . JoBeth. Like Madonna."

"I'll take it! From now on, please address me only as 'JoBeth,'" she buzzed.

"I think I can handle that. Hey Jobs?"

"I'm sorry, there's no one here by that name."

I smiled. "Excuse *me*. JoBeth?"

"Uh huh?"

"I'm so glad you're going with me. I'm going to need all the support I can get."

"Me, too. Everything is going to be so amazing. I can just feel it!"

"I'll talk to you in a little while! Hurry . . . but don't speed!"

"Next stop? Nashville, Tennessee!"

Click.

★ 3 ★

Nashville, Tennessee. Music City USA. It sounded so much more sophisticated than Mobile, Alabama . . . home of the what? Former country star Lily Black? And now that I would be back in Nashville, it couldn't even claim that!

Goodness gracious, I thought while I sat in traffic to get off my new exit, people were everywhere! And that was one of the main reasons I couldn't wait to get to my new place—it was smack dab in the middle of everything!

The Bristol, at 1803 Broadway, was a beautiful building. It looked like a New York place, kind of like what I always pictured Monica and Chandler from *Friends* living in, just smaller. I parked on the street next to an old run-down market called Virginia's. It looked a tad bit out of place in the nice surroundings, but I wasn't going to complain.

There were probably groceries in there, which would save me a trip in the car to the nearest grocery store. Wherever one of those even was.

Finding "Carson, Lilah" on the electronic keypad at the door was easy. But as soon as I did, my cell phone rang, and I realized I couldn't remember which number my landlord told me to push to let myself in. *Crap!* I thought. What was that number?

But I didn't have to worry for long. Someone was coming out of the door. Perfect. And he was hot. Like real hot. And weirdly enough, he looked familiar, but I had no idea why or where I would've seen him before. I hadn't even moved in yet!

"Hi, there," hot guy said.

"Hi," I said, my eyes cast down, flattered but hopelessly lame. "Thanks," I said as I took the door from him, hoping he lived in the building and I could work up the nerve to actually talk to him again. Fat chance. I could feel him staring at me, most likely my rear end—the side that couldn't act like a total fool—as I walked inside. *I could get used to Nashville.*

Fishing the keys out of my over-packed purse, I was prepared to be thrilled at what I found inside. But I wasn't. I wasn't at all. It was dark, empty, and dirty. The owners *had* said they'd been gone for a little bit and that I might need to spruce it up some, but my goodness. Sprucing wouldn't cut it. It needed a full-on renovation.

The paint was chipping. The concrete floor had a crack in it; there was dried food in between the granite counter tops and the oven. The microwave was filthy and sticky. The blinds on the door out to the teeny, tiny balcony were bent. The windows looked like they had never been cleaned. The light bulbs were all removed in the bedroom. The bedroom was *tiny*. Tinier than tiny. Ironically, the bathroom was the cleanest, only the corner of the mirror broken off.

I needed to send the sweet owners a dictionary. Spruce? I didn't think so.

What did I get myself into? I panicked as I subconsciously reached back inside my purse to find my cell phone.

"Hello?"

"Natalie?"

"Hey, girl! How's it goin'! Mama told me you were on the road today."

"Well, I'm here now, actually."

"And?"

"It's great!"

"What's wrong?"

I could fool most people into thinking I was fine (as long as I was on the phone), but not my sister Natalie. Natalie Carson Baylor was a kindergarten teacher by trade, but I had always sworn she had the powers of a medium. She could see right through people. And it was awesome until she was looking through you.

"Does Judd actually *like* when you do that?"

"Do what?"

"How you're always right?"

"Oh! Haha," Natalie giggled. She and Judd had been married for years, but they still acted as though they were newlyweds. "Judd hasn't mentioned it, but that's probably because he knows if we argue about it, I'll probably win."

"How's 'Summer-Sault?'" I asked about my adorable niece, trying to stall. I had called my sister instinctively, but I didn't really know how much to actually tell her yet. If I told her about the condo's crappy condition, chances were good that Natalie would go run her mouth and tell our parents. And then, my parents would call and tell me all over again how it was a mistake to be renting a condo in the first place, and that the U of M dorms were clean and tidy and blah, blah, blah. But, on the other hand, I wanted to tell someone. And it couldn't be JoBeth—I didn't want her to change her mind and go back home, especially after I found out Mr. and Mrs. Miller were against her moving, too. I knew they would get over it fairly soon—they were total workaholics—but it was the first day! So Natalie would have to do.

"My child is covered in paint right now, though we *discussed* that she wasn't allowed to get into her crafts until after dinner. Didn't we, Summer?" Natalie said, half to me, half to her three-year-old daughter.

I pictured Summer in Natalie's "craft closet" at their perfect little cottage in Mobile drenched in (hopefully) water-based paints. And yet, Natalie sounded calm as a cucumber.

"Enough about Sum. I'm serious, Li, what's wrong?"

"I don't know if it's as big a deal as I'm makin' it, but—"

"Out with it."

She had powers. Kindergarten witch-doctor powers or something.

I sighed, trying to empty my lungs of all my pride so that I could just say it. "The condo is awful!" I cried.

"What do you mean awful?"

"It's so gross! There's stuff on the walls!"

"So paint it."

"There's a crack in the floor!"

"Put a rug over it."

"There's grime in the microwave and in between the counter and the oven, and the windows are fil—"

"Use some 409. Windex. Look, Li, my house looks like what you're describin' every single day before I get my hands on it. As long as it's not on fire and there's no poisonous gas, all you have to do is a put some elbow grease behind it. You'll be amazed. And I'm about to sound like Mama, but this is a perfect example of what a 'deal' looks like. There's always a catch. But the good news is that this catch is totally doable. You can do this."

It wasn't a deal. I was paying an arm and a leg for the place, but I wasn't about to say anything. For some reason, I felt relieved to know that my perfectly put together sister had some of the same problems I did. Natalie (named after Natalie Wood) had always been all planned out. Kindergarten teacher? Check. Married? Check. Perfect daughter? Check.

And Natalie, like JoBeth, didn't go through an awkward phase like I did. Though she had been tall like Daddy and me, her body had gradually filled out, her hair had remained tame, and her teeth were the quirky, real kind of crooked—not the kind that desperately needed braces.

"Ok. You're right, that's all I need to do. Just clean up," I said, nodding to myself, convincing myself.

"I wish I were there to help. I love cleanin' other people's houses!" Natalie chirped. "Oh, hey, the oven's beepin' in the kitchen."

"What are y'all havin'?" I asked, suddenly hungry, suddenly just a twinge homesick—if just for a home-cooked meal. It hadn't even been one day! Buck up, Lilah!

"Enchiladas and strawberry pretzel salad."

"Mom's favorite meal." I smiled.

"And mine! Ha!

"I love you little sister, and Li?"

"Yeah?"

"Your place is going to be just fine. Just give it a little TLC."

"Thanks, Nat. I love you."

"Love you too, little sis. Call us when you can! Summer's been askin' about Aunt Wiwah," Natalie giggled.

"I will. Night."

"Night."

I let out a big sigh after we hung up, and looking around, I saw my sister's point. It was nothing a little Walmart couldn't fix.

★ ⭑ ★ ⭑

A drive to the nearest Super Walmart, four trips to and from my car, and a Sears delivery man later, unit 414 started looking like an actual home. My parents could keep me from using my money to buy the condo (another stupid fight), but they couldn't keep me from using it on the inside. I found candles to take out that dingy smell and a rug to sit on top of the big crack in the concrete floor. The bed I'd picked out from Sears made the small bedroom feel cozy, and the semi-cheap futon I'd gotten for JoBeth's "bed" covered up the dings in the paint on the living room wall. I bought light bulbs, groceries, bath towels, toiletries, and laundry detergent. Everything I needed, except one thing: JoBeth.

I tried calling her cell phone a couple times while my Kraft Mac and Cheese cooked in the microwave, but I got her dang voicemail every time. By the time I finished my own home-heated dinner, I was way past worried. I was pissed.

I need to get out of here, I thought, so I walked outside. It was a warm spring night, sticky—but not nearly as humid as Mobile—and I knew I probably shouldn't be walking alone (I could practically hear my parents rattling off a list of what-ifs), but it was a Saturday night and tons of people were walking around. Starting on the street next to Virginia's Market, I walked up to the infamous roundabout with the naked, very un-Nashville-like statues. *What about these naked men scream Music Row?* I wondered. *They should at least be holding guitars or something, right?*

ASCAP, BMI, and other studios I'd seen (including Masterfonics, off in the distance, where I'd first met Faith Hill) lined the streets I had only vaguely remembered until now. It was like a song you hadn't heard in years. Right until the moment it played, you couldn't be sure you'd remember the words. But once you heard the melody, you realized that your memory picked up where you last left off.

Nashville was like that for me. A deep-rooted memory—a memory I'd buried but kept fully intact. And now that I was back, I could feel myself beginning to unwrap each piece and remember it like it was yesterday.

Walking up Sixteenth Avenue South, I saw the place I remembered the most: Slaughter House Productions. There was something comforting about the fact that it hadn't changed a bit. Maybe it was a sign of things to come, I hoped.

There was a light on upstairs in the house-turned-office, but for the life of me, I couldn't recall ever going up the stairs when I was younger. Jake's office was downstairs, right inside to the left. I wanted to go in sit on Jake's couch—or on the floor beside the couch . . . where we had discovered the song that changed everything. But I restrained myself and kept walking.

★ 4 ★

(Slaughter House Productions, 1999)

"Have you heard this one yet?" Jake said with a yawn as he held up a cassette tape. We had been at the office all night listening to demo tapes in search of the perfect first single for me, and I was about to fall asleep sitting up. Three large boxes labeled "It's a Hit," "It's a Dud," and "Possibly Maybe" sat on the floor next to us. Unfortunately, there were more tapes and CDs in the dud pile than in any other box.

"What's it called?" I said, yawning back.

"'Burning Blue.'"

"No, sir, I don't think so. When can you take me back to the Chambers' house? I'm so tired."

"Lily, this is your future. Your career. Sleep when you're dead, right?"

33

"Right," I groaned as I leaned back into the bottom of the couch, crunching some of the CD cases and lyric sheets around me.

When word got out that Jake needed some songs for a new artist, the whole Row sent them in. And from listening to a handful of them, he could tell that the minor details that I was *female* and a *child* (just barely nine) had either skipped their attention or else they didn't care—hence the amount of songs in the dud pile. It was most likely the latter. Nashville publishers and song pluggers were mostly aware of their song submissions (it was their job), but lone, unpublished songwriters were known and prone to take every opportunity to have their "babies" listened to by managers, entertainment laywers, producers, or anyone else associated with an artist. And so, we were stuck at his office on a Saturday night, listening and sifting through song after song—mostly crap. But finally, Jake heard "the one," and it made all the crap worth it.

It was a song on a cassette rather than a CD, which meant one of three things: the song might have been written a long time ago and had yet to see the light of day, the writer could claim to be "old school" and only record on cassettes to preserve some weird "vintageness," or the writer was broke and couldn't afford to get his or her demos put onto a CD. In other industries, all this might matter, but not in Nashville. What mattered on Music Row was the song: the lyrics, the melody, the dynamics, the heart, the passion bleeding from the speakers. And of course, it needed radio appeal and commercial reach.

Jake couldn't write the song himself, but he could recognize a hit immediately. And this song had it all. Bingo. It was going to get me the label attention I needed, hopefully a deal. We'd been working so hard on everything else. (I'd finally gotten used to answering to Lily . . . and with a lot of practice, my new signature was finally starting to look natural).

Jake said I sat with the Walkman headphones on and closed my eyes for so long that at first he thought I had fallen asleep. But then I started humming the chorus . . . and he said I gave him chills, the good kind.

"I like it! Can I take it home?" I asked, all of sudden wide awake.

"Yes! Yes! All right, let's get you to Brentwood, shall we? Can you learn this song by tomorrow afternoon?" Jake woke up a little too.

(Whenever I was in Nashville for an extended period of time, I stayed with my daddy's friend's family, the Chambers. They had three daughters, and one was close to my age.)

"Will that get me out of church?"

"Yeah, sure."

"Good."

"I thought your dad was a preacher?"

"Yeah, but I hate wakin' up early."

"I know all about that. Here's the lyric sheet if you need to figure out some of the words."

"Thanks, Mr. Slaughter."

"Jake, please, Lily."

"Oops. Jake."

"Now, that's more like it. Let's go."

the
HOOD

D.O.C. : 12.15.98

BURNING BLUE
{B. HOOD}

I REMEMBER HOW YOU FOUND ME
SITTIN' IN THE DARK
LIKE SUNSHINE ALL AROUND ME
LIT ME UP WITH JUST A SPARK

AND WE WERE BURNING BLUE
FANNING FLAMES & FLYING THROUGH
WILD AND ALL CONSUMED BY YOU
& WE WERE BURNING
WE WERE BURNING BLUE

I SHOULDA KNOWN IT WHEN I TOUCHED IT
SHOULDA KNOWN IT'D LEAVE A MARK
HELL IS REAL THE WAY I'M FEELING
SMOKIN' EMBERS, MELTING HEARTS

{CHORUS}

ASHES, ASHES, WE BURNED DOWN
WHAT STARTED HOT IS FROZEN NOW

{SOLO}
{CHORUS}

(February 22, 2000: Los Angeles)

"Jake? What's a go-see?"

"Heck if I know. Ask Anali," he mumbled absently from the front seat of the town car.

"It's a . . . umm . . . it's where we go to different places and try on dresses for the show this week," Anali said, dumbing it down.

Anali was my stylist when I was in LA. Originally from England, she had moved across the pond to work with some of the world's biggest pop stars, which made her a perfect selection in my eyes. Anali was very good at her job, but she wasn't as good with "children," as she called us. She was one of those types who would probably never even think of procreating for fear that her wardrobe might change.

I nodded silently and continued to look out the window of the town car. I might have been ten, but I had grown up in the one and a half years I'd been thrust headfirst into fame. I had nearly mastered the craft of being enough of an adult with everyone who expected me to be mature and enough of a child when I was in front of the press and during interviews. My brand was well protected.

Inevitably, Jake had explained to me during media training, *people will ask you if you feel like you've lost your childhood. It's your job to say no.*

At the time, I hadn't thought too much about it. "I like my job!" I'd answered. I got free everything, was tutored for three hours a day, and had no homework, unlike the rest of the kids my age. I got new clothes every week, got to wear makeup years earlier than my parents would have allowed back home in Mobile, and ever since "Burning

Blue" had gone double platinum, I had been nominated for all kinds of awards and asked to sing my hit single on the Grammys. So, yeah, I was all right with the growing up I had to do.

The Grammys! Not just in front of my country music peers. Nsync, Christina Aguilera, Britney, Destiny's Child! The Grammys for musicians were the equivalent to the Oscars for actors. Go-sees were forever in my future if I kept this up, Anali had nonchalantly said with a tight, British smile.

And once I saw the "ensemble" I might get to wear to the show, bedazzled and pink with sparkly shoes and jewelry, I was hoping Anali was right.

"I LOVE THESE DRESSES!" I squealed as I twirled in my third BCBG gown.

"The dress you wore to the Country Awards or whateva' . . . you need to fire that stylist immediately. It was horrid and you looked fat," Anali confessed, even though no one had asked.

Jake shot her a look. Had Anali not been a child once? Not had a brain or a heart once?

"I picked it out. And I won," I shyly defended myself.

"It figures. Leave it to a five-year-old to pick out an ugly frock from Baby Gap," she said, rolling her hoity-toity eyes.

"A word, Anali?" Jake said with a pained smile. He led Anali out of the room, leaving me a little confused and downtrodden in my sparkling princess dress.

When they came back, Anali was smiling and oddly chipper, squealing, "I think that's the one, darling! You look absolutely ravishing!"

And that was the beginning of the "yes" period.

Everyone said "yes" to every single word, every single request I made. And if they said anything but "yes," they were let go on the spot.

Of course, I had no idea at the time that people were being paid (with my money) not to tell me the whole truth. I honestly thought everyone loved me, loved my every move, my every thought, my every breath. I mean, some people had gone as far as telling me I had the Midas touch. What was I supposed to think? *Maybe I do*, I thought at the time, and there was no one there to tell me otherwise. I'm not sure I would have believed them if they did.

I was on top of the world. I got a brand new bus to cart me around the country in style. Jake insisted that I needed it in order to look the part, to make fans believe I really was "all that and a bag of Doritos." Of course, the money had come out of my pocket, and of course, it didn't touch Jake's ten percent, but that was standard, apparently. My tour rider demanded—seriously—purple and white towels that smelled of lavender in my dressing room's bathroom, purple and white flowers at my makeup table, watermelon Bubble Yum, two bags of Rold Gold pretzels, peanut butter M&Ms, and a six-pack of orange soda in the glass bottles. I know, I know, a little diva, wasn't I? I didn't know any better! Jake asked me what I would want if I could choose . . . so I told him. And, voila!

He'd even arranged a photo shoot of me in my new custom bedroom in the back of my new custom tour bus for *People* magazine. The article was aptly titled "You Wish You Had Her Life," and it proceeded to tell the magazine-reading, celebrity-loving world all about how lucky Lily Black was. And I agreed. I had it made. Well, I thought I did.

Technically, I was still an opening act for the Dixie Chicks, but in my own mind (no doubt with the help of my handlers), it was my show, my tour, and the Dixie Chicks were good, but they were living in *my* world. Basically, I was your typical bratty child with a bank account. Sound familiar? And because of my instant fame and sizable fan base, Jake had been able to negotiate a forty-five minute set (while most newcomers got fifteen to twenty) and a $30,000 cut of the sell-out sales for me for each show. A number one song and seemingly endless potential for additional sales justified the upgrades to my tour status. To offset more of the tour's cost, the Chicks brought in another opener who was a twenty-four-year-old guy, and in my eyes, an old (but cute) man. His name was Blake something.

As I kept walking down Music Row, I wondered if I really had had it made or if I was just under the impression I had because of what I had been told. You tend to hear only what you want to hear when you're that age (famous or not)—and I wasn't sure all that much had changed. Because when I lost my record deal, it was as if my life was over. Within seconds, the people who had said "Whatever you want, Ms. Black" had disappeared, never to be seen again. Anali was on to bigger and better clients in no time. The Grammys didn't call me again the next year, not even for a spot as a presenter. And by the time I got the invitation to attend the show (probably just out of pity), I had already moved back to Mobile. All good things must come to an end. But, why?

More flashes of the recording studios, my first trips to the local radio stations, my first music video shoot, and the photo shoots for my album's artwork whipped around in my brain like a blender as I retraced my steps as a former superstar. The stylists (the good ones and the rude ones), the long flights, the red eyes, the interviews, the fan mail, the hate mail, the award shows, the red carpets. It all came back.

If I was going to do all of this again, I was going to need to change some things. And since I was seventeen now, a fully licensed adult (well, almost), I figured it wouldn't be too difficult. The hard parts were going to be getting Jake back, getting a record deal, and finding another "Burning Blue" for lightning to strike twice. Piece of cake, right?

My phone rang in my pocket. I pulled it out to find "Home Sweet Home" flashing across the screen.

"Hello?"

My dad answered back, booming (almost chanting), "Hello?" into the receiver. I could hear bags rustling in the background and pictured him unloading somewhere near fifteen Walmart bags in the kitchen. It was his Saturday tradition to go to Walmart and pick up everything he figured we needed—and that included some stuff we *didn't* need. His reasoning: it was on sale!

For example, it was now May, a month or so after Easter. My dad had walked in last Saturday with about eighteen Easter egg decorating kits. "They were just fifty cents apiece! Plus, Summer will love it!"

Mama saw all the loot and said, "Cole, honey, she's one little girl. How many kits does she need?"

His answer: "She's got friends, doesn't she?"

Mama and I laughed and laughed, picturing Natalie

and Judd trying to round up seventeen people who had a kid in effort to use all the kits they had. Mobile wasn't *that* big of a city!

But that was my daddy, and I wouldn't trade him for anyone in the world.

"Hey, Daddy," I said.

"You safe and sound in your place?"

I was not about to tell them I was walking around by myself. But I wasn't going to lie either. Not fully.

"I made it to Nashville!"

"Oh, good to hear. I was startin' to worry a little. Someone forgot to call us!"

"Oops."

"It's OK, sweetie. You called us three other times. I thought four was overkill anyway. You know your mother. She's always worryin.'"

"Daddy! That was *your* idea!"

"Was it? Oh, yeah," he said, laughing. "Well, tell me everything! How's your place? Is JoBeth there, yet? What's the weather? Have you eaten dinner?"

"Whoa, partner. Sloooooowwww down. My place is good. JoBeth is still not here yet. The weather is about the same as home. I'm still in the South, you know. And mac n' cheese."

"Kraft?"

My daddy was a bit of a food connoisseur, specializing in junk food mostly. And Sun Drop soda.

"Yep!"

"Mmm, mmm. That makes me hungry. Did you stop at Priester's and Clanton's on your way?"

"Yes to Priester's, but I decided to skip Clanton's this time."

"Rookie mistake. I bet you're kickin' yourself now."

"Yep. That peach cheesecake ice cream would go good with my healthy meal of champions right about now."

"Oh, you're young. You can afford to eat that stuff. And let me tell you one thing: enjoy it. It gets tougher to get away with it later."

"Whatever you say. Hey, where's Mama?"

"She's out back on the porch, readin' or tendin' to her garden, I think."

"It's dark!"

"You know that doesn't stop that woman."

"Is she still mad?"

"At you? No, honey, she was never mad."

"She was awful quiet this morning."

"That's just how she gets when she's sad. You know that."

"Does she think I'm makin' a mistake?"

"By moving to Nashville? I don't think so. But you should ask her yourself."

"That wasn't super convincin', Daddy."

My worry-meter started creeping back up.

"Well, it's been an eventful couple months, Li. I mean one minute you were going to college and picking out your classes, and the next, you come to us after singing at a baseball game and say you're not going at all. Then you stormed out of the house when we weren't as thrilled as you wanted us to—"

"I'm sorry about that. I shouldn't have done that. And I said things I didn't mean. I was just—"

"We all say things we don't mean. It's done, it's over, and I don't want it to change the fact that we are rootin' for ya, honey, no matter if we disagree on this right now."

"Well, I, for one, hate that you disagree."

Daddy chuckled. "Oh, here's your mother. Sandy, it's Lilah on the phone."

I heard my mother's tiny voice getting further away, no doubt going to pick up the other phone in their bedroom.

"Hey, baby," Mama said.

"Hey, Mama. How's your garden?"

"Slowly but surely gettin' back to what it was. I just can't *believe* someone would come and uproot everything! Some people just have nothin' else to do, I guess."

"I know. I thought we lived in a safe neighborhood."

"We do," Daddy chimed in. "Bored, idle folks with nothing else to do is all it was."

"Probably a kid," Mama said.

"Anyway," I said, trying to steer the conversation back to where it came from, "Mama, I am safe; my place is great. I ate dinner. The weather is perfect. Oh, and I'm sorry."

"Sorry for what, darlin'?"

"The way this whole thing went down. I know I'm kind of wrecking you and Daddy's plans for me, but I promise I can handle it. I'll be safe and careful and always lock my doors."

"Oh, honey, it's not about you being mature enough. We know you are. It's just that you're only seventeen, and even though we trust you . . . we just don't trust others. Lilah, you're our baby girl. We want you to be safe and happy."

"I know, and I want to say sorry for somethin' else."

"For what?"

"For yellin' at you. For actin' the way I have been for the last couple weeks and pretendin' I wasn't sad this morning when I drove away."

"We knew you were sad, Li," Daddy said. "It was your eyes."

I threw my head back, just for a second. My dang eyes gave me away, always. Ugh! I would have to work on that if I wanted to make in the music business again. I couldn't have people smellin' my fear!

"Ugh, you guys know everything. Anyway, I'm sorry."

"Stop saying you're sorry, sweetie. Kids and parents fight. It's the way of the world. We are over it! You're there, and we're happy for you, OK?" Mama said.

"OK. Hey, Mama? I have one more question. And be honest."

I stood on Music Row, trying to think of a way not to sound like a baby.

"What is it, sweetie?" Daddy asked.

"Do you think I'll make it again? Am I even good enough?"

"I think so," Mama answered weakly.

"Wow, you sound so certain," I said with blatant sarcasm. One of my charming gifts.

"Of *course* we think you are," Daddy reassured me. "What your mother is trying to say—I think—is that we know how talented you are. You've always had a voice of an angel. But sometimes fame has nothing to do with talent. You remember how all this went down last time. That music business ate you up and spit you out."

"Thanks for reminding me."

"No, Lilah, hear me out. Hear *us* out."

"We know you will do a great job; we just don't want you to be disappointed if things don't work out exactly as you plan. Last time you came back, you were so devastated that your mother and I thought you were going to fall apart."

Here we go again.

"I know, but I was eleven years old then. I'm an adult now, and I can take care of myself."

"Technically, you're still a minor, according to the law."

"Dad, I'm seriously not in the mood."

I really wasn't. It was just a replay of every other talk we'd had lately.

"What? Can't blame me for trying to hold onto my baby girl as long as I can!"

"Excuse your daddy. Are you gonna call Jake?" my mom asked.

Saved by Sandy.

"Yeah, I thought I would."

"He definitely knows Nashville. The good *and* the bad."

"So I should?"

"I think it couldn't hurt. At least see what he says."

"Yeah, I think I will. Well, what are y'all's plans for the rest of the weekend?"

"Well, we have church tomorrow. I guess someone is excited she won't have to go *every* Sunday now?" Daddy asked, knowing I had always begrudged that requirement of a preacher's daughter.

"I'm just not a morning person," I answered.

"Yeah, especially when you're hung over," my daddy joked."

Busted. I had definitely been hung over last week when I rolled into church thirty minutes late after staying out at a fellow classmate's graduation party, my hair still dripping wet from my last minute, thirty-second shower. I had *had* to though, or else I would have smelled like beer, smoke, and Waffle House (even though the smoke wasn't my fault, the bar we went to was full of it.) Man, I thought I had played it off just fine, but obviously, I hadn't done a wonderful acting job. Whoops.

"You didn't think we knew, did ya?" Daddy asked.

When I didn't answer, he continued, "I saw you from the pulpit and I knew. Your eyes were dartin' all over the place in search of an exit strategy in case you had to throw up."

"Oh, gosh," I turned red, but luckily there weren't very many people out and about to notice on Music Row. (Which also sort of scared me.)

"Oh, Cole, stop trying to make her feel bad," Mama said.

"San, she knows I'm kiddin'. I don't love that our baby girl's drinkin' before she's legal, but as long as it was just a one-time, last-hoorah graduation thing, I can let it slide. We were all seniors once."

I said nothing, knowing I should tell the truth—that it *hadn't* been the first time—but I froze.

"I don't even want to know if you have a fake ID," Mama said, and I pictured my mother sitting in her bedroom, shaking her head in worry.

I, again, said nothing. There was nothing I *could* say without implicating JoBeth's under-the-table operation. And I needed JoBeth to be in the clear. Whenever she decided to freaking show up!

My dad sensed the awkwardness, and knowing him, he probably already knew it was JoBeth. Either way, he changed the subject, saving me from further embarrassment. "Well, have you talked to Natalie since you left?"

"Yep. Earlier."

"You like her better than us?" Daddy joked.

"Yeah, Daddy. So much better."

"Well, we love you, kiddo," he said.

"I love you guys."

I felt a catch in my own throat, but pushed on.

"I love you, sweet girl," Mama said, clearly sniffling.

"Bye, baby," Daddy said.

I knew my parents well. And once they hung up the phone I knew my daddy was going to walk into their bedroom and let Mama cry in his arms. Just the thought made me want to start crying, too. I wouldn't say it out loud, but I knew how lucky I was.

Taking Edgehill, one of the side streets, I found myself on Seventeenth Avenue South, equally considered to be "Music Row" in the music industry. And there was one really good reason why: RCA B was on Seventeenth. Elvis had recorded in that studio (among many other artists, but come on, *Elvis Presley!*). If I remembered correctly, it was right up there on the right . . .

I stopped walking, like on a dime. My heart skipped a beat or two and then picked up speed. How in the world had I forgotten what else was on Seventeenth Avenue? Selective memory?

The radio station. *The* station that did it all. Or more specifically, the man who ruined my career.

(2000)

Eleven was an awkward and unfortunate age for some girls, but it seemed especially awful to me. Not because

I had everything I had ever wanted, but rather because of how quickly I lost it. Looking back, there seem to be somewhat of a life trend: At eight, I was discovered. At nine, I got my first record deal. By eleven, I got a number one, won multiple awards, and performed on a world tour. Where else was there to go when I turned twelve or thirteen?

Some celebrities declined with time and age. They slowly drifted out of the spotlight. Me? Not so much. I didn't drift as much as nose-dive. And it all started with a phone call.

"Lily?" Jake said on the other end of the phone.

"Hey, Jake. What's going on? What's the news?" Jake always had good news for me: another deal, another endorsement, another great song.

"What are you doing?"

"What do you mean? I'm on the phone with you, silly!"

"I mean, who is with you?"

"Everyone—I'm at catering."

"Can we talk later or do you want to talk now? Your choice."

"Go ahead."

"Ok," Jake said hesitantly. "Dane Kimmel's not going to play 'Knocked Out.'"

"What?" I was shocked, instantly flushed. I stood up from the catering table and walked out without an explanation to anyone there. Luckily, the other guys were much too interested in their food to notice. My bus was far away from the arena's room designated for catering, so I took my new purple Nokia cell phone (remember those?) and walked into the stage area where I was playing that night: Philips Arena in Atlanta.

"What do you mean?" I said again, once I finally could hear myself think.

"I mean, it's been eight weeks. I've called, the label's radio promo team called. Kimmel said every time that he needs time to get through Faith, Martina, Shania, and JoDee's new singles first, and then he'll play your song. But now, he's saying he's not going to play it. Ever."

This is when my personality split into two—not in a weird way. I (as Lilah Carson) might have been eleven, at the beginning of my awkward stage, entering into physical jungle of womanhood—though not there yet—but I (as Lily Black) was an artist, and I'd developed a complete sense of professionalism. It was almost as if I could flip a switch from my dramatic, confusing, attitude-giving tweenage self when my business and career were on the line. But I was the business, the product, so when someone didn't like it/me, I took it personally.

"But I don't understand. He told me he loved it. He told me over and over how much he loved it, and he used the F-word and everything. And he promised, didn't he?"

Promises. They meant something to a preacher's daughter from Mobile, Alabama. They meant something to eleven-year-olds in any place, even Nashville. But promises in the music industry were less . . . real.

An agent could tell you one thing and be flat out stroking your ego (or theirs). A manager could tell you that you sing like a sparrow when you sound like a turkey gobbling. A radio PD (program director) could swear up and down that he couldn't wait to put a song on the radio.

That he *looooved* it, that he'd definitely put it on the air—it's a smash hit—if you would just give him two weeks . . . OK, maybe two more. And then he just needed a couple more till he could play it.

And then, three months later, still no play. He might think (and he knows better) he's one little ole radio station in little ole Nashville and that someone else will play it first. Then he can play it, when he knows it's "safer."

What he doesn't know (actually he probably does) is that every single other PD in the nation is waiting for the Dane Kimmel to play "Knocked Out" first. So, by him not playing it, the song has no chance. I might have been a "child," but I knew this much.

"Lily? Are you still there?" Jake asked.

"Yeah, I'm just . . . mad."

"Me, too. I'm liable to walk over to his office on Seventeenth right now and tell him how I feel."

"I don't know why he promised me," I said, still in shock.

"Sweetheart, you'll learn faster than anyone how wretched some of these guys can be. They think they own the world because they can choose whether your song gets played or not. They all have God complexes, Lily."

"What's that?"

"Never mind. Anyway, they're not all bad. Just a handful of 'em. Why don't you go back to the bus and take a nap before your show tonight?"

"What does this mean?"

"What do you mean, honey?"

"I mean . . . for me? For the tour? Should I call my parents?"

Jake skirted around his highest-grossing client's

question as best he could. "Let me make a few phone calls, and then I'll call you back."

"OK," I replied, defeated.

"And, Lily?"

"Yes, sir?"

"Knock 'em dead tonight."

"You got it," I said, trying to sound like I was just fine.

After I hung up, I stared at the big black stage in front of me, unlit and unexciting. I turned around and looked out at all the empty seats. In a few hours, those seats would start filling up. And I would perform, but this wasn't my tour yet. And at that moment, I realized I might not see that day. All because one guy didn't keep his word.

I had asked Jake what it meant for me, but I was worried that I already knew the answer. Without radio play, it was almost impossible to promote yourself. Jake had explained it that way when we'd had first gone around on the radio circuit with "Burning Blue" just one year before.

"In a nutshell, we need radio . . . *bad*. They can make your career soar or fall flat on its butt. People'll try to tell you that radio's old school, but ask 'em how their record sales are doin' without radio support. They won't have an answer that makes sense, not unless they're underground, and really, how many people buy CDs out of the back of a van? So, when you go in here, show them how sweet you are, how polite you are, and then knock 'em dead with your voice, darlin'," he'd said.

"You got it," my nine-year-old self had responded, holding a small thumbs-up and wearing a huge smile.

Jake had also said that once we got the radio PDs' attention the first time, it would be "smooth sailin'" for the next song(s). He'd said we would be able to skip the radio tours if it went well because they'd already know and love me.

"You have to kiss their butts first, but when you bring 'em a gem like this here song, it'll be no time before they will call *you* up wanting *you*, begging *you* to stop by."

It was all true, up until the part about them actually playing my second song . . . or my third.

I stood there in the big black arena and suddenly felt embarrassed. I wanted to climb into my expensive custom tour bus and never come out. No, actually I wanted to crawl into my mama and daddy's arms and fall asleep while we all read the Bible by the fire. I wanted to sit next to my daddy in the Lord's Chair and listen to him up in the pulpit at church. I wanted to call someone, but I couldn't.

How could I explain to them that I might not get to be Lily Black anymore? That this was over? All our work and sacrifice? How could I let my team down? My bus driver Larry was the sweetest man ever. Would he have to go back to working at that country gas station? My stylists, my road manager, my band! What would they do?

I didn't want to be the reason they lost their jobs. That wouldn't be fair. They didn't do anything wrong . . . *I* didn't do anything wrong. Hmm, I thought, maybe I could try. Suddenly, I got an idea that could fix everything.

I left the arena and basically ran to my bus, passing a parking lot full of screaming fans on the way. Being the professional I was—I'd been trained well—I dutifully stopped to take pictures and sign autographs. Since I smiled like usual, nobody suspected I was falling apart inside. And just as I was about to lose my grip, a Dixie Chick came out and stole the spotlight away from me, giving me enough time to slip away into my bus. Phew.

Logging onto my Internet Explorer on the bus, on my purple MacIntosh Notebook, I looked up 91.5 NASHVILLE and found a phone number at the bottom of the webpage.

"91-5 The Twang, what's your vote?" someone answered in a really annoying DJ-wannabe voice.

"My vote for what?" I asked, caught off guard.

"Your vote for your favorite artist!"

"Who are my choices?"

The "DJ" seemed a bit annoyed that I didn't know, but he kept on.

"Martina McBride, Tim McGraw, or Lily Black?"

Without thinking, I impulsively said, "Martina."

"Thanks. Have a twangy day," the voice said in a completely normal voice.

I hung up the phone, confused as to why I hadn't voted for myself. Wondering whom everyone else was voting for. Wondering if anyone even liked me anymore.

I speed-dialed my road manager, Teddy.

"Hello, Miss Black. What can I do for you?"

"Hey, Teddy? Can you find a phone number for me?" I said. Normally, I loved the feeling that I had someone to help me out, like I was a princess. But not that day.

"Anything you need. Who's number?"

"Dane Kimmel. He's the PD at 91.5 in Nashville."

"I'll get right on it, Miss Black."

"Thanks, Teddy," I said, getting more and more nervous.

The dial tone was extra loud in my ear. "Hello?" a lady answered, obviously not a DJ.

"Hi, this is Lily Black. Could I speak with Mr. Kimmel please, ma'am?"

"Umm, just a minute." Forty-five seconds of the worst

hold music I'd ever heard later—this was a radio station!—
Dane Kimmel answered.

"Hello?"

"Hi, Mr. Kimmel. It's Lily. Lily Black?"

"Hi, Lily. What's going on?"

If he knew why I was calling, he didn't let on.

"I just wanted to . . . you don't have to answer if you
don't want, but I was just . . . wondering why you didn't
play 'Knocked Out?'"

For a minute, I thought he had hung up. But then, he
exhaled, and I knew he was still there. I could picture
him in his office with all the posters and autographs and
records littering the walls. Magnets and bumper stickers
clung to his filing cabinets, T-shirts were stacked in the
cushy chairs, and backstage passes from hundreds of
concert experiences hung on the door-knobs. Signed
guitars sat in the corners of the room. I thought about all
the framed pictures of Mr. Kimmel and the artists who
had come through Nashville, and I remembered first
sitting in that very office, dreaming of my picture being up
on the wall one day.

That dream had come true and then some. There was
one of the two of us at my private concert at the Ryman
Auditorium, one backstage at Fan Fair (Nashville's outdoor
country festival), and if I had to guess, there was probably
one taken after my opening set at the GEC (Gaylord
Entertainment Center) on the same Dixie Chicks tour
just three months ago. The last picture was probably still
waiting to be framed. I wondered if it ever would be now.

Dane Kimmel finally cleared his throat.

"I don't think anyone has ever asked me that before."

"Like I said, if you don't want to . . . wait, *no*." I got bold.

"You promised me you'd play it. You said you just needed a couple weeks."

"Lily, it's just business," he said in a patronizing tone.

"Is the song not good enough? I can ask Jake if we can go back into the studio. Or we can give you a different song if you want."

"No, honey. It doesn't work that way. I wanted to play your song, I really did. But we have competition."

"Competition?"

"Other stations here in town. We compete with them for the most listeners. And when Martina, Faith, Shania, and JoDee's singles came out all at the same time, I had to play them first. They've been out for years. And to be honest, your song didn't beat what they had."

"But why couldn't you play mine, too? You decide what goes on the radio. And "Burning Blue" did so good!"

"Like I told you, it's business. By the time I could play it, the window had passed. Besides, I'm sure other PDs are playing it, right?"

I wanted to know more about this so-called "window," but instead I said, "Actually, no, sir. They were waiting on you."

"Really?" Dane Kimmel answered, sounding a tad bit surprised, but then again, he could have been trying to sound surprised. Mr. Kimmel was like everyone else: he treated me like I was still a little kid.

"What if we go ahead and give you another song? Any song on the album you want. You can choose."

"Like I said, it doesn't work that way."

"Why not? We have like eight more you can play."

"Lily, I think I need to explain something to you. I didn't want to have to say this, but you're giving me no choice."

I felt like I was about to be punished by one of my parents. Not my favorite feeling.

Mr. Kimmel continued. "You had a big song, and it did really well for you. But it's not going to happen this time. I have listened to the rest of the album, and none of the songs are as good as 'Burning Blue.' And to be honest, you're not testing well anymore."

"Testing?"

"Focus groups, listeners that call in . . . people aren't requesting you anymore. Look, I'm sorry I can't give you a better answer."

Don't cry. Don't cry. DON'T cry, I thought.

"Well thank you for answering my questions, Mr. Kimmel. Have a nice day," I said professionally. How, I don't know.

"Goodbye, Lily."

Lily could remain calm, but *Lilah* couldn't hold it in any longer. I took off my shoes to crawl into my bus bed and saw the faded "chick feet" I'd drawn on my foot at the beginning of the tour. The Chicks called it my initiation. I had no idea it would end so soon. Pulling myself under the peach colored quilt Mama had given me so I'd have "a piece from home," my tears hit the pillowcase. I had wanted Mr. Kimmel to change his mind; I had stupidly thought that if I could just talk to him, he would realize that he'd made a mistake. He said we were friends! And if nothing else, I expected a better reason than to beat other stations. He promised to play it, and now none of the songs are good enough? And no one requested me anymore? I knew I should've voted for myself. What was happening?

A few minutes later, my cell phone rang from the table

across the narrow bus, and I perked up. Maybe it was Mr. Kimmel changing his mind after all! I wiped my eyes and took a deep breath, snapping back into professional Lily Black mode.

"Hello?" I answered in my best regular voice.

"Hey darlin."

It was Jake, not Mr. Kimmel.

"Hi, Jake," I huffed. My throat stung from the lump that was forming.

"I just got a call from Dane Kimmel."

Oh no, I thought. *I'm in trouble.*

"Yeah?" I croaked.

"He said you called him and asked why he didn't play your song. Why'd you do that?"

"Because I wanted to know why he broke his promise. What did he say?"

"Well, he said it was fine that you called him, but that not all PDs would see it that way."

I was a swirling pot of embarrassment, pity, sadness, disappointment . . . and sheer anger. Teenage anger, even though I wasn't a teenager yet. What Mr. Kimmel had *really* meant was that it *wasn't* OK that I called him either.

"Why not? What's so wrong with me asking them? I get questions all the time. People ask me if I have a boyfriend, if I want to go to college, if I like having a preacher for my daddy—*he*, Mr. Kimmel, asked those questions on the air the last time I visited the station—and I can't ask him anything? I can't ask him why he lied to me and won't play any of my songs?"

Jake sighed, understanding my frustration but also knowing that music industry doors rarely swung both ways. "We'll try to figure something else out, OK? I'll call the label and talk to them. It will be just fine, Lily. Shh, don't cry. I'll call you later. Good luck with your show to-night."

I still had to perform—I'd forgotten all about it. And right at that moment, when I wanted to crawl under the covers and never wake up, there was a knock on the little door that separated my bedroom from the rest of the bus.

"Lily? Are you ready to start hair and makeup?" It was my makeup artist, Arielle. And there went the rest of my "personal time" for the night . . . and the rest of the weekend.

★5★

I shuddered. It was one of those memories that chilled me to the bone. To think that *that* man put the snowball in motion, that Dane Kimmel could—*would*—even do that, still bothered me like it had happened yesterday. I was a kid, for goodness sake!

But snowball it did, and the next thing I knew, I had been dropped from my record label.

"How could she be this . . . big and have the record label decide to drop her? She's got a whole lot of other songs on her album she could put out, right?" Daddy had asked Jake.

"The problem, well, there are a couple of problems. And they all stem from perception pretty much," Jake had answered. "First things first: Radio is important. Nashville radio is the most important—it's our backyard, Music City, the capital for country music. Nashville's most respected station needs to play Lily's songs in order for us to get the rest of the nation on board. I know it seems silly, but it's the way of the radio world. Dane Kimmel is the one all other PDs look to for "what to play." So if he won't play this one or the other songs on the album, no one will. Which means the album is dead. Which means the label is done."

"But what about all the money she made with the album? My daughter toured around for years and gave the label a percentage of her earnings, did she not?"

"Yes, they made their investment back and then some. But you have to understand one thing, Mr. Carson. And just so you know, I don't like this any more than you do. But your daughter, whom I love like a daughter myself, is a novelty. The music industry—here, LA . . . heck, across the world—loves novelties when they work out. But not all of them have staying power. Some of them, like LeAnn Rimes, have enough momentum to propel themselves to the next chapter, the next age, but that part has nothing to do with how sweet, how talented the child is. It has everything to do with luck, timing, and the music that happens to be out when the expiration date approaches. It's not fair, but it's reality. It's a small opening, and I want to be completely honest. Lily Black didn't make it through."

At that moment, my mama started crying. I had been asked to wait outside Jake's office, but I couldn't help but listen. When I heard my mama cry, I felt so terrible. I'd let my parents down.

Jake had gone on to explain that not all one-hit wonders were children. He mentioned songs like "Who Let the Dogs Out?" by the Baha Men, "Mambo No. 5" by

Lou Bega, and a couple other songs I'd had never heard of (as if that would make us feel any better). When you're in the middle of a storm, it's hard to feel comforted at all, especially by someone else's failures. I think it just makes you feel worse at the time.

Afterward, we drove the seven hours home in near silence, only talking about stopping for bathroom breaks and what to get for dinner. It had been the only time we hadn't stopped at Priester's Pecan Company or Clanton's Peach Park. And that's how I (who instantly demanded to be called Lilah again) knew that my world had changed.

Looking at the building for 91.5 The Twang now, I stuck out my tongue. It was childish and stupid, I knew, but it was how I felt. And honestly, I should've done it years ago. The fact that radio was still so relevant somehow pissed me off, considering I'd had unholy hopes that the old school radio business would collapse with all the new competition. No such luck.

I wondered if Dane Kimmel still had his program director title. He probably did, I thought, because he played by all the rules so much that he would keep it forever. He didn't keep promises to a pre-teen back then, which meant he definitely wouldn't keep one to a seventeen-year-old.

It was still crazy think that one person had so much power. To play or not to play. And when Dane Kimmel chose not to, every other country station had followed suit, and my career was dead in the water. Like Jake had said, perception was a one of the biggest parts of the music industry, and just like that, I had joined the ranks of "Who Let the Dogs Out."

So, I would steer clear of Dane Kimmel for as long as possible. But assuming I'd run into him eventually, I mentally tallied a mark on the name chart under "Lilah Carson" instead of my former stage name. It was very possible that Mr. Kimmel wouldn't even recognize me now. I mean, I had kind of grown into my body. I was still tall, but boys were finally taller, so it didn't look strange anymore. My brown hair had grown to be naturally wavy, and with the right Chi care and expensive hair product, it looked like a million bucks. My freckles were still there, but less pronounced, and I think they actually added to my Southern charm. Less threatening. So with a little help from a stylist—maybe not too much this time—I could really shine. That is, if I was even able to get a record deal again.

When I looked back down Seventeenth Avenue South, I realized that the radio station's building was at least four blocks away. I'd broken a sweat! But now that I had thought about Mr. Kimmel, I realized I would have to make a decision on which name I wanted to use, and soon.

To be completely honest, Lily and I had always been two different people. I was a human being with faults, insecurities, chicken pox scars, zits, and a period. Lily, on the other hand, had enough confidence to sustain an entire Girl Scout troop on a weeklong hiking trip by *themselves*. Lily had perfect pitch; never missed a note or an ad lib; had tiny, perfect pores; and was always a mature, professional woman (no matter her actual age) who had absolutely everything under control. The problem was that Lily Black didn't actually exist.

Who would I try to be this time? Perfect Lily or imperfect me? We both had our ups and downs, so why couldn't I just choose, already?

Coming up on my new home, I figured the decision,

although very important, could stand to wait one more day. I'd only been in Nashville for a couple hours.

In the elevator, my thoughts took an unexpected turn to the boy who had first let me into the building a little bit ago. He had been so cute! It had been a while since I'd felt *anything* for anyone other than Michael (my first real . . . anything), and I was delightfully excited about the prospect of having a pretty little distraction. How I would go about finding him again, I didn't know. But I had time.

As I turned the corner down the hall, I saw something at my door, but I was too far away to see exactly what it was. When I got closer, I saw that it was a *who*, not a what.

Jo-flippin-Beth. Finally.

"How did you get in the building?" I said as I got closer.

JoBeth was texting while she sat on the floor surrounded by enough bags and cardboard boxes to fill up our entire condo. I was pissed that she was so late—*five hours*—but at that moment, I was more interested in knowing if JoBeth had met my helpful hunk. *Already possessive of a new boy with no name—great*, I thought. *I'm officially desperate.*

"Someone was walking out when I was walking in."

"Was it . . . a guy?"

"Who?"

"The someone who let you in."

"Oh, it was a girl. Cute though. She looked like a potential party-thrower. Wow, it's gonna be awesome not to live at my stupid parents' house of horror. We can have boys over and drink whenever we want!"

"You did that anyway, Jobs," I huffed as I made my way through the crap to open the door.

"Ha! You're right. But this time I won't be worried about getting caught! Aren't you so glad I talked you into gettin' that fake ID?"

I rolled my eyes at my overly party-fied friend, but JoBeth didn't seem to notice. She was too busy oohing and ahhing. "OH MY GOSH, THIS IS AMAZING! I can't believe we have our own place! Ours! We can do whatever we want with it! And it looks so good. This will do juuuuust fine," she yipped as she plopped down on the futon that I had plunked down two hundred dollars for.

I hadn't wanted to be *that* roommate, the one that nickels and dimes the other—money wasn't the issue. But to keep some semblance of boundaries alive, I had agreed on giving JoBeth a rent-free situation as long as she split the groceries every week and paid for half the utilities. But that was before. *If I had known JoBeth was going to be like this, I might have made different arrangements,* I thought to myself. Plus, her parents could afford it.

"Li, what's wrong?" JoBeth asked.

"It just . . . it just would have been nice to have had some help around here. I've been waiting for hours."

"But you did a much better job without me!" JoBeth got up and ran over like Fred Flintstone to give me big bear squeeze. "I love it, I love it, I LOVE it! HEY! Why don't we go out and celebrate! I saw some good lookin' bars on my way in! There's one called Tin Roof, and this super hottie was standing outside. He might be fun," she winked.

"You want to go out? You just got here! Don't you want to—"

(I wasn't actually surprised. JoBeth *always* wanted to go out.)

"NO! Let's get out and work our legs a little bit! I've been driving all day, and I want to have some fun for once!

Whoo-hoo!"

If I hadn't known better, I would have wondered if she wasn't already drunk. But this was JoBeth. Totally high on life. Never liked to sit still or be alone. Reluctantly, I got ready to go out and "have fun," only to find JoBeth rummaging through the fridge and eating my leftover mac and cheese when I got out of the bathroom.

Let it go, I thought. *She is my best friend, and I love her.* And I did. We walked hand in hand (with our fake IDs in the other hand) to the nearest, hottest bar: Tin Roof. On the way, I thought about the half lie I'd told Mama earlier, but hushed it. *I'm a mature adult . . . practically,* I told myself.

"Holy mess!" I yelled the next morning. If my place had been small and cramped before, it was tiny now. The contents of all JoBeth's boxes and bags were strewn about, no rhyme or reason.

"What?" JoBeth slurred.

"What happened?" I couldn't help my shrill tone; I'd had little sleep, and my patience was paper-thin.

"Five more minutes," JoBeth murmured from her pillow, her hair stinking of beer from ten feet away. And cigarette smoke. And possibly, vomit.

"No!" I screamed as I dropped the laundry basket full of plastic cups and plates and towels on the floor next to her head. JoBeth shot up and gave me a drunken death stare. The look kind of freaked me out, but I chalked it up to hung over anger—who wouldn't be pissed if they were woken up with a loud bang?

JoBeth cursed, loudly.

I gave her a look.

She quickly snapped out of it. "Sorry Lilah. I know you don't curse. And I don't, either. You just scared me, that's all."

"It's OK, Jobs." I felt bad for snapping at her. She was sleeping. "It just looks like our old cheerleading squad moved in. Where did all of this *stuff* come from?"

JoBeth looked around the condo, equally surprised at the mess she'd made in the middle of the night.

"My room . . . I guess I pulled more of it out of the car last night. You know I do weird stuff when I'm drunk."

"I know, but holy mess, JoBeth! We don't have room for all this. I only brought what I *had* to bring. My makeup, hair stuff, clothes for shows, some good books, my computer, and my Bible. That's it!"

"Well, what do you want me to do? Sell it?"

"No! Just get a storage locker or something . . . and then take whatever you don't need back to Mobile when we go next time. Is that doable?"

"Yeah, I can do that. Sorry. I was just excited. And I didn't know what to bring."

JoBeth rubbed her forehead. She was definitely hung over. So I tried lightening the mood a little.

"I am kind of impressed you fit all this into your 4Runner. Well done, madam. What time did you leave the bar last night?"

"Umm, I can honestly say I don't know. I was dropped off. It was late though," she said with her eyes closed.

"Late? No, really? I wouldn't have guessed that."

She opened her eyes, looking smug.

"The question is what time did *you* leave?"

"That's easy. Midnight. On the dot."

"How did you get home?"

"I walked."

"With?"

"No one. Myself. It's right down the street. Took me seven minutes, and it would have taken less if you hadn't made me wear heels."

"No self-respecting Southern woman wears flip flops to a bar. And I thought I saw a guy with you."

"Pretty sure I was alone. Unless you count the guy you were sucking face with . . . I was with him *with you* for three hours land-locked in a booth next to the bar. You were trying to make the bartender jealous."

"Did I succeed?" She looked hopeful.

"Of course you did."

"What was the guy's name?" JoBeth tried to smile, but I saw her wince a little. Still, she was satisfied with my report. Good gracious, she stank.

"Which one? The bartender or the guy you made the bartender go crazy with?"

"Either." She threw up her hands half-heartedly.

"You swapped spit with both of them at some point before I left, so I'm sure you still have their DNA in your mouth. You probably have it in that vomit in your hair, too."

JoBeth jumped up from the futon like she'd seen a snake.

"Gross! Why didn't you tell me?"

"It blends in with all the stuff you brought." I followed JoBeth to our bathroom where she jumped into the shower.

"Could you?"

"Here . . ," I passed her shower supplies—shampoo, conditioner, body wash, a loofa, and some Clorox bleach for cleaning up the shower afterward. I left my smelly friend in peace, only to be summoned back for a towel.

I was really putting on my grown-up pants this morning, and I was proud of how I'd pulled myself back together and that I hadn't thrown up from the stench. I didn't want to fight, but I also didn't want to feel like a mother. Were we going to go out all the time now because there was no curfew, no parents, and no more grades or tests?

Not for JoBeth anyway. Forget college; I had the biggest test of my life coming up. The rest of my life. I was starting to see everything so clearly since I'd gotten out of Mobile. It probably made the most sense to go back to being Lily Black, to try to resume my old career. Eventually, when I got to my thirties, I would start *thinking* about settling down and finding a husband, then maybe kids a little while after. And if my biological clock had run out by then, who cared? Artificial insemination was getting more and more popular with stars, and I would definitely have the money. I already did.

The small town I came from didn't get me like Nashville did. Here, people were definitely Southern, but they weren't as country or as traditional—at least not in my opinion. Careers were allowed to come first here, and no one thought there was something fundamentally weird about it. People already seemed so much more city-like here, and yes, they had churches. Steeples popped up everywhere just like in Alabama . . . I hadn't left the Bible Belt yet. Nashville was considered the "Buckle"! But the difference was that I wasn't known as a preacher's daughter here. I wouldn't even have to go to church here (though I wasn't against it). I wouldn't be watched like a hawk, because people wouldn't be waiting for me to fail. Slow down . . . maybe they would run to Daddy and tattle? No, this place would be professional.

Being here might not have been my parents' (or Natalie's) idea of perfect, but it definitely had its upsides. And it catered to my kinds of ducks. Musical, record label kinds of ducks. Let my timeline commence. Yee-haw!

* 6 *

On Monday morning, bright and early, I woke up without an alarm clock. And I was ready to get to work. Slaughter House Productions would be my first stop. Since JoBeth had been out all night again, I decided to let her sleep. I would tell her all about it when I got back.

A quick bowl of Lucky Charms (I needed all the luck in the world), a cup of black coffee, and I had enough of a sugar buzz to fly to Jake's office. I liked my little place, I decided as I walked down the hall. I loved it, actually.

The elevator took forever to get to my floor, and the wait was brutal. It gave me a good long chance to worry about what might not happen with Jake, with anyone, with Nashville altogether.

How could I go back home to Mobile so soon? It had

only been one weekend! What would my parents think? They would be so disappointed in me. Not for not making it again, but for being so darn proud and renting an expensive condo in a city that hadn't asked me to come back. My parents would try to convince me to go to U of M after all. They hadn't gotten my tuition back ("just in case, sweetheart," Mama had said hopefully) anyway, so it was totally possible. And, oh, how happy they would be to have me back on "track." How could I even go—

"Well, hey there again."

There he was. The guy from Saturday. My good omen, not bad. That sugar rush might not be crashing after all. And this time, I wouldn't waste the moment.

"Hey there back," I answered with a shy smile.

"I saw you the other day. Do you live here?" he asked.

"I just moved in. Fourth floor."

"Well, lucky me. I'm on the fifth. What's your name?"

"Lilah."

"You look familiar," he said as we reached the first floor. "Where are you headed?"

"Sixteenth Avenue." I tried to sound like I was a native—or at least a college student who just switched spots from campus to a real place. Well, that part was kind of true. I *had* gotten into U of M.

"Great. I'll walk ya."

He was so cute. And charming. And as far as I could tell, he was in some part of the music business, maybe an assistant to someone. He knew all the same studios and publishing companies that I'd pointed out to JoBeth the night before. I realized I could simply ask him what he did, but I didn't want it to seem like I was just using him to have another contact. I really didn't! I wanted this—

this walking side by side, possibly turning into something more—and I couldn't let any hastiness ruin what I'd packed up and moved to a new state for. Maybe he was my lucky charm. Plus, I didn't want to ask and interrupt him while he talked about his first internships at that little publishing house over there. "Teracel," it was called back then, and he had sorted tapes for hours.

I wanted to ask if he'd sorted through "Burning Blue" and possibly couriered it over to Jake Slaughter for an artist named Lily Black, but I quickly realized that he probably wouldn't have been old enough. He looked older than I, but not that much, and I didn't remember anyone even close my age in the business back then. And revealing my stage ego was not about to happen. I wasn't ready for that just yet. First I needed to talk to Jake and get his unfiltered opinion on what to do.

"Well, here we are," he said.

I was confused.

"Did I tell you where I was going?"

"Oh, no . . . sorry. This is my stop. I am so rude. I've been going on and on, and I never even asked where you were going on Sixteenth."

"You're kidding."

"No, I really am sorry. Where should I walk you?"

I laughed; my luck was getting better by the second.

"Here. *This* is where I'm going."

"Shut up."

"I'm serious. I came to see Jake Slaughter. I used to know him many years ago. What do you do here? Another internship?"

"Oh my gosh; you're *Lily*."

"How did you—"

"I'm Owen! Owen Slaughter! It's nice to finally meet you!"

"Hi! You're Owen? As in Jake's son?"

"Guilty."

"Well, no wonder you know Music Row! You practically grew up here!"

"You could say that. I spent more time here than anywhere else. Guess you kind of did, too."

"Wow. So you work for your dad now?"

"I do. I joined the family business instead of finishing college. I manage a couple small acts on my own now."

"Oh my gosh, that's amazing! Anyone I know?"

"Not yet. They aren't signed yet. That's the goal."

"Well, you learned from the best."

"That's debatable," Owen joked. "So, what are you coming to see ole Jake for? Lodging a formal complaint?"

"Yeah, after all these years, I decided he didn't treat me right," I joked back. Owen was even more charming now that he had a name.

"So your real name is Lilah?"

"Guilty."

"I like that. Why'd you change it?"

I pointed to the sign that read Slaughter House Productions.

"Shoulda' guessed. Did he give you some bullcrap reason? Like Shania isn't Shania's real name, either?"

"It's not?"

Owen laughed and shook his head.

"Eilleen."

"Huh?" My face contorted.

"Crazy, right?"

"It is! Well, your dad was pretty straightforward. He

76

said Lilah Carson sounded like a grandmother. He was right . . . it *is* my grandmother's name. You should have seen my mama's face when he said it. She about fell out of her chair."

"He can be a little gruff. He's mellowed out a little over the years."

"Really?"

"No."

I burst out laughing, making Owen chuckle at his own joke. He got cuter by the minute!

"Well, is he around, your dad?" I asked.

"Should be. He's an early bird, unlike me," he laughed. "Come on in."

The place looked pretty much identical to when I was last there. Maybe a couple new pieces of furniture, but otherwise, it was the same.

We talked for a few minutes, and I found out why, exactly, we had never met. Apparently, Owen, who was twenty-one now, had been going through a weird phase emotionally back then. Without his mom around, he'd basically set up shop with another friend (who *did* have a mom), moved right in, and found reasons to stay for days, weeks even. Jake promised he would stop going out of town so much, but he was continually gone for three to five days out of the week, no matter what he'd said. So Owen quit believing his wheel-and-deal dad. And although Owen thought it was awesome that he worked with Lily Black, he stayed away. At the time, he had thought Jake was using my name to get him to come back home and pretend everything was all right when it wasn't. But by the time Owen had given up on his rebellion, I was back where I'd come from, and he never got the chance to even say hi.

Owen checked his cell phone. "I hate to stop this, but I have to go. I have a call in about thirty seconds. But my office is upstairs. Once you're done with Dad, come up and see me, all right?"

"I wouldn't miss the chance."

"Terrific," he said as he scaled the old creaky stairs three at a time.

Alone in the hallway, I gathered myself and finally knocked on the door of Jake's office. Game time.

"Come in," I heard a familiar voice say. Opening the door, I saw that Jake was turned around at his desk, staring at Billboard.com. Chart-watching. Charts obviously still ruled the town.

"You got it," was all I could think of to say, and an older, grayer version of the Jake I remembered froze before turning around slowly.

"Oh, my," Jake said in awe.

"You're supposed to say, 'Knock 'em dead.'" I was totally faking my confidence level. My palms were sticky and my toes were curling so much into my high heels that I almost lost my balance.

"Lily?"

"I go by Lilah now, but yes, it's me. Ta-da!" I said as I did a little pose.

"What are you doing here?"

"I think I want to . . . find . . . Lily again," I answered as I put my hands down by my side, unable to look Jake in the eye.

"Well," he said. But that was all he said, and it made me a little nervous. He was going to turn me down. Tell me to go elsewhere this time.

This was what I feared. Oh, why had I just blurted it

out? I should've learned *something* from the last time I worked with Jake. He didn't like desperation. He said it looked weak. And here I was looking as desperate as I ever had.

Just as I was about to walk out, he started talking.

"Sorry, I was just thinking. Please sit, Lilah." I did as I was told. "I think this is a great idea."

"You do? I mean, what were you thinkin' about?" I really wondered, but I was also trying to take the focus off my wobbly knees as I sat down on the couch in my yellow sundress.

I looked at the spot by my feet. It was the exact place we'd been sitting when we first heard "Burning Blue" all those years ago. That memory had once been buried so deep, but now that I was in Nashville, it felt more like yesterday, just like all the others.

"I'm just trying to think of how to spin this. He put his arms up as if tracing a headline. '*LILY BLACK: ALL GROWN UP AND READY FOR A COME BACK.*'"

"I like the sound of that. Do you think we have a shot?"

"It'll be tough to get the labels back on board."

"Why? Did they stop likin' me?"

"To be honest with ya, honey, no. They forgot aboutcha though. It's been too long. And times are different now."

That stung, but I was more curious than hurt.

"What do you mean?"

"Well, we're about to go head first into an economic crisis for starters. And the music industry is already having a rough go. Labels are cuttin' back on signing— and development deals are no more. And now there's that dang *American Idol,* which takes all the slots labels have open."

"Even in country music?"

"Yeah, they argue that even the top ten on that show have built-in audiences that they can count on. There's just no time for anyone to get good. You have to be a quick success nowadays. Shame, if you ask me."

"So it's basically a long shot?" I panicked (on the inside).

"Have you ever known me to back down from a fight?"

"No, sir." And that was true. When radio stations didn't play my song, Jake did all but ruin his relationship with the industry.

"Well, I don't intend on lettin' my little Lily Black down now!"

I sank back into the couch, able to relax for the first time in what felt like weeks. Jake Slaughter was on board. And Jake Slaughter hated losing as much as I did.

"I met Owen finally," I changed the subject, trying to enjoy my first small victory since the move.

"Oh, fantastic. He's becomin' quite the manager these days."

"That's what I hear. And I think he lives in my building off Broadway and Division."

"You live here in town? When did you move?"

"Last week." I didn't want it to seem like he was necessarily the first stop I'd made, even though he probably figured that was the case. Whom else would I go to? He'd been my only window into the Nashville music scene. My babysitter, my chaperone, even my surrogate father back then!

"Well, that's great. All right. Let's do this. Let's get back together in a few days and come up with a plan of attack. I need to put my thinkin' cap on. In the meantime, be thinkin' yourself about songs, and do your homework on all the competition. Lots has happened since you were here last. Labels'll want to know what makes you different, what makes you worth investin' in."

"You trained me well, Jake. I've already been researchin'. Can I ask you a question, though?"

"Sure, honey."

"Do you think I could do it . . . again?"

I knew I'd asked my parents, but I *really* needed to hear it from the expert.

"As long as your voice hasn't gotten any worse and you stay as gorgeous as you've gotten, I don't see why not. Have you been writing any?"

"I haven't, but I want to. I feel like I finally have something to say now that I'm a little older, you know?" Truth? I did want to, but I hadn't thought about it that much until now.

"That's what I wanna hear. That go-getter attitude! I'll get you with some co-writers in the very near future. I got some people. In the meantime, be compilin' song ideas. 'Burning Blue' is still the one to beat."

"Right, will do," I nodded. "Well, I'll be back—let's say, Wednesday-ish?"

"Perfect, and Lil—I mean, Lilah? Glad you stopped by. It's great to see you. Tell your family I said hi!"

I smiled, but I didn't want to lie and say yes to his request. I wouldn't be giving my parents a play-by-play just yet, not until I had concrete news. Career-changing news. The kind of news they could be proud of. No-college-needed news.

On my way out of Jake's office, I took a detour and stopped by Owen's office like I'd promised. Just to tell him goodbye and that I was glad to have finally met him . . . and see his adorable face.

"Knock, knock," I said as I leaned in the doorway.

Owen turned and smiled. And of course, I melted a little.

"Hey! How'd it go?"

"Pretty durn amazing. Are you slaving away up here?"

"Phone calls out my butt. But that's life when your bands need connections and have absolutely nothing."

"Sounds fun." I laughed.

"Nah, but it pays off. 'Look at the big picture, son,' Big Jake always says."

"Does he now?"

"Yeah. Hey, so, I wanted to ask you something, but I don't want you to feel obligated or anything."

"If you want me to help you make calls, I totally can. I was going to be a communications major you know—if I was going to go to school—so I can be your temporary assistant!"

Owen laughed. "No, that's not what I meant. Although, I'd love that, too. I was going to ask if you wanted to maybe go out with me sometime. I know we technically just met today, but I feel like I've known you for years."

I wasn't ready for that. Plus, I was figuring that JoBeth would call dibs on him way before I could convince Owen that I was more of his type. JoBeth had always gotten to the boys first, literally first, because she would walk right up to them and flirt, flirt, flirt. Now I wouldn't even have to worry about it! Nashville was really feeling like home— more every second.

"I think I could fit it into my overflowing schedule."

"Oh, is that right? I'd feel so honored to be penciled in

to the great Lily Black's schedule."

I walked home by myself, even after Owen protested that I shouldn't be walking alone. But he had another conference call with the members of one of his out-of-town bands, and I told him I couldn't wait around. Plus, it was daylight! I needed to get back to my place to catch JoBeth before she freaked. It wasn't that she would be mad once she knew where I'd had been, but JoBeth really wasn't a big fan of being left alone. And who would in a new city? To make it up to her, I decided to take her out to lunch, my treat. We could go to the sushi joint over on Demonbreun. It would be perfect for our first real lunch in Nashville. Support the local eateries!

On my walk back home, I tried to think more about what to say to JoBeth, but I had trouble focusing. The hot, charming guy was Owen. Owen was Jake's son. It was all too perfect.

7

JoBeth, true to form, had been more than a little peeved that I had left her alone all morning, but once the sushi arrived at our table on the patio at Sushiyobi, she seemed to change her tune a little. Phew.

"This looks nothing like what we have back home," JoBeth said, staring at our shared plate of colorful sushi rolls. I instantly knew we ordered too many. "It's so fancy! Look! This one's called 'Nashville.' I thought it was appropriate. And this one's called 'Pink Lady.' Like *Grease*!"

"It's so yummy," I said with a mouthful of the one called 'Dragon.' "I'm starved. All I had was dry Lucky Charms. I was too nervous to eat any more."

JoBeth looked up from her now cold bowl of miso soup, as if she were going to comment. So in effort to stall the inevitable, I kept going.

"Hey, see that building down the street?" I pointed.

"Yeah, what's that?"

"Remember that picture on the mantle at my house? The one of me with Faith Hill? Well it was taken there. That's Masterfonics Studio."

"Oh my gosh, can we go in there?" JoBeth was easily star-struck.

"I mean, we probably could, but she wouldn't be there. She only used that studio for that one album, as far as I know. Maybe just that song!"

"How did you get to meet her? I mean, you weren't Lily Black then, right?"

"Not yet, but my manager Jake knew her and worked with her or something, so he like called her when my mom and I were at his office for the first time and asked her if she wanted to hear the next country superstar."

"No way. What did she say?"

"Well, I guess she said yes because a couple weeks later, Jake took us to Masterfonics while she was recording 'Love Is a Sweet Thing'—remember that song?" JoBeth nodded. We knew every song of Faith's. "Her producer let me sing a couple passes of my own while Faith was eating lunch. Oh my gosh, it was so cool. Anyway, she gave me some tour T-shirts, and she taught me to wear a scarf in the studio, no matter what season."

"Why?"

"She said it warmed her vocal cords."

"Was she nice?"

"Who, Faith? She was the nicest person ever. Exactly like I always thought she would be. And let me tell you, it's not always like that. I met some people back then who were nice on TV and everything. But in person? Not so nice!" I laughed.

"Wow. I want your life."

"Oh, you've seen me in my darkest days. You do not want my life, and you know it!"

"Speaking of your life . . . since you decided to go see your old manager without me, tell me all about it," JoBeth said with a slight chill in her voice. My stalling with her always had an expiration date.

"I said I was sorry, JB. I didn't want to wake you up. You were like a brick!"

"I would have woken up for that! This is why I came, you know!"

"I'm sorry. I should have at least told you I was leaving, but you kind of looked dead to the world."

JoBeth sighed. "You should have stayed out longer last night. You're becoming quite the party pooper, you know? It's not like we're *old*. We are young and hot and we can do it all!"

"Maybe you can, but not me. If I'm really serious, I can't be out all night, drinking and ruining my voice."

"Hey! I'm serious, too. And for the record, I don't ruin my voice. Unless you count kissing boys. Come on, Li, at least find a boy to play with."

I hesitated at that. "Umm . . . I'm not really on the market these days. Like I said, I really need to focus."

JoBeth rolled her eyes. I felt a surge of guilt course through my veins, but something inside told me not to mention Owen yet. It was too soon.

"Ok, boring-face. This better not be about Michael still. It's been like six months! He was dead weight. No good for you."

"It's *not* about Michael."

JoBeth bit the side of her cheek. "Well, if you're not going to have any fun here in Nashville, at least tell me what Jake the Great said. Is he on board with resurrection of Lily Black? Or did you tell him you were thinking of going by Lilah?"

"Well, I didn't really go too much into name-changing—or changing my former stage name to my real, family name—oh, whatever. He *did* say it would be more difficult to get a record deal nowadays though. Economy and *American Idol* and stuff."

"Well, that sucks. Maybe your old name will be a help then. You already kind of have a fan-base right?"

"Who even knows? I've been so far out of all of this, my fans have probably moved on by now."

"Why didn't you send stuff out to your fans back then—telling them that you loved them all, but you needed to go back to being a kid or something? I found out you were done singing by seeing you alone at the lunch table!"

"For starters, I was only eleven and didn't even have access to my fan mail. Some department in the label handled all that and signed my name for me on all my letters. I didn't even know I had been getting fan mail until later. And secondly, I was too ashamed to face any of it. Why are you saying all of this?"

"Oh, just trying to think of ways to keep fans . . . and let them know you still value them and their support. Maybe you could've been sending out updates all these years. Then you would definitely still have the fan base you need to compete."

"Well, I can't do anything about that now, can I?"

I was . . . well, yes, I was a little annoyed. JoBeth was

talking about changing history. If it were that easy, I would go back and change Dane Kimmel's mind altogether so that he would play all of my songs and propel them to number one. *Just* because he kept his promises. If it were that easy, I would've changed a lot of things: my twelfth birthday party, the Conner twins, Amy and Lauren, my rebellious phase, my slew of terrible boyfriends, my once warm and now lonely night that I lost my V card, and eventually losing Michael *altogether*. I was sure there was plenty more I could add to the list. Sometimes, I wished I could have just skipped my teen years altogether.

"Sorry, geez," JoBeth answered defensively.

"No, I'm sorry. I just can't change it, you know? The past? All I can do is look into the future."

"Ok, I got it. No more living in the past."

"Thank you. Let's talk about something else? So, what's new with you? Have anything in the works?"

"Like what?"

"Like with your job search, what you're thinkin' now that we've been here for a couple days? What about a place like this?"

"Oh that. Mmm . . . not really. I don't think I want a serving job. Too stressful in this big city. Too many people in a big hurry. I did see a few boutique-type places up by the bars we went to the other night, but I don't know if they're even hirin'. Plus, I don't like people that much."

"You're one of the most social people I know!"

"Yeah, but serving people? Seeing fat people in the dressing room? Yuck."

"JB!"

"What? You're my BFF. If I can't be honest with you, who can I?"

I shrugged it off. Just another day in the world of Jo-Beth Miller.

"What about that bar?"

"Tin Roof?"

"Yeah."

"I want to go there, not work it! Plus, then I'd have to tell them how old we really are."

"Good point."

"Have any other ideas?"

I thought for a second. Then, going against my selfish judgment, I blurted out "Slaughter House. I noticed they didn't have anyone manning the front desk. I'll call tomorrow."

"A secretary? I was thinking of something like singing or something . . . ," she trailed off.

After a few seconds passed, and it got awkward enough, I said, "Well, maybe you can start there . . . at Jake's. He knows all the right people, and who knows? It could lead to something!"

"That's an amazing idea! You'd do that for me?"

"Of course! It's always been JB and Lilah!"

I saw the wheels in her head turning, and then she popped up in excitement. "Oh my gosh, I have the *best* idea. Probably the best I've ever had."

That wasn't the first time she'd ever said that, but I didn't mention it.

"What would you think about asking Jake if we could be a group? Like a duo? The Dixie Chicks minus one!"

I had no idea what my face was giving away, but I really hoped it wasn't showing my true feelings. Just this one time! I *wanted* to get excited about it, for her sake. JoBeth was an amazing singer, and she totally had the right look, but I had a feeling Jake wouldn't go for it. Still, I couldn't crush my best friend's all-of-a-sudden dream just yet.

"I'll ask him."

JoBeth threw her arms around me in a tight hug, and I almost fell out of my chair. "You're the best. We could be called JoLily! Or LilyBeth."

I smiled, not totally liking either name but knowing I did the right thing.

"Can I ask you one question?"

"Of course, best friend. You can ask me any question you want."

"I didn't know you wanted to be a singer."

It was more of a statement.

"What do you mean? I sang all through high school. You were the one who refused, remember?"

"I know, but I didn't know you wanted to like *sing* sing. I mean, it's great! I just didn't know."

JoBeth shrugged. "Well, now you do!" She tossed her chopsticks on the empty plate. "So, what's next on the agenda?"

We were hungrier than I thought.

"Agenda?" I asked.

"I mean, what are we doing the rest of the day, LC?"

"Please, you know how much I hate that nickname! Lauren Conrad just *had* to make *my* initials into the worst thing ever."

"I liked *Laguna Beach*, thank you very much!" JoBeth said.

"I did too, but *The Hills* is annoying."

We looked at each other and said "Heidi" in unison and laughed until our stomachs hurt. Out of the corner of my eye, I could have sworn I saw Dane Kimmel eating with someone, but I wasn't about to let anything ruin the afternoon.

"Hey, why don't we go exploring? We can drive by the studios and see if anyone famous is at Masterfonics today. Ooh, and I've never been to the Country Music Hall of Fame!"

"Me neither! Let's do it!" JoBeth said excitedly.

"Great! Check, please!"

As it turned out, Slaughter House was in need of a receptionist, part-time. JoBeth, with my recommendation, could start training next Monday. And with JoBeth set, I could focus on my next meeting with Jake, which happened to be in three and a half hours.

I had no idea what to tell him, though. Besides the fact that I was leaning toward going back to Lily Black. What JoBeth had said about me having somewhat of a built-in fan base would be a good point to raise . . . if the fan base still even existed.

Did I sound like anyone out there right now? Taylor Swift was young, too, but she was more of a self-proclaimed songwriter. Carrie Underwood was older, but a powerhouse vocalist, and was always spot on! (Hard to beat.) Kellie Pickler was also younger (not as young as Taylor, but still older than me), but she wasn't anything like me.

Coming back to Nashville as Lilah instead of Lily had some upsides. It was new, fresh, different . . . and people, the industry, and the fans wanted that, right? No, well, not always. They wanted different at the right time—not just at any moment. Case in point: how many Madonnas were out there?

Jake used to tell me that the record labels and the radio PDs, they had a job to do, too (and he said it in a much nicer way than Dane Kimmel). They sometimes couldn't afford to try something that wasn't already known to work. Another case in point: How many artists out there in the pop world tried to recreate boy bands? Girl bands like the Spice Girls? The music industry liked tried and true. They liked track records and statistics. One more case in point: Dane stinking Kimmel not playing "Knocked Out."

Coming back as Lily, I would have *some* kind of track record in my back pocket, even if it hadn't ended well. That could be blamed on age. Now that I was older, more mature, prettier, sexier (even though it wasn't something we spoke of in the Carson house), maybe someone on Music Row would see a glimpse of the goldmine I used to be.

Oh, who am I kidding? I thought. Jake Slaughter would tell me whom to be, when to be there, and what to say— and I wouldn't object for a second. Jake knew what he was doing. He was the decision-maker, and I was the talent. I could go back and forth all I wanted with this Lily v. Lilah stuff, but deep down, I knew that I wouldn't even have to ask. He would tell me before I even had a chance.

"All right: let's get to it," Jake said as he sat down at his desk, messy with EPKs (electronic press kits) and flyers and folders of all his artists. I noticed he had pulled an old manila folder with "Lily Black" written on it. The ends had curled and yellowed with time. It was nice to know that he didn't chuck it, though. Maybe that meant he still believed in me.

"That folder looks like it's seen better days," I said.

"Yeah. Unfortunately, there's not much in there we can use. The industry has changed so much even since last year, much less seven. I teach a management course at Belmont University every Tuesday and Thursday morning, and the dang textbook changes every single semester, it seems. They have to update everything. For example, marketing didn't include social media like it does now. Facebook and MySpace and all that crap. Anyway, let's get you a new folder, shall we?"

I smiled, happy to start over on some things. "Sounds good to me."

"Great. Stand up."

"What?"

"Stand up."

I did was I was told.

"Sing 'Burning Blue.' Go," Jake commanded.

"Right now? A cappella?"

"Go," Jake said again.

Here goes nothin', I thought as I stood up and closed my eyes to try to summon the right starting pitch. I hadn't even warmed up! But that didn't matter, not to Jake. You could either do it or you couldn't—black and white, no gray.

As I sang, any worry I had fell to the floor. It felt good to sing in front of someone. I was at home in Jake's office, at home in Nashville. This is where I belonged, with Jake by my side.

By the last lyric, I heard not one but two sets of clapping. I opened my eyes to see Jake *and* Owen, Owen smiling wide.

"Oh, I didn't know you were here," I said, a little out of breath and a lot flushed. "Could you hear me all the way upstairs?"

"I was walking by. You sound like absolute heaven. Even better than the recording from back then."

"I agree with the boy. He has an ear I trust."

"Thanks, Pops," Owen said as he winked at me. I blushed even more.

Jake stared at a hole in the wall behind me, and for a second, I wondered if he had noticed the tension between Owen and me. But then, he blinked and sprang into action, Gold-Miner style.

"Ok. Here's what I think. First, you're going to be Lily Black. Lilah still sounds like a grandma's name. More than ever, we need you soundin' young. Taylor Swift is out there now, and her name sounds as cool as it gets. All right, second. I think we should get you into the studio to get a version of this on tape. I like how broken down and organic it sounded just now. We don't have time to get you into songwriting at the moment—it's an undertaking—but I need something I can take to the labels *now* to get their ears buzzin' and get a couple meetings. We'll want new, original music for the showcase we'll have, but this will be good enough to start us off. Got it? Owen, get Brandon Hood on the line. Let's get a session set up. Guitar-vocal."

I (now Lily) nodded fervently saying, "Brandon Hood? I haven't heard that name in years! How is he?"

"After 'Burning Blue' went number one, his career took off. Now he owns his own publishing house and has three killer writers and a studio right off Seventeenth. You should drive by it on your way home. The Hood, it's called. Funny, ain't it?"

"You guys and your names." I rolled my eyes, respectfully, of course.

"We can't help that we have amazing last names," Owen chimed in, his seductive smile radiating into my bones. I smiled back, but quickly took my focus away from him in an effort not to raise any suspicions with Jake. I didn't want to mix business with pleasure. And Jake was business. But luckily, I wouldn't be working with Owen, so he could be the pleasure part of the deal—just not anywhere near Jake's office . . . or Jake.

Judging the room and the awkwardness, Owen made himself scarce and went upstairs to call Brandon Hood.

"I know we're about the same age, but do you think I look as young as Taylor Swift does?" I asked Jake.

"Taylor's got the young look on lock-down, but I don't think that's such a bad thing. We don't want to be copycats. You look more like a woman. A young, curvy woman. Have you ever considered modeling?"

"No!" I laughed nervously, but I was very flattered. Even if it was a fifty-year-old man who would be paid 10 percent if I did indeed model for anything. It was his job to squeeze the lemon for as much juice as possible.

"Well, I think we should aim high . . . start small but aim high. CAA's got this new department for sponsorships and endorsements. You know Faith and Tim's Soul 2 Soul tour? They got Jeep to sponsor it. Cool story actually. Faith and Tim borrowed some crew guy's old red Jeep back in '96 when they were doing a show together in Pennsylvania. And in that Jeep, they talked about their future as a couple. They had the 'relationship talk.' So Marcie Allen at CAA really nailed it. She reached out to Jeep, and now, Jeep is sponsoring the entire thing. Unbelievable, isn't it?

That said, do you have any particular products you'd see yourself endorsing? Like hair products or makeup stuff or something?"

I was trying to listen to Jake, I really was. But he'd lost me way back at Faith and Tim's Jeep. Would I ever have a cool story like that? It would be awesome to meet another artist on the road and make memories. When I was ten years old, the reality of dating was six years away, so it was stupid to even dream about it. And I couldn't have dated any of the guys on the tour anyway. They had been in their twenties and thirties, even back then. The youngest person I knew in Nashville was probably . . . Owen.

"Umm, hello?"

"Oh, sorry, Jake. Memory lane creeps back into my head a lot these days. Coming back here probably doesn't help me. Anyway, yeah, I think I could do makeup or a hair de-frizzer like John Frieda. Saved my life," I laughed twirling my long, un-frizzed, shiny brunette locks of hair.

Jake was writing every word down, presumably because he had no woman at home to tell him about beauty brands. I noticed he still didn't wear a wedding band. Speaking of love (or something like it), I wasn't sure how Jake would react if he did find out about my feelings for Owen. Sure, when we were kids, he was all for us being friends, but probably only because his wife had left a gaping hole in his son's heart. I never thought to ask Jake about the circumstances when I was younger—remember, I was ten—so I still had no clue about that whole situation. *But who would want to leave Owen?* I thought now. Not me.

"And do you have any ailments, like diabetes or anything?" Jake continued.

"Random. Are you going to have me pee in a cup for

drug testing?"

"Ha! No, no, but I sure hope you aren't doing drugs or anything. I can't imagine your ole dad would like that. I'm just thinking of all types of endorsements. You know the youngest Jonas brother is a type 1 diabetic? He's all over the diabetes websites, and I'll bet he does some national PSAs soon. Great exposure, and the way those boys' careers are going, they don't even need the extra help."

"I hate to disappoint you, but I just have plain ole allergies. Doesn't everyone in the South?"

"That they do. Or if they didn't before they got to Nashville, they will eventually. I remember when my ex started to develop them. Good lord, was she pissed. At me! That may be one of the reasons she left us," he chuckled.

I could see a little hurt—or bitterness—in his eyes, and it made me sad for him. I wondered if he still loved her, if that was the reason he hadn't remarried. I wondered if it had been something that simple and petty that had driven her away. I wondered if she had ever tried to contact Owen and make peace with him. (I wondered a lot.)

Wow, I thought. Everything kept circling back to Owen. I was acting like a lovesick puppy. I couldn't stop thinking about our upcoming date. It was still considered upcoming because we hadn't even set a time or day yet. But when I was done with Jake, I intended to change that.

While we waited for Owen to come down with a studio time, Jake laid out the beginnings of the "new Lily Black schedule": I would start taking vocal lessons with Janet Kenyon twice a week and train with a European man named Don every other morning at six. Pretty soon, I would go shopping with a new stylist to create my new image. And most importantly (to me), I would take boxes of CDs home and get ideas for songs to write myself. I needed to immerse myself in the music of the present if I was going to write. Jake ordered me to go to all the writer rounds I could. Owen would help me weed out the bad ones, and he was already going to a bunch of them anyway, so I could just tag along with him. Jackpot. Jake had no idea he was setting up our first date.

"So, tonight at the Bluebird? I've been ordered to go hear Hilary Lindsey and Gordie Sampson play, and you supposedly have two tickets for us?" I said as Owen walked back down the creaky stairs. I'd excused myself from Jake's office when he got an important call from another one of his artists.

"I guess this makes our first date for real."

"Shh! Don't say that so loud!"

"Oops, sorry. I'm excited though." He held my gaze for a couple seconds until we heard Jake's door handles and turned away from each other. "And Brandon said he could do Monday evening for 'Burning Blue,'" he said, quickly trying to cover up our moment. How sweet.

"That song's in my head all over again already, Champ,"

Jake said. "Monday night when?"

"Oh, 7:30 p.m. at his place."

"Confirm it. That's good for you; right, Lily?"

"You got it!" I responded with my usual phrase.

When Jake went back into his office, Owen and I burst into quiet laughter, doubling over in the small hallway.

"Well, should I come pick you up or would you like to meet there?" Owen asked.

"You're serious?"

"No! We live in the same building!"

"I was about to say."

"What's your unit number?"

"It's 414, but I actually don't want to mention this to my roommate. I don't want her to feel left out. She's new in town. You don't have any extra tickets, do you?"

"Doubt it. Hilary and Gordie are the best of the best these days. Major hot streaks."

"Oh, all right. Well, I'll just tell her I have a business dinner or something. Meet you in the lobby?"

"Great, and I can take you to dinner before the show if that will make you less of a liar."

"It's a deal."

On my way back home, I felt like dancing in the streets. Of course, I wouldn't—I wasn't completely nuts—but I thought about it. A "Burning Blue" remake? I hadn't even thought of it! Genius. But it didn't surprise me that Jake had. It didn't surprise me that he made me sing on the spot either. He always did that back then, when I'd least expected it. But, thankfully, I had delivered, and right in front of Owen. Two birds with one song (and I got a date out of it). A date with Owen!

If I had harbored any reservations about Jake's current relevancy as a manager (which I hadn't), they were long gone now. Jake was on it, just like he had been back then. He'd told me the same spiel that he had given seven years ago: "It's my job to get you in the door; it's yours to sing your butt off. So you just worry about that, all right?" Alrighty, then!

To have someone like Jake in my corner meant I *could* simply do as I was told. I could show up and rest assured knowing that everything was right on target, whether it be a rehearsal, a show, a night in the studio, or plane ride. He was the Gold Miner, but he was also a bit of a Willy Wonka, too.

I was very excited about the idea of writing my own songs. Hopefully, I'd end up penning *the* tune that would make me great again. I could write about growing up. About being a star and then being a nobody.

Wait, no. No one would relate to that at all. Was I crazy? Hadn't I learned anything? People want to feel included in the songs; they want to go on the ride with you. Understand, commiserate, laugh, cry, and feel with you. Wish for you.

But, sadly, that was all I had. What else did I have to offer in the way of life experience? How it felt to be screwed over by your first love? Failed relationships? When I was ten, I was just trying to hit notes and stay in tune. I learned the hand movements, how to open my eyes, how to work the stage, work the audience, make *them* feel the song. Except I'd had no idea what the song was even saying.

But when I sang "Burning Blue" in Jake's office, the whole song had sounded different. Purer, somehow. It was as if the years had packed on an edge . . . hold on, was that real emotion I heard? The song was about something real. Passion that burned so hot it burnt out. Ten-year-old me didn't know about that, but seventeen-year-old me did. Boy, *did* I.

I met Michael at a party—JoBeth had known where all the parties were, official and unofficial. Public school and private. The public school ones were always way better— more alcohol and less worry about the cops showing up, getting kicked out of school, or my daddy finding out. Michael Kimsky was a year older (a senior), and he went to the public high school, which instantly made him hotter than the boys I'd dated from my own school. I was a junior and had just recently "gotten hot." I'll never truly believe that, but whatever. Anyway, Michael noticed. He swept me off my feet in every way possible. We talked about marriage, what we'd name our kids, how he would add all of our names to each point of the massive tattoo of a cross on his upper back. Mikey Jr. and Anna Kay. Cute, huh? But everything fell apart when I found out that he'd been cheating on me with someone else.

I didn't know her apparently, and it was probably for the best, because I didn't even want to put a face with a body, the body I pictured writhing under the sheets in his stupid dorm room at the University of Mobile, the dorm room I had helped him move into . . . and decorate. Stupid.

The whole reason I had ever even wanted to attend the University of Mobile was Michael. We were going to find an off-campus place and get married when I was a junior and he a senior. Four years to the day we had met—it sounded sweet at the time. But by the time I found out about his wandering penis, I had already applied and gotten in. And like a committed idiot, I hadn't applied anywhere else.

Ever since the beginning, JoBeth told me it was never going to last. I was "too good for him." I "didn't need to settle." I was "too young for love." But until he cheated, I didn't believe her. She said she could spot a wandering eye a mile away (whatever that meant) and that I should stop sulking around and date other people. "Show him what he's missing" and all that. I tried to go out with boys from my own school again, but it wasn't the same.

Luckily, I had only seen him once since the break-up. It was Easter (just a month or so ago), and JoBeth had dragged me to a party he shouldn't have been at. Michael was just standing there with a cup of foamy beer right when we walked in, and I felt like I had been punched in the gut. He just looked at me—no smile, no nothing—then walked away. It was like he didn't have a heart, and for the first time, I wondered if it had always been that way.

That's why that national anthem felt like such a big . . . gift. Like God was giving me a reason not to have to see him in class or around campus while also showing me the anxiety I would feel every single day. The national anthem saved me—I found a new pride in it. I loved that song now.

The lyrics of "Burning Blue" popped in my head.

And we were burning blue
Fanning flames and flyin' through
Wild and all consumed by you
And we were burning, we were burning blue

Gosh, I thought, *this song was pre-ordained to fit my life in so many ways.* And it was there all along—I just hadn't

ashlyne huff revolette

taken the time to listen. All I heard was the past, the failure. But dang, this song was really, really good! *Burning so hot it burns out*. It even sounded like my career, something I was determined to undo the spell on (with Jake's knowhow) and keep burning for years to come. I stood in the elevator in my building, humming the melody, ready, itching to get back into the studio to sing it again. I was ready for my comeback. And my date.

"So, how old are you now?" Owen asked as we stood still in a long line outside the Bluebird Cafe. It wasn't moving because the first show hadn't ended yet. The nine o'clockers were outside waiting patiently, though, because nights at the Bluebird were worth the wait. Worth it to sit in the room with average-looking songwriters who wore average, department-store clothes rather than designer duds, who brought old beat-up hand-me-down guitars instead of the latest releases because they were more comfortable, like a security blanket. These regular joes and joe-ettes were responsible for most every word, every note, and every feeling in the songs that you heard on the radio that topped the charts. It was magic in there, and therefore, totally worth the wait to hear the stories behind the songs: what they were going through the day they walked in to write each one, what they were thinking about, and whom they were writing them for (the artist aside). Most times, you figured out that the best songs were not written with any artist in mind at all. It was the intimacy, the access, that made the Bluebird so incredible.

"Lily?"

"Yeah, umm, sorry. I was just caught up in amazement." I giggled. I'd never actually been here before, even though

106

I had heard about it for years.

"I asked how old you were."

There was no point in lying now . . . Jake could corrob-orate my age in a split second if Owen wanted to question my answer.

"Seventeen, about to be eighteen. Oh, and by the way, thanks for dinner."

Vague, but still true, I thought, considering my birthday was quite a ways away.

"You're very welcome. Do you—"

"Yes, I have a fake ID. Wasn't that what you were going to ask next?"

"Wow, you know me so well, and you don't even know me . . . yet."

"I know I shouldn't have one, but my friend got them for us in high school, for prom night, so we, well, now it sounds stupid . . . but we thought we could get away with anything. And I thought I was cool enough to hold my alcohol."

"Were you?"

"No." I laughed.

"Well, for the record, I am not trying to turn you in for having a fake. I just wanted to know our options for later on."

Owen reached out for my hand without looking away from me. I figured we would be kissing at that moment, maybe more if we weren't in public. But we couldn't leave the line because that would mean giving up our spot; so we stood there, gazing into each other's eyes, gulping down the butterflies toward the lust that buzzed around in our vital organs.

My lust spoke up without my approval. "And to answer

your next question—or the one you're thinking about but won't actually ask me—is no."

Owen raised an eyebrow, confused but intrigued.

"No, I *still* can't hold my alcohol," I said in a low, flirty voice. I had some game when I wanted to.

Owen's confusion gave way to a mighty, sexy smile, and he grabbed my arms, then stopped himself, and breathed out heavily through his teeth as if he was going to ravage me right then and there.

I felt my "preacher's daughter-ness" wag its finger of disappointment at me, but I'd blocked the guilt and shame before, and I could do it again. For someone this attractive? Heck, yeah, I would. It felt good to be wanted by someone I wanted in return. Someone who knew me as a person, knew my true circumstances, knew about my past, and still wanted me. Good gosh, I was tempted to drag him away from the line, lie to Jake about seeing the show, and let him have me in the backseat of his car. We couldn't go back to my place. JoBeth couldn't know about us, not yet. We could go to his, but what if she saw us in the hall or elevator? No, we couldn't risk it.

"Oh good, the line's moving," Owen said. The buzz was fading, but only because we had a show to catch. Probably for the best, I thought, because I really didn't want to have to lie to Jake. Nothing good ever came of lying.

"So, how was your meeting last night? It went late," Jo-Beth said as she folded up her blanket on the futon, one of her morning routines since her "bed" doubled as the only proper place to sit in the condo. I needed to go shopping again.

"It was great. We went to the Bluebird after the dinner to check out some writers."

I couldn't lie, but I didn't have to give all the details. Privacy wasn't a sin, was it?

"The Bluebird?"

"Yeah, you know, the place where songwr—"

"I know what it is. I'm not dumb."

I looked up from the coffee maker at JoBeth, who had a terrible look on her face. A look of disappointment.

"I'm sorry, JB. I promise to take you next time. Last night was kind of last minute."

JoBeth said nothing. Instead she passed right by me to make her cup of coffee in silence. Hmm.

"Are you ok?"

"I'm fine," JoBeth answered coolly. She was obviously not fine.

★ ✦ ★ ✦

JoBeth started her job as a receptionist/assistant at Slaughter House the same day I was scheduled to go The Hood to rerecord "Burning Blue" with the original songwriter, Brandon Hood. It should've been a happy day, but it was strained.

I couldn't figure it out, but ever since "the Bluebird incident," JoBeth had barely said anything to me beyond one-word answers. What had I done that was so wrong? The Bluebird wasn't somewhere I had *ever* heard her talk about, so why would she care about not going? She loved music and singing, but I didn't think she gave one hoot about songwriters. JoBeth was into the glam, or the glam she thought existed. I hadn't exactly gotten around to telling her that the music business was the opposite of glam. I figured what was the point?

Could she know about Owen? And why would it even matter if she did? I'd had boyfriends before, and JoBeth had never cared one bit. Like Michael, for example. JoBeth had always said he was so cute (a blind person could see how hopelessly adorable he was), but she had always loved—well, accepted—that he and I were together. Plus, she had always had enough boys of her own.

And that's why I didn't mention him, right? Because JoBeth got everything. All the guys, just by default, just by being there. Just by saying hello. She was just so darn flirtatious, and the boys just ate it up. Except for Michael. And what was wrong with Owen being my little secret for a couple of weeks? Nothing. It wasn't like I was telling everyone but her. I wasn't ready for Jake to find out yet, either. I wanted to keep things professional (or look like they were anyway.)

But I had another problem at hand. A bigger one. I had forgotten to mention anything to Owen about JoBeth, about her being the friend I'd ever so briefly referred to before our date. And I hadn't mentioned that the same friend was going to become the new receptionist at his office, either. And now JoBeth and I were walking together toward the office, like two schoolgirls. Like the old days, and yet nothing like it at all. At home in Mobile, JoBeth had been the one to bring me into the fold. Now it was the other way around. Here in Nashville, I was the popular kid in school, and JoBeth was the new girl from a different city. Well, sort of. She was more like the hot, could-flirt-with-a-brick-wall, talented new girl. And instead of feeling good about it, I was freaking out.

By the time I even started to think of ways to cover my butt, we were walking through the front door of Slaughter House Productions.

"This is nicer on the inside than outside," JoBeth said, the first full sentence she'd spoken all morning.

"The nicer the outside, the more temptation for people to want to break in or something. Most of the places out here are studios with lots of expensive equipment and whatnot."

"Uh, are we in a bad part of town?"

"No." It was a struggle not to roll my eyes. We stood awkwardly by the old dusty desk in the foyer.

"Let me go get Jake so you all can get acquainted," I said as I turned away from JoBeth toward Jake's office.

"Is there like a studio in here?"

"For what?"

"You know, recording. I've always wanted to hear what I sounded like."

"No, that's at a recording studio. This is a management office."

"Sorry. Some of us didn't get to be a superstar before they grew boobs."

She was pissed. I was pissed. But before I could say anything to diffuse the situation, Jake burst out of his office with a giant BMI mug of steaming black coffee, probably his third or fourth of the day already.

"Morning!"

"Hey, Jake. This is my friend from Alabama, JoBeth. JoBeth, this is the infamous Jake Slaughter, manager extraordinaire."

"Nice to meet you, young lady."

"You, too, Mr. Slaughter. Thanks for the job. I hear you're known as the Gold Miner around here?"

A JoBeth specialty: turning up the charm around adults.

"Once upon a time. And thank your friend here." He motioned toward me. "She argued on your behalf, said we needed help around this ole place."

I *had* argued with Jake, but I regretted it a little now. She was kind of being a brat.

"Thanks," JoBeth said with a half smile as she barely turned toward me. What was her problem? She was never this moody.

"No problem!" I said, though I really thought it was kind of becoming one. "Well, Jake, I'm going to head back to rehearse for this evenin'! Feels like yesterday you gave me that work tape to go practice with!" I laughed, trying to get the heck out of the office.

"Owen's upstairs. I know he'd like to see ya. He said y'all had a great time the other night. Learn anything from the writers?"

"Oh my gosh, they were amazing. Definitely inspiring. I'm definitely interested in setting up a time to write with that guy you mentioned. Definitely."

"Clint. Yeah, he's great, too. I'll give him a ring and put a bug in his ear. He's super busy, so we'll have to wait a while, but it'll be worth it. Trust me."

"Whatever you say! Well, you guys get acquainted! JB, don't let Jake push you around!"

And there it was again, that half smile. Someone had obviously woken up on the wrong side of the futon.

"I'll send Owen to the studio tonight," I heard Jake say as I was one foot out the door.

"All right." I waved as nonchalantly as I could, knowing it was only a matter of time before Owen bounced down the steps and laid his dreamy eyes on a blonde Southern beauty. And suddenly, I was embarrassed to realize that I didn't want to be there to see it . . . or be compared to.

Some insecurities never died.

Outside Slaughter House, I took a deep breath and walked back to my place, even though all I wanted to do was turn around and see if Owen was in the window, beckoning me to come upstairs for some reassurance and a couple kisses like some a weird (and hot) reversed version of *Romeo & Juliet*.

★ ⋆ ★ ⋆

Two hours later, my phone buzzed from inside my purse. Owen.

But when I looked at the screen, it said "MAMA & DADDY." I had barely even called them since I'd gotten to Nashville, something I wasn't necessarily trying to do, but still, it had happened. Oops.

"Lilah! How's the big city?"

"Hey, darlin!"

(They always called together.)

"Hey, Mama! Hey, Daddy! All's good. How's the small town?" I joked.

"We're managin'. The house sure feels empty," Daddy said.

"I was going to be movin' into the dorms anyway!"

"Your daddy's just kiddin' around. We do miss you though—"

"So how's everything goin'? How's JoBethie-Beth?

How's your place?" he jumped back in. He had more energy than my niece!

"How much coffee have you had?" I laughed. "Everything is good. Jake is gonna work with me again, which is good. My place is gettin' there—haven't had much time to spruce, but so far, JoBeth is the messy one out of the two of us!"

"Is she with you now, honey? You shouldn't say things like that," Mama warned.

"Mama, re-lax. I got her a job at Jake's, answerin' phones and stuff."

"Oh, oh. I'm sorry. Well, that's good. Very nice of you to take care of your friend like that."

I rolled my eyes. "Yeah, I guess. She's been actin' a little strange though."

"How so?" Daddy asked.

"Just moody and stuff ever since we got to Nashville. And she's all of a sudden gung-ho about us starting a band."

"A band?"

"Well, a duo thing," I mumbled.

"Do you want to?"

"It's not that I don't want to, but I don't know, Daddy. It could get complicated—"

"Lilah? If I may, could I say something?"

"Sure." He didn't have to ask, but he always did.

"You don't have to want to sing with her just because she's your best friend."

"I know, but I feel guilty!"

"You can be friends and not do everything together. Just don't make any decisions now. You just got there."

"OK," I sighed. I totally trusted him, but *he* didn't

have to break that news to JoBethie-Beth. Easier than it sounded.

"She also might be moody 'cause she's homesick," Mama said. "This is the longest she's ever been out of Alabama, I bet. You remember how tough it was for you to get used to bein' in Nashville and goin' on the tour bus all the time. You would cry and cry."

"I was *ten*, but thanks. Maybe I'll find us Cracker Barrel. Comfort food always helps, right?"

"Sure does!" Daddy chimed in.

"That's a great gesture," Mama said. "Well, I'm gonna go lie down. I love you, Lilah Marie."

"What's wrong, Mom?" I asked, but my dad answered instead.

"She didn't sleep well last night."

"Because of me?"

"Oh, no, no, sweetie. Her back was givin' her some trouble's all."

"You sure?"

"Yeah! But while we're on the subject, are you still happy?"

"We aren't on the subject, Dad!"

"Just humor your old daddy, huh?"

"Yes, I'm still very happy. I love it here."

"Just making sure cause you don't sound like my little girl today."

"Just the JoBeth stuff, I guess."

"OK. Well, be sure to tell ole Jake we said hello. And your mama and I are hopin' to find a time to come up there and catch a show or somethin'. Love you, Lilah."

"Oh, about that . . ."

"Back to Lily?"

"For now, yeah. Jake's orders." I giggled.

"I'll tell your mama, but you know her. It'll take her three whole years 'fore she gets it right."

"Haha, she *finally* called me Lily when I was a sophomore in high school!" I laughed.

"You were mad as a hornet. You didn't want to hear that name ever again. You *yelled* and everything."

"I was a little bit dramatic that way."

"Nothin' like your sister was."

"Oh, Daddy. I miss you."

"We miss our favorite daughter, too, honey," he joked. "Call Nat soon. She's been asking aboutcha."

"Why hasn't she called me again since I got here?"

"Said she wants to give you space, let you get settled or whatever. So, just call her when you're ready, all right?"

"Was that Judd's idea?"

"He told her she could be a little overly maternal sometimes."

"He told her she could she could be a little overly maternal. And then! Then she punched poor Judd in the arm and blamed the burnt brownies on *him*!"

"What?"

"Well, she got so mad when he said she was too maternal that she left the kitchen and forgot all about finishin' dinner. So the brownies burned and set off the smoke detector. She blamed it all on poor Judd!" he cried out.

"Some things never change. Hopefully, Summer-Sault wasn't there."

"Oh yeah, she saw the whole thing. Now she asks why Natalie 'buwwnt the bwownies.'"

Daddy and I laughed until our bellies ached, and when it was finally time to hang up, I suppressed the tiniest bit of homesickness I felt. I had a hit to remake.

★ 9 ★

The Hood was shiny, new, and way more my style than Slaughter House, probably because Brandon Hood was only in his early thirties. He'd been really young when "Burning Blue" made it big.

"Lily?"

"Mr. Hood?"

"Brandon, please. 'Mr.' makes me feel so old."

"Sorry, old habit."

"Gosh, last time I saw you, you were what . . . eleven?"

"Barely. Looks like you've been doin' all right." I looked around. "This place is awesome!"

"Pays the bills," he said.

"And then some, it looks like."

"Do you need any coffee? Tea? Throat Coat? Honey?"

"Some tea and honey would be great. Thanks."

"I see you have your scarf on. Just like back then. Who did you say taught you that trick?"

"Faith Hill."

"Oh yeah, that's right. She's cut a couple tunes of mine, thanks to you."

That made me feel good. At least my short career helped someone else back then. Look at him now!

"I intend to repay you someday you know," he said as we walked back to the kitchenette.

"For what?"

"Giving me all this. If you hadn't gotten my song—"

"Someone would've discovered it, Brandon."

"Well, actually, I sort of snuck my work tape into your pile. I mailed it insinuating that it was from a signed writer from Sony."

"Wait, you didn't write for Sony?"

"Well, I *did*, but I had been dropped from Sony months before I wrote it. And my girlfriend broke up with me as soon as I lost that job, saying I had no future. I oughta thank both of them now, I guess."

"Why?"

"Well, since I didn't write it during my short stint at Sony, I owned one hundred percent of the song, which meant I made all the money from it. And, *she* was the one I wrote it about."

"That's funny. I never considered it being about a girl. To be honest, I didn't even know what it was about when I sang it," I said.

"I never thought you would actually cut it. And I had no idea who Jake was pitching it to at the time. I just tried to find any way I could to get my song heard. It was my last shot at being a writer—I thought. It's crazy what you'll do when you get desperate."

"Well, I'd say your plan worked. Did you know I was just a little kid when you heard the song all finished?"

"Not at first, no. Ha! You sounded so mature. Here's your tea and honey, madam. Let's go back into the vocal booth and get you set to rock, shall we?"

"Are you OK to redo it all over again?"

"Are you kidding? This song is my baby, my first number one; I've missed her! Owen said you wanted a stripped-down version of what you did back then? Guitar-vocal?"

"'Organic' was the term Jake used," I joked.

"Oh, I hate when people use that term. It means nothing and everything at the same time. Sometimes 'organic' means that a producer won't put as many instruments into the song, and people are so wowed. But to be real, sometimes that means they just didn't have any more ideas!"

"Do you think this will be all right soundin'? Just me and a guitar?"

"Oh yeah, this will be magic. If you're anything like you were back then, your voice will sell the words and make it where you don't need nothin' else on the track."

"Isn't that lazy?"

"Not if it's good. I think each song should be treated differently. Some songs need a full band, lots of BGVs (background vocals), overdubs, auto tune—if the singer can't sing—and sound effects. Some don't need a thing . . . and for those, all the bells and whistles can actually hurt the end product."

"And here I was thinking it had something to do with me!" I laughed, realizing how much I didn't know about the music industry.

"It does. It does. But sometimes other factors and egos can get in the way."

I know about egos, I thought. Speaking of egos, I hadn't run into Dane Kimmel just yet. But I was sure the time would come, and when it did, I would be ready. Cue the *Rocky* theme song.

Owen arrived as we were wrapping up for the night.

"Well, hey there," he smiled at me, and of course, I instantly blushed.

"Hey, man," Brandon stood up to shake hands, "Take a seat. We were just about to listen to a rough comp."

"Studio lingo . . . you'll have to dumb it down for me. I'm just a manager, you know." Owen winked at me. Blush.

But Brandon didn't skip a beat. "Sure thing, O. It's a rough compilation of all Lily's vocal passes she sang tonight. See, on the computer here," he pointed to a screen that was filled with different colored sound waves, "all these are times she sang the song. Then I go in and choose the best word from all of them and make a rough comp—which, as I said, is short for 'rough compilation.' Later on, I'll clean it up so that it can be mixed."

"You do that with every word?" I asked, shocked.

"Every syllable."

"Whoa, that sounds like it would take forever."

"It's a bit tedious, but it's worth it in the end. And I like it for whatever reason. It's like a big game of Tetris—does that show my age? Anyway, it can be challenging with most singers—but not Lily. She probably had it perfect by the second pass, but she insisted on going until she got hoarse."

"Perfectionist," I copped.

"Can I hear what you got so far?"

I made a face, unsure if I was ready to hear it myself— much less let the boy I was kind of dating hear all my clunkers.

"Yeah! Keep in mind, it's not finished yet," Brandon warned.

"Oh, sure. I bet I'll love it," he smiled.

I smiled back, calmer. And when Brandon swiveled his leather boardroom chair around to press play, Owen reached out and held my hand. He didn't even take it away when Brandon turned back to listen.

Once we heard it, Owen started clapping, giving me a standing ovation in the middle of the tracking room. It was a little embarrassing, but I was thrilled he liked it for two reasons: First, because I liked him. A lot. Second, if *he* liked it, Jake would. And if Jake liked it, maybe, just maybe, I had a chance.

"You wanna go somewhere?" Owen asked me as we walked out of the studio still hand in hand. It was dark, and I was instantly relieved he was there to keep me safe. I hadn't thought about how long it would take when I'd walked there earlier.

"Like where?"

"My place?"

I knew what that meant, and I *liked* what that meant. I was interested . . . really interested. But I needed to call JoBeth and make sure she was fine to get her own dinner. I would promise a Cracker Barrel breakfast for tomorrow to make it up to her. Hopefully, that would buy me some time.

"Let me just call my friend first, OK?"

"JoBeth?"

"Yeah, how was she today?" I pretended to be nonchalant about it.

"Oh, she's fine. Just learning her way around. Dad's never had a proper secretary, and I don't know if he really knows what to do with her." He dropped my hand to get out his smart phone and return a quick email. Music was seriously 24/7.

I wanted to ask if he thought she was pretty, but I said nothing. Not the time.

"Hello?" JoBeth answered, sounding a little less crabby, thank goodness.

"Hey, girl! How was your first day?"

"Good. That office is in the dark ages. And that chair sucks. But Jake and Owen were nice."

I had to cut to the chase.

"That's great to hear. What are you doing tonight?"

"I'm out walking, trying to get the lay of the land a little. I met some Belmont students earlier."

"Boys?"

"Why, of course! But they all wore super tight jeans. One of them said his were women's jeans! I don't know, it could be creepy, but maybe it's hot."

I rolled my eyes. Finding a silver lining for the male species was JoBeth's real calling in life. She could find any reason to like a boy. Too bad it wasn't an actual profession.

"Well, be careful walking around at night. What are you thinkin' of doin' for dinner?"

"Oh, I don't know, what about you?"

"I . . . I'm not hungry just yet, so I'm going to explore a little myself. Maybe I'll run into you later?"

"OK, that's fine." JoBeth seemed a tiny bit disappointed.

"Hey, JB?"

"Yeah?"

"How about Cracker Barrel tomorrow mornin'? My treat?"

"Fine."

"I promise we'll spend more time together. I know I've been a little busy."

"A little? You've been avoiding me since we got here."

Oh, boy; here we go, I thought.

"Jo, of course I'm not avoiding you. I just work." I walked a little further away from Owen, feeling my face warm up.

"You swear you're not hungry?"

"Huh?" I was confused.

"I mean, you swear you're not avoiding me?"

"YES! YES!"

"OK," she said after a second. I couldn't tell if she believed me or not. "Bye."

And we hung up.

"You're not hungry?" Owen said as I walked back to him. Now *he* was confused.

For a second, I had forgotten he was there. I hoped he didn't hear the petty girl argument we'd had, so I kind of changed the subject.

"I don't know if I'm hungry for just *anything.* Are you a good cook?"

"Do you like Ramen noodles? Chicken flavor?"

"Mmmm, sounds nutritious."

"I'll eat anything after a good workout." He smiled, his

eyebrows rising, and he kissed me. Holy crap.

"Did you want to get that workout in now, or . . . ," he said in between long, drawn-out kisses. They were the kind you saw in romantic comedy movies. The kind that made you *want* a boyfriend. But I was that girl!

"YES!" I panted, out of breath. And just like that, I let myself be led to apartment 503.

Sunday school, the Bible, the teachings at Cherry Hill, and my parents all told me that I wasn't supposed to have sex before marriage. "Pre-marital" was the term they used. And maybe it was all the repetition, but I always felt consumed by guilt and shame immediately after sex. I knew it was a rule for a reason, but I had already broken it before—back in high school during my token rebellious preacher's daughter days—so what was the harm in doing it again? It wasn't like I could reclaim my virginity or something, so I might as well enjoy myself, right? Then why all the guilt?

I probably wouldn't have even done it in the first place had it not been for Michael. Before him, I'd been pretty inexperienced, and I probably still would be today had I not *truly* believed that he was the one. Not like the "one" silly girls gushed about in stupid TV shows. Like, the actual one.

I wondered now, after all that happened, if Michael only talked about getting married because he knew I would let my guard down. And if that was the plan, it worked. He had been so gentle, so sweet, and I hadn't thought for one second that I was doing anything wrong. How could it be wrong if it was true love? That's what marriage was, right? Love and commitment. I'd had both—I thought. All I was missing was a piece of paper (and a ring), but in my mind

I was as good as Mrs. Michael Kimsky.

After my first time (not his), I'd promised God that I would marry Michael, so it really wouldn't be considered "pre-marital" in a few years. I thought maybe it would cancel out. But once I found out that he'd cheated, I couldn't help but think it was some sort of punishment for breaking the rules. You don't get to bargain with God.

I was a mess for weeks, months, but after a little while, I realized I couldn't take back what happened, so I let it happen again. And then again with another boy—it was Senior Slide. And now, here I was again, with Owen. Being craved by someone, that was my favorite part, usually, but with Owen, it was different. With Owen, I felt more like I had with Michael. I actually wanted to be with him, for me. Finally, I thought, I was getting something and someone I wanted. And judging by what had just happened (and his enthusiasm), he really wanted me too. Michael who?

Owen was really good at it. He knew how to make me feel special and said all the right things. And the Ramen noodles were better afterwards, just like he'd said.

"I still can't believe we never met," I said when we were wrapped up watching Jay Leno's "Headlines."

"I know."

"You seem tired."

"I am. Sorry. Long day."

"Are your bands getting somewhere?"

"Slowly but surely. I hate Mondays."

"Well, maybe now you can hate them a little less?" I was thinking how much more I loved Mondays with our new potential tradition.

Owen yawned and smiled tiredly.

"Maybe I should go. You need some sleep."

He didn't argue. He only said "OK," which wasn't exactly what I had hoped for. I kind of wanted him to maybe fight me just a little, beg me to spend the night, maybe, even though I really did need to get back downstairs before JoBeth suspected anything.

The next few weeks were uneventful, in a sense. JoBeth worked at Slaughter House while Jake and I checked everything we could off the list to get me ready to play a showcase for record labels. A stylist named Darla owed Jake a favor, so she took me shopping in Green Hills for some new stage clothes. She told me the ones I'd brought from Alabama were "fine," but we wanted better than fine, didn't we?

Besides my school uniform (which I'd joyfully burned the last day of school at the senior bonfire), I basically only wore one thing when it was nice out: Sundresses. I had lots of them, in every color. It's what I wore to church back home. It's what I wore out to the bars, too. It was what I liked, felt comfortable in, what I felt confident in choosing without the know-how of a stylist. My sundresses were cute, no doubt, but Taylor Swift wore sundresses, which meant they had to go.

When I was ten, I didn't really need a signature "look." My young age did the trick. But that signature had fully expired, and the new Lily Black had to stand out.

Shopping could be fun. But it was a whole new ballgame with a stylist. I swear, I had never tried on that many pieces of clothing in one day. Darla kept passing more and more over the dressing room doors in every store and literally asked to see every top with every bottom before she made any decision on what to keep and what to chuck. I'll stick to singin', thank you. It was long, but five hours later, my new Lily Black look was complete.

I would always wear darker clothes from now on, for three reasons. One, it would accentuate my lean, feminine figure. Two, it would contrast with my porcelain skin. And three, it would automatically make me look different than Taylor Swift. That was the key, to differentiate. I would wear only high heels, no more flats or cowboy boots. I needed to be seen as a woman, not a girl, and high heels could make that happen instantly. I had never really worn heels because I'd had always been so tall, taller than the boys, sometimes. But once Jake reminded me that Faith Hill was also tall (and wore heels), I started working on my balance. Books on the head, the whole nine yards.

My hair would be styled in one of two ways. During performances, it would always be worn down, straight and sleek, for more drama. During red carpets, interviews, etc., it could be pulled back into a low ponytail or a high bun. Anything but big curls was fine, because big curls made me look younger, and not in a good way—not for Lily Black purposes.

My jewelry would be sparse but effective. Instead of big, flashy, dangling earrings, I would always wear classic diamond studs. My rings and bracelets would be simple: silver or black and always with just enough bling to sparkle in the light while I held my microphone. There was only one piece of jewelry I was required to wear during every performance. A local designer had handcrafted a one of a kind necklace specifically for me. It was a cross, made from black Swarovski crystals, and it was the perfect amount of boldness and style. My stylist referred to it as the glue that held the new "Lily Black brand" together. It was true, it was amazing, and it was totally me.

And, last but not least, my makeup. I had never worn a lot of it on a regular basis, but the new me would wear it, and always in a particular way. My eyes, like my wardrobe, would have a darker, smoky look to contrast with my pale skin. Not so dark that I looked gothic, but enough to pop, especially on stage. My eyeliner would be in the shape of a cat eye. It would further complement my big blue eyes and create a subtle drama. (Drama, in the right amount, was always good.) Bronzing powder and blush would be used minimally for contouring, because too much bronzing would fight my natural skin tone. And the biggest adjustment for my Chapstick-wearing self was my new lip shade: crimson red.

According to Jake (since I could never say this with a straight face), the new Lily Black, Lily 2.0, was hot, sexy, and a full-blown woman who wasn't afraid to strut her stuff. I didn't know about strutting my "stuff," but I definitely felt a lot more confident and a lot more beautiful. Needless to say, Darla got the job, full-time.

Jake and Owen put the word out at Belmont University and Middle Tennessee State University that a "young, hip" country band was needed. What they *didn't* advertise was that they needed to be cheap, but with college kids without a union affiliation, it apparently wasn't bound to be an issue. "Those kids are paid in opportunity—and that's priceless," Jake said.

The audition was packed with musicians, all with a great deal of talent. That was how Nashville was:

ridiculously talented. Most, if not all, were well trained and disciplined, and the others were just plain "naturals." And that made it especially difficult for me to narrow it down. All I could decipher was "cute" and "not so cute" . . . and none of them compared to my Owen. Jake, on the other hand, had a very specific vision of what the band should represent. For him, it wasn't as much about their ability-level as it was about their stage look.

Jake wanted edgy. Not necessarily "LA edgy," but country music, Nashville edgy. Most of all, he didn't want the band I had last time: a hodge-podge of young and seasoned guys. No rhyme or reason, no uniformity. I'd nodded in agreement, but I honestly thought my band *did* have a theme back then: old.

After the audition, Jake and I sat in the empty rehearsal hall with a list of the top players.

"The band should be an extension of you, Lily, and an extension of your new, older, more sophisticated brand. Your new wardrobe? *That's* the look, the feel we're shooting for! And we got 'em. Lily Black is going to rival the likes of Shania Twain!" Jake said.

And I liked the sound of that, even if it did mean pushing the boundaries. I was getting used to that, and I wasn't as safe as I looked. My brunette hair would only set me apart even further from the brood of blondes like Taylor, Carrie, and Kellie.

Jake kept talking about how I could be an even bigger star this time around, how we could explore avenues of branding outside of music, like a fragrance, a clothing line, or shoes . . . the sky was the limit. And that was great, but I had really stopped listening at the name "Shania." She had been my lifelong dream since . . . ever. When the other little girls wanted to be Disney princesses, I had dressed up as Shania, and now, I was actually going to get to *channel* her! For my job!

Surrounded by all the new Lily 2.0 ruckus, I still found myself feeling guilty I hadn't gotten around to at least mentioning JoBeth's duo idea to Jake. No, I didn't want to do it, but I promised her—kind of—that I would look into it.

I finally worked up the nerve one day when JoBeth was out of the office running an errand.

"Hey, Jake? I got a question."

"Sure. What's on your mind?"

"Umm, well, it's about JoBeth?"

He made face, but I didn't know what to make of it.

"She's a really good singer . . . ," I started, trying to make sure I didn't show my true feelings until he gave his two cents.

"Is she?"

"Yeah, and I think she's possibly wanting to . . . maybe . . . do a group thing? Like a Dixie Chick minus one." I couldn't think, so I used her description.

"No," he said without any hesitation. I was a little relieved, but I still asked him why he thought so.

"Unless you're willing to give up everything you've worked for, back then and today, I don't think you need to entertain it a second further."

"OK," I answered. But he kept going.

"I like your friend. She's good at running the place and gettin' me up to speed with all these shared calendars and stuff. But she's a wild one. Comes in some days lookin' a little worse for the wear, if you know what I mean. You're not out with her every night are you?"

I noticed he didn't mention anything about her being too young to drink, and I was grateful. I didn't want the conversation to go there.

"I couldn't if I wanted. Don's 6:00 a.m. workouts make me want to barf as it is." That was unfortunately true.

"Good, good. Well, it's a no for me on old Jo. Sorry kiddo. If she keeps on the ways she's goin', she's a train waiting to wreck. I see it all time. You know better than anyone, this business takes a lot more than just talent."

And that was that. He moved right on to the next item of business without so much as taking another breath. And I already dreaded breaking the news to her, but I literally didn't have time to think about it right now. Jake was already talking about my showcase for all the labels in town. He decided it would be held at Twelfth and Porter downtown. Some acts did theirs at soundstages like SIR or Soundcheck where they rehearsed, but Jake said that mine should be more intimate, more like a real show to set me apart, a running theme. And having an open bar helped—record execs seemed to stick around when there was alcohol. The show was tentatively set for July, August, or even September, depending on when Jake felt the labels' interest was strong enough. If they seemed lukewarm at the prospect, he would postpone the show until the temperature changed.

"We only have one chance . . . well, one more this time. And it has to blow 'em away. You're not a child prodigy anymore. You'll either blend in with the Carries and Taylors, or you'll stand alone. We have to make sure you stand alone."

With a new band, a new wardrobe, and a targeted image, "standing alone" seemed as though it would be easy. But for some reason, my doubts rushed in. The voices in my head screamed "You've failed before and you'll fail again," "You're not as talented," "You're not a true musician like Taylor," or "It's been too long, you're a has-been," And the worst ones were "You should just go to college and forget about all this," "Be a good daughter and quit," and "You don't belong here."

I knew it was the devil trying to break my spirit, my confidence, my will. When things were good, there he was, always trying to ruin everything. And I also knew that no matter how much that devil tried, I would *not* be moving back home, even if my pride was the driving force. Either way, the devil would not win. I was doing this.

But ironically, when those doubts crept in, I got homesick, of all things. And when I got homesick, I liked to talk to someone *from* home. I rarely had to even pick up the phone, though, since my parents called like clockwork, every six or eight hours, always on speaker with both of them yelling into the phone, always just being themselves, the salt of the earth. But when the ESP didn't happen one day, I decided to call Natalie instead.

Before Nat could even say hello, I heard Summer running through the house in the background, screaming.

"What did you do to my niece?" I gasped, joking.

"She just saw *E.T.*"

"That movie still scares me."

"Oh, well Judd thought she would be fine. I told him he gets to deal with the nightmares."

"Serves him right."

"Amen. So, how's everything? I hear you're movin' right along? How's your place?"

"My place is gettin' there, thanks to your tips. And yeah,

I guess. I have a couple things in the works. Showcase for labels comin' up in a month or so."

"Good. I want to come see what you've done with the place soon, but Summer has vacation Bible school in a few weeks. What's the hold up?"

"Hold up on what?"

"On the showcase? Why a couple months?"

"I need to practice with my new band, for one. And I have to get more original songs so we have more to play at the showcase. . . ."

"You gonna write one this go 'round?"

"That's the plan. I want to write. I always have." I paused, doubting myself again. "But what if the song is bad?"

"You never know till you try. Boy, do I sound like Mama, or what?" Natalie laughed.

"Sometimes I wish all I wanted to do was to go to college and be a kindergarten teacher. Like you."

"What's that supposed to mean? Don't get all Lily Black on me now."

"Oh, shut up, Natalie. I didn't mean it in a bad way. I just wish my dreams in life weren't so complicated."

"Who said being a kindergarten teacher was easy?" Natalie's vocal pitch raised.

"No, Nat, I never said that either. Would you just calm down?" My voice matched hers in intensity. "I mean there are steps to your job, obvious ones. If you go to this school for four years, pass these tests, you get into this master's program. If you get a job, you are a teacher. There are just no steps to mine. It's all about luck, timin', and who you know."

"But I thought you knew everyone."

"I thought so, too, but apparently, seven years is an

eternity in the music business. I don't feel like I know anyone."

Natalie was quiet for a few seconds.

"Come back to Mobile then. We miss you. Summer misses you." Thank goodness she'd calmed back down a little bit.

"I miss y'all too, but I can't be a singer there. Gigs at Felix's are hardly considered 'makin' it.'"

"I know. And I'm happy you're there. Honest. Mama really misses you, you know. She seems a little bit depressed these days. But you didn't hear that from me."

"Oh, don't tell me that. Is she still sad I'm not going the typical route?"

"I don't think it has anything to do with any route, but she hasn't said anything to me either way. I'm just speculating. Eventually, she'll be all right. Me and Daddy'll take care of her."

"I promise I'll come visit in a little bit."

"Do you think you'll *ever* move back to Alabama?"

I paused, knowing what Natalie and our parents would want to hear, knowing that my answer would go straight back to them as soon as we got off the phone because Natalie had most likely been encouraged to ask this very question. I had to proceed with caution.

"Well, I signed a year lease. It's kinda permanent," I answered finally, hoping the insinuation would answer for me. "At least three hundred sixty-five days, but I'm kind of thinking of buying it. . . ."

"I had a feelin'."

"What?"

"Look, I don't know what you have against Alabama, but I happen to be proud of where I come from."

"Nat, I don—"

"It's fine, really. I get it. I'll talk to you later."

And she hung up the phone, leaving me alone with my metallic pink Razr on my ear. What in the heck was going on! It was like the flippin' twilight zone around here!

I wanted to call my parents and tell them how rude Natalie had just been, but I figured I'd be receiving a call soon enough anyway once Natalie spilled the buying beans. Plus, I had a bad feeling that Natalie wasn't the only one back home who felt the way Natalie had reacted. And at that moment, I wasn't really in the mood to be berated, told, or "encouraged" in any direction besides the one I had in front of me. I had just gotten off that roller coaster.

Did I think I was better because I was here and not there? Had I given that off in the weeks leading up to the move? Was that what made Mama and Daddy so sad? What my mom was depressed about and not the fact that I'd skipped college? Had I acted like that when I was ten and famous?

I really didn't know the answer. I liked Alabama—it was where I was born and raised. And sure, I was a bigger fan of a bigger city like Nashville. But didn't everyone want to travel and be somewhere they weren't? Something along the lines of the grass is always greener theory? Tons of my friends went to University of Alabama and Auburn, and some even went to Samford in Birmingham. No one accused them of hating or being too good for Mobile. What was wrong with a little curiosity? A little ambition?

Natalie didn't understand because she could do everything she ever wanted in Mobile, fifteen minutes away from where she spent her childhood. Kindergarten teachers were everywhere.

Singing careers had to be right here in Nashville. I couldn't be driving seven hours every time there was a meeting or a show at Tootsie's or the Ryman Auditorium.

Gosh, I had to make it now, more than ever. Make it big and then everyone back home would understand me. Then they would respect that I was just simply different from rule-following Natalie. They would encourage my dreams. They would applaud my efforts and the risks I took to give up a degree, a safety net, to do what I loved. They would understand that I didn't want to get married right after college, have babies immediately, and go to Parent-Teacher meetings or soccer games. A lot of girls I grew up with wanted exactly that, and good for them! But I wasn't like everyone else. My aspirations were . . . different.

OK, maybe they were a little better, in my opinion. I'm allowed an opinion, right? JoBeth would get it. Owen would too.

Owen. His name—that's all it took for me to calm down. I had been dating him for weeks now, and we had been able to keep it away from Jake, thankfully. And while JoBeth knew we went to shows together (she went half the time anyway), she most likely didn't know anything yet, either—at least she hadn't let on if she did. Owen and I had never held hands in front of her—or at least not until the lights went down. And we only kissed, among other things, in the privacy of Owen's place, the elevator, the hallways in our building, and sometimes even in Owen's office while JoBeth was on her lunch break. Those were my favorite moments.

I had gotten extremely savvy at "going to the market." I took my purse and everything, but once I was in the elevator, I went up to 503 to meet Owen for a quickie.

It felt dangerous, exhilarating, even criminal, our little love affair. And I knew we technically could just come clean. Jake might frown upon it, but he would eventually realize it was actually his idea that we met in the first place. And he would have to remember we were adults (let's just hope he rounded up), capable and free to like (or love) anyone we wished. JoBeth would be happy for us; I had spent an entire last semester hearing over and over that I should move on from Michael, already. Still, the excitement of it was fun. I'd never had anything like this back home. Even Michael hadn't been dangerous. He'd been safe—or so I had thought.

All of a sudden, I really wanted to text Owen while he was at the office. Tease him a little.

<Hey hot stuff>

About a half hour later.

<Hey Lily. What's up>

<What are you wearing?>

<Clothes. N a meeting. Call later.>

Did he mean *he* would call me or I should call him later?

<Me call you? You call me?>

I got the answer roughly three hours later when he called. My heart raced at the sight of his name on my screen.

Owen said he wanted to meet at his place in two hours and have a glass of wine or something before we went to a show downtown at Third & Lindsley. I had to admit to myself that I was way more interested in what "or something" meant than the show. What was he doing to me?

On my way up the elevator, I thought about how much I'd changed in the last month and a half. I had gone from a lame high school senior to someone with a *lover*. I had been dragging around a broken heart, and now I had a Super Glue by the name of Owen Jones Slaughter. He made me forget the past, believe in love all over again— think about marriage, even. Kimsky was old news. Mrs. Slaughter? Oh, how crazy awesome would it be to have Jake as a daddy-in-law? It would be what he called a "PR dream," a story every news wire would pick up. A story I'd love to tell our future children. And then, I'd definitely get to stay in Nashville forever. It was settled—in my mind.

Owen was waiting at the door, wine in hand. *What a host,* I thought as I added one more check mark on Owen's husband-able traits. After a couple sips of chardonnay— not my favorite, but wine was wine, alcohol was alcohol— he led me to my favorite spot in apartment 503: his bed.

I could do this forever. I would have bet anything that Natalie and Judd had never had anything like this back in Alabama. There was just something in this Nashville air.

Umm, we never made it to the show.

When I tiptoed back into my place around ten o'clock, I found JoBeth sitting on our tiny balcony with a beer, staring off at the Batman building in the distance. I discreetly dipped my head down and sniffed myself, praying I didn't smell like all the love I had just made.

"What are you doing?" I asked JoBeth, cautiously, nonchalantly.

"What about you? Shouldn't you still be at a show?"

JoBeth responded without looking back, her feet curled up under her shirt on our cheap, hard plastic outdoor chair (that I paid for).

"Oh . . . yeah, it ended already . . . it was great. Real fun," I lied. I hadn't meant for it to, but it just came out.

"Who'd you see?"

Oh, no. I couldn't remember whom I was *supposed* to have seen. I coughed a few times so I could think.

"Craig Wiseman and Tim Nichols, right?"

Right! I thought. "Yeah!" I coughed again. And then it occurred to me that JoBeth was in charge of not only my calendar, but also Owen's. I had to tread lightly and think about what I said.

"Did they sing 'Live Like You Were Dying'"?

"Of course!" I lied again, starting to sweat a little. I walked to the kitchen to get a glass of water for my throat, which was now burning from all my coughing.

"Ooh, I love that song," she said as she hummed some of the chorus. "What else did they sing?"

Crap, I thought. I was not prepared. But JoBeth bailed me out again.

"Any Chesney hits?"

"Wow, JB, you really are getting good at this music business thing! Is that where you were this afternoon so late? At the office? I feel like I never see you anymore!"

Gain sympathy.

She took another long swig of her beer, and I could tell she wanted to ask me if I had spoken to Jake about us, about our future as JoLily or whatever—I was glad I didn't tell Jake the names she picked out. But I didn't want to break it to her just yet. She needed some fun.

"Let's do something tonight. Something fun. Your

choice!"

JoBeth almost instantly perked up. I thanked my lucky stars for easy fixes.

"Maybe we could do a little karaoke tonight?"

I had to say yes. I had to turn this night around and mend things with my best friend, my roommate, my champion. We lived so close in this condo that I couldn't stand to live another day in fear of a fight.

"Ok, let's go. Where?"

"There's a place called Wanna B's. It's on Broadway downtown."

"Let's go!" I cheered.

But really, I despised karaoke. It was the worst ever pastime for a true singer. I didn't want to sing to low caliber tracks with stock BGVs. Karaoke was fun when you *weren't* serious, and how could I not be serious now? In Nashville? How could I be seen drunk (and you had to get drunk to do it properly) pretending I didn't care how I sounded? I most certainly *did* care.

But I went anyway, in the name of stability. I went because I couldn't handle any more mood swings. I went to appease the dragon. Normal JoBeth, sweet JoBeth, wasn't a dragon . . . but this other side, I didn't want to poke. Plus, I didn't want to be the one who had to crush her dream. Not yet. And honestly, it wasn't that she *couldn't* make it as a singer at all, just not with me . . . or with Jake, judging from our conversation.

With my good attitude dragging behind me like a cranky three-year-old, I trudged through the gobs of tourists downtown, all wearing the "tells" of a Nashville tourist: cowboy hats and boots. New ones. You could spot them by their dress and their leisurely pace, stopping every couple steps to take a picture of an Elvis statue or the Ernest Tubb Record Shop and darting into the souvenir shops to get Music City USA T-shirts and mini plastic Tennessee license plates with their names on them. OK, maybe not every tourist, but some! I could find the name "Lily" on a license plate . . . but not "Lilah." I never found it on anything, much less spelled the way Grandma Lilah did.

Maybe that was a sign, I thought, that I should become Lily for good. Gosh, would I consider legally changing my name? What had Faith Hill done? She had gotten famous before she married Tim McGraw, and she hadn't changed her stage name. But what did it say on her Tennessee driver's license? Speaking of, I needed to get one of those to further prove that I was serious about staying (to myself and my family). There were probably laws about how long I could live in Nashville without updating all of that stuff anyway. I didn't know the laws exactly; I had never lived outside Alabama before. Sure, I had traveled the country and some parts of the world, but I had never actually lived anywhere but Mobile.

My mind was spinning with factoids, details, grown-up stuff I hadn't thought about before. It was so wildly out of control that I didn't even see Owen until I ran straight into him.

"Hey there, where you going so fast?" Owen smiled.

"Whoa! What are you doing here?" I gasped.

"Surprise!" yelled JoBeth. Owen smiled again.

On the outside, I tried to look happy, like this was just another normal night, but on the inside, I was freaking out. I said it again to myself, *What was he doing here? What if JoBeth saw us together—no, no, wait. This situation wasn't that abnormal, all three of us went to shows all the time.* Then again, this wasn't a show.

"I figured Owen might still be downtown from that show at Third & Lindsley so I took a chance! So glad you could make it, O!"

Crap, I thought again, lying was kicking my butt. I looked at Owen, then JoBeth, then back at Owen as I said, "Yeah, me too! I had *no idea* JoBeth was going to invite you! If I had known we were coming back out, you and I could have just come straight from the show we *both* went to! Oh well!"

Hopefully he got the gist.

By the way, when exactly had this cutesy nickname started? "O." *Really?* It was kind of annoying. JoBeth blew cigarette smoke in my direction. She had picked up the habit somewhere in the last month, and thankfully, she'd kept it out of the condo so far—it was against the rules in my lease. But it was still gross. And just another testament of how much JoBeth had changed.

As I stood there, my anxiety started to rumble. I could barely handle karaoke without my boyfriend watching me. Gosh, what was JoBeth thinking? She was very aware of my feelings on the subject. I wondered if she was doing it to get back at me for being too busy for her. Or maybe it was punishment because I didn't gush about the idea of us becoming JoLily. And then my thoughts rushed to a more time-sensitive issue: Did Owen expect me to sing? Would he like me more or less if I did? Would he find it trashy or hot—or confident, maybe? And what would Jake think about my ability to sing in "every possible situation"? That was all he had stressed when I was first starting out back then. It was one thing I had hated . . . just because I liked to sing and was good at it did not mean I liked to sing at any given moment. Did Kobe Bryant want to play basketball in the middle of the mall? While shopping? Probably not. He was a human, not a machine. Okay, he was a very gifted human, but still a human.

Breaking the awkward silence, Owen spoke up. "Awesome." He clapped his hands together. "Can't wait to hear bad music!" he cheered, obviously joking . . . I hoped. "Let's g—"

"Are you coming?" JoBeth did her signature strut toward the door of the eighteen and over bar, fake ID in hand, like a pro. Shoulders back, lips parted, confident stare, just like she'd taught me a few years ago.

"Yeah," I said, fishing my own fake ID out of my purse, not wanting to show either one of them how I really felt about the situation. I wondered how close JoBeth and Owen actually were. How often they "chatted it up" at the office without me, whether he'd told her we were a couple, maybe more.

But no matter what, I couldn't show panic. Panic wasn't the kind of attention I wanted; especially when two of the three of us were sleeping together, and one of us, possibly, still had not been informed. I could never really tell with JoBeth—especially these days.

Inside Wanna B's, it was smoky, or maybe it was just an old building and *JoBeth* smelled like a giant cigarette. Either way, it stank to high heaven, it was dark, and was full of bodies and their drunken brains. And how could I forget the terrible rendition of a classic "Boot-Scootin' Boogie"? Someone was destroying Brooks & Dunn, and people were *clapping*. Why was I here again?

Once we got past the bouncer to the main room,

JoBeth was greeted by like six people. One of them handed her a beer. It begged the question: was JoBeth a regular at Wanna B's? But then I remembered what Jake had said about her coming in looking "worse for the wear," and it made sense. These were the friends she'd replaced me with ever since I'd started turning down the invitations to go out. *Wow*, I thought, *I don't know any of these people.* I took a look around at the place. Wanna B's couldn't be any further from the Bluebird (probably by nature), even a honky-tonk bar like Tootsie's. This was a terrible idea. Thanks, Owen, for playing along, but I wanted to go home now—preferably together. Taxi! But before I could even figure out the logistics of an escape without blowing the cover I'd lied to protect earlier, Owen yelled over the noise. Well, to be fair, what that "singer" was doing was worse than plain noise. It was horror. It was garbage. Out-of-tune garbage. It should be illegal to sing that badly. Especially in Music City.

"What are you gonna sing?" he said.

"I don't think I want to sing tonight." There. I said it. Now, I just had to wait for his reaction. But it was JoBeth who chimed in instead.

"You're so above karaoke; right, Lilah?" she teased.

"I didn't say that," I said hotly.

"Well, I'm not! Here, O, hold my beer," she said as she bounced up to put her name on the sign-up sheet.

"Wow, she's a character," Owen said watching her flirt with the emcee, no doubt getting him to move her name up the list.

I agreed with Owen, but for some reason, I felt like he meant something else by the word "character." Like it was a good thing, an endearing quality. Maybe sometimes it

was, but in this instance, certainly not. For the longest
time, I just put up with her antics because I felt like I owed
her the benefit of the doubt. She had been my absolute
savior in high school. But now, I don't know, I felt like
maybe it was time I started thinking about myself a little
more. I didn't owe her forever, did I? I would bite the bullet
and tell her tomorrow, tell her everything. I would come
clean about Owen, about the fact that I wanted to stay the
course as just Lily Black, no Jo. If we were as close as I
thought we were, she would have to understand. I started
to feel a sense of calm until the loud, annoying host who
spoke too closely into the microphone yelled, "NEXT UP
. . . WE HAVE JOOOOOOOBETH!"

All her "people" cheered like it was a real show. Yes, she
had definitely been here before.

The distraction was probably the best thing to happen.
Goodness gracious, I was all over the place tonight! No
more white wine for me; it obviously went straight to my
head. God must be punishing me for keeping my relationship a secret from JoBeth. For lying about the show
at Third & Lindsley. Secrets and lies never ended well, and
this was the outcome: confusion, jealousy, and karaoke.
The perfect, well deserved kind of torture.

I remember how you found me . . .
Sittin' in the dark . . .

Oh my gosh, I thought, *now I'm hearing things.* My career was flashing in front of my eyes. But no, wait, it . . .
was JoBeth. She was singing "Burning Blue" at a karaoke
bar in front of me, the real Lily Black—and Owen. *Of all
the songs in the entire world . . . what a mean joke.*

But I was in public, so I tried to laugh it off, tried to be a good sport and joke with Owen about the "coincidence." I was happy my best friend was an amazing singer, but did she have to sing the one and only song my career rested upon? The song binder up on the table was like five inches thick! Hundreds of songs to choose from! I was about to make a lame joke about it when I looked over at Owen. His mouth was slightly open with a look of pure awe in his eyes.

What is going on here? I screamed inside my head. What happened to JoBeth? What had Nashville turned her into? I thought bringing her would be fun, like a permanent vacation for us. But I didn't know she was going to be like this. I didn't know she was going to all of a sudden expect to be my business partner. I thought she would *maybe* try to do her own thing after she'd been here for a few years, but really I thought she would eventually go to Belmont. Everything was just wrong, all wrong. We were falling apart.

"She sounds just like you," Owen said, still in his stupor of awe. "I didn't know she could sing."

What could I say? "I'm better, though, right?" Or "This is the first show she's ever done beside a talent show"? When I realized there was really nothing I *could* say, I turned around on one heel and walked out of the bar, leaving my precious star-struck Owen to watch a true wannabe sing my song. And sing it just like me.

⋆10⋆

Before I even opened my eyes, all the emotions from the night before came flooding back. I was mentally exhausted. I was hurt. I couldn't believe JoBeth was ballsy enough to sing "Burning Blue" in front of me, like she was taunting me. JoBeth was known to be bold, sure, but not toward *me*. And what was worse, my boyfriend was impressed by her act of boldness. I was so mad at him that I'd refused to acknowledge any of the texts he'd sent last night.

<Come back out!>
<Where'd u go?>
<We miss u>

I was so mad at both of them. But that was last night, and today was a Sunday, which changed things. I could almost hear my daddy saying "forgive them" live from the pulpit in Mobile, Alabama. And so I would.

But when I opened my eyes, I was alone. JoBeth's "bed" was empty. And not like the "oh, I woke up early and went for a jog" empty. It was still in its futon-as-bed position, and the blankets were still folded on the floor. My first thought was to panic, as usual. JoBeth was different these days, less careful. I had no idea who those people were from last night or if they were safe.

I sat up, my skin feeling instantly hot. What if she had been taken? What if one of those frat-ish looking boys took her home with him and took advantage? I texted her. No answer. I texted her one more time, just to make her phone ding again, hoping. Nothing.

Then I saw it was only six in the morning. JoBeth was a late riser, something we'd shared before I started my 6:00 a.m. workouts. Now I woke up without a clock and couldn't go back to sleep no matter how many hours I'd gotten the night before. JoBeth wouldn't be answering at this hour anyway. *Ok*, I thought, *I should give it another few hours before I really worry.* Everything was probably fine. She'd probably be walking in the door soon anyway.

In the meantime, I was going to enjoy my morning. I brewed a big pot of coffee and sat down on my balcony to read my Bible, trying to imagine which sermon Daddy would be giving in about two hours from now.

Being a preacher's kid, I had heard 'em all, so I randomly selected a dog-eared passage in my Bible (one of dozens) and started reading. I suddenly wished I was at home in Mobile, getting ready for the eight o'clock service with my mama. We always rode together since Daddy had to be there even earlier to prepare. It occurred to me for the first time—well, ever—that she would have to drive alone today, like she probably had for the last weeks since I'd moved. She'd always be alone from now on. I was the youngest. Her "baby," she said.

I wanted to be there today, which was funny, because that never used to happen. I never got away with it, but I always would whine and beg on Sunday mornings to sleep in just once. All my other friends whose dads had regular jobs got to! But not the Carson girls. So, of course, now that I was here in Nashville, becoming an accidental early bird, I didn't even have to leave my condo. Wasn't that the way? Right when you stopped being expected to do something, you wanted to.

I prayed hard at the end of my reading . . . for patience with JoBeth and her general safety, for the right words to tell her the truth about Owen, and about our future as a duo. I prayed that the news wouldn't put too much of a strain on our friendship. I didn't want to hurt her. And I prayed for my own heart. It needed some softening, especially after last night's drama.

I tried to convince myself that I was just mad at JoBeth for stealing my thunder, for being so moody, for trying to embarrass me. But I knew, deep down, it was more than just being angry at her. I was afraid. Afraid she not only tried but *succeeded* in outshining me, just like she had throughout high school. I was afraid I'd lose the only thing I felt like I had that she didn't: music.

I tried JoBeth again, but of course, I got nothin'. It was still too soon to worry, though, so I made some interim plans. I washed my coffee cup, put my Bible back on my nightstand, put a bra and underwear on underneath my barely there pajamas, threw on a stitch of makeup (thin eyeliner, a touch of mascara, and a dab of concealer to cover up the crater on my chin), and hustled to the elevator.

While I was on the compassion train, I needed to apologize to Owen and ask for his forgiveness for storming out and being so rude as not to text him back. I was going to make it up to him in person. It was better that way.

I pushed the button for the fifth floor before readjusting myself in the elevator. I wanted to look like I "just woke up" when I slid into his bed.

Without thinking, I burst through the his never-locked door, figuring Owen would be either sleeping or sitting on his couch with messy hair, drinking from one of his old coffee mugs with Jake's slogan "We Slaughter The Competition," watching GAC or CMT videos or *SportsCenter*, with just shorts and mismatched socks on.

I was wrong. I was more wrong than I'd ever been in my entire life. If there was a contest for being the most wrong in the history of man, I'd won it. By a landslide.

JoBeth wasn't with some bartender or Belmont student in his dorm. She wasn't dead either. Not at all. She was alive and naked. She was naked in Owen's bed. She was moaning instead of silent. She was *with* Owen, not alone, also naked, wrapped up in a tangly mess of sheets.

They were doing it, yes that, what Owen and I had done only hours ago, on the same sheets, in the same bed, in the back corner of his loft-style condo. Six hundred and thirty-five square feet never felt so small. Or awkward.

"Oh my gosh!" I shrieked, putting my hands over my mouth. I should have put them over my eyes, but I couldn't look away. It was a like train wrecking in front of me, someone falling in the middle of a cheerleading stunt.

I had to look. I had to make sure I wasn't seeing things, that I wasn't in a no-good, very bad nightmare where crazy, unreal, unfathomable things went down.

I blinked as long and hard as I could and then opened my eyes with extreme caution. Still there. My "best friend" and my "boyfriend" . . . together, intertwined in each other's skin. Naked. Together. Touching. More than touching. Way more than touching.

"Oh my gosh," Owen whispered, frozen stiff.

But JoBeth just stared at me, like I had interrupted her in the middle of something.

Owen, on the other hand, could be read like a book. His eyes were wide like a six-year-old who just got caught sneaking a Nutty Buddy out of the freezer when he'd already had dessert. Or a thirteen-year-old boy caught looking at dirty magazines by his mother. He looked ashamed and guilty. Good.

"Lily, I—"

"How could you . . . either of you . . . ?" I looked back and forth at Owen and JoBeth, looking for an explanation, *anything*, to make the cruel joke end.

"It was a mistake," Owen sputtered, untangling himself from JoBeth, who had been silent until now. Her eyes looked a little bloodshot. She could have just been hungover, but part of me wondered if she was still a little drunk.

"Excuse me? A mistake? Then you must not learn from yours, because you made that one a lot!" She sat up and looked at him.

Owen gawked back at JoBeth, and I hoped it was because she was lying about how many times they had hooked up.

"Is this true?" I looked at Owen only, still in complete shock. I could barely feel my arms.

Owen looked down, another rush of guilt washing over his face. My stomach dropped along with my Razr phone, which made a loud clunk when it hit the concrete floor, sounding way too loud in the silent, tense room.

I was frozen, unable to form a lucid thought, unable to make sense of what was staring me in the face. "My" Owen had been screwing—and that's what it was—JoBeth for weeks, who knew how long?

"How long?" It was all I could manage to say, and this time, I looked straight into JoBeth's eyes, fully expecting a blunt answer. I was ready.

"Uh . . . the day after I started at Slaughter House. But he hit on *me*!"

Ok, maybe I wasn't ready. My heart joined my stomach near my wobbly ankles and my phone. And I felt stupid in my cute pajamas and makeup. It was almost July. Almost two whole months that the boy I secretly hoped and dreamed would be long-term marriage material had been lying to me. Pretending not to even really notice JoBeth when the three of us were together at the office, writer rounds, rehearsals, the number one parties, or the dinners Jake treated us to.

This is something out of a flippin' Lifetime movie, I thought. This wasn't real life; it wasn't what a small town girl from Alabama had to deal with. Cheating . . . not just a boyfriend but also a *best friend*! And together! And wait a minute, if JoBeth was defending herself, it could only mean one thing. . . .

I knew what I said earlier, about forgiveness and all that, but how could I forgive this?

"JoBeth, can I talk to you alone?" I said weakly, wishing I was stronger.

"Anything you want to say, you can say it in front of Owen," she said flatly.

I was embarrassed to get into this kind of conversation in front of Owen, even if I didn't want him anymore. There was no telling what would come out of JoBeth's mouth. But I had no choice.

"Did you know I was dating Owen?" Luckily Owen was staring down at the floor, basically burning a hole through it. I didn't want to look at him.

JoBeth stifled a laugh. "You weren't very good at hiding it. Next time you try to lie to your *best friend* and say you're going to the market . . . you probably should bring back some actual food. And you forget, I knew where you and Owen were at all times. Perks of being the secretary. An idiot could fill in the blanks."

I was caught. I knew I shouldn't have lied, but this right here seemed so much worse than lying about groceries. JoBeth *knew* about Owen and me and still slept with him!

"Why would you sleep with him if you knew I liked him so much?"

Of course, there were a million questions I wanted to ask, but that one summed it up pretty well. I thought about all the times I'd blindly given my so-called BFF the benefit of the doubt, all of which were up in the air now. The only thing that remained was doubt itself.

"You don't own him!" she yelled.

"I never said I did! I asked *you* why you did that to me."

"Oh, boo hoo. You'll find another guy. You always do."

"What? What do you mean?"

"I'm never enough for you! You're always trying to find

153

a guy to replace me. And I wasn't going to let it happen again! Not for *this* loser." She nodded at Owen, who looked miffed. "IT HAPPENS EVERY FREAKING TIME!"

I was getting mad now. Before this morning, I would have tried to talk JoBeth down, tell her that no boy could replace what we had. But now? I didn't even know *what* we had—or if I wanted to keep having it. Still, I couldn't help but dig a little deeper.

"WAIT. I've only had one other real boyfriend." I felt queasy even saying the word "boyfriend" about Owen now. "So NO, it doesn't happen every single time."

"And he had to go, too! He was such a pansy."

"What are you talking about?"

She looked away, forcing me to figure it out on my own. There was no way. No way in the world she was trying to tell me that. But then, all the little things I could never quite make sense of finally came together.

JoBeth had been the one that called Michael *for me* to ask who it was that he was cheating on me with. *JoBeth* had been the one who reported the news that I "wouldn't know her." *JoBeth* was the one who relentlessly pushed me to go out with every single guy I could find so I could get over Michael.

"*YOU* were the one Michael cheated on me with?"

JoBeth shrugged. "I had to!"

"But you—"

"Oh, get over it. I saw him first. That's why we went to that freaking party in the first place. But you got him and had to freaking fall for him. You left me out of everything!"

"I did not!" I screamed. "I told you everything! Even when . . . we had . . . ," I started, instantly reminding myself that we were not alone. We were still in Owen's condo. Gosh, why was he still here?

"All you ever talked about was Michael this, Michael that: we're going to get married—blah, blah, blah; we'll never move out of Mobile; and it's going to be so great! But you never even thought about how that would make me feel!"

JoBeth, wrapped in a sheet, was standing on the bed, trying to keep her balance.

"Why is everything about you?" I asked.

"I'm your best friend!"

"So? Best friends can have boyfriends! Husbands even! My mom has—"

"Oh, don't bring your perfect family into this!" she snapped. "You always have to remind me how perfectly freaking perfect they are!"

I was shocked. I thought she loved my family.

"I'm not!"

"Oh, shut up, Lilah. I'm so sick of you and your innocent routine. And by the way, I'm not calling you Lily. You don't deserve the title."

"I'm outta here," Owen finally piped up. "You chicks are crazy." He stood up, wobbling the mattress and JoBeth, and started for his closet. Since JoBeth had the sheet, he was totally exposed. I wanted to vomit at the thought of his you-know-what touching JoBeth's you-know-what. And the whole place smelled like sweaty beer, which didn't help matters. It was like they brought Wanna B's home.

I glanced down for a split second—I couldn't help it. Owen's "thing" was no longer, ya know, up and at 'em, and in the midst of all the nonsense, a part of me almost wanted to laugh. They say things look better in the dark.

Yep, they did. But it didn't matter now. I was through with Owen, but JoBeth obviously wasn't.

"Hey!" she barked. "Don't you dare put this all on me! You're the sex addict! 'Anytime, anywhere': isn't that what you said in your office?"

Owen stopped at the door to his closet, but he said nothing.

"I'll take that as a yes. He *never* told me to stop," she said directing the word "never" toward Owen, who took the opportunity to disappear into the closet. Twenty seconds later, he left his own condo in a hurry.

I was at a loss for what to think about him. I felt dirty. I felt stupid. But mostly, I felt played. I couldn't believe my fantasy had been so wrong. The only good news was that Jake still didn't know our relationship status . . . or did he?

Regardless, Owen was not the biggest problem in the room. The problem of the century was the blonde chick who was now sitting on Owen's bed with her hair a matted mess, eyes of steel, and clearly, a heart of stone.

"I just don't get it. Why would you do this—if you knew I liked him?"

I wasn't going to even utter the word "love", or what I might have mistaken for love.

"Are you still on that?" she sounded put out. "Look sweetie, I saved you from falling for a man whore— Owen—and a bum—Michael. You owe me!"

My feet felt like they were burning on the cold concrete.

"Owe you? For ruining my life? Not once but twice! No, no, no: I don't owe you anything! If anything, you owe *me*!" I paced.

"For what? Bringing me here to be your secretary? To be your groupie? Your personal cheerleader? I told you I wanted to do a duet with you, and you lied to my face. You said you would talk to Jake about it, but I have waited every dang day for him to call me into his office to tell me the good news. But he hasn't. All he wants is his stupid crappy coffee or for me to take a message! Sorry, but I'm so much better than that."

"I *did* talk to him. And I was going to tell you today!"

"Bullcrap."

"I was! And about Owen! Gosh, I can't believe I was trying to spare *your* feelings."

"If you talked to him—and I don't believe you did—then what did the old man say? Not that I even want to sing with you anymore. I could go out on my own. Owen said so last night, after you made a huge scene and left in the middle of my performance. Thanks for taking me out for some great fun."

"You call that a performance? It was karaoke and my song. Why would you sing my song in front of my boyfriend?"

"It's a free country, and he wasn't your boyfriend—clearly."

My feet got hot again. I wished I had worn shoes.

"Fine, if you want to know what he said, I'll tell you. Jake said he didn't think we should work together."

"He did not. Jake loves me."

"You don't believe me? Ask him yourself. Be my guest. He said you were a train that was waiting to wreck."

I didn't want to use his phrase, but she was killing me. I had to get out of there, or I was going to lose my mind, if I hadn't already. And my vocal cords were buzzing. If I'd known I was going to be screaming all morning, I would have warmed up my voice.

"You're so freaking full of crap it's scary. You always have been. I can sing and you just can't handle it. You're so jealous that I'm prettier and God forbid, more talented than you are. I guarantee if I had been at Bayfest back then instead of you, Jake would have picked me and left you behind."

That stung. Maybe more than anything else she'd said. But it didn't matter what she said. Jake *had* picked me. Yes, JoBeth was good. She was great, in fact. But I was Lily Black. And I knew better than anyone else that making it in music had so much more to do than having a pretty face and a good voice. It was about the whole package, one Jake didn't see in oh-so-beautiful JoBeth.

I was done talking about it. I was done with the whole thing.

"You need a new place to live."

JoBeth threw her hands up, as if she didn't see this coming. "Well, that's just great. Throw me out because you don't like hearing the truth."

"What truth?"

"Look in the mirror. I made you who you are, and this is how you repay me? Were you ever my friend? Or did you use me back then just like you're trying to use me now . . . to make *you* look good."

"Just be out by tomorrow morning," I said as I turned to leave.

JoBeth picked up a half-empty cup of water on the floor by Owen's bed and threw it at me as she screamed. "I hate you!"

I ducked. It smashed on the floor, splashing water on my foot. But then I smelled it. There was no water in that cup. It was pure vodka, still cold. Gross, but it explained a lot.

As I got to the door, I turned around and said one last thing. "Good luck, JoBeth. Nashville might be bigger than Mobile, but it's a small town at heart. Everyone finds out about everyone."

"Nice outfit by the way," was all she said. I let the heavy door slam on its own, hoping the neighbors wouldn't complain. Oh wait, what did I care? This was Owen's place.

Just when I thought I was safe, I saw Owen sitting in the hallway (he'd obviously stormed out without his car keys). I wondered if he would go back in any time soon. I wouldn't have.

"I'm sorr—" he said, but I put my hand up and kept walking past the elevator toward the stairwell. I didn't want to be there any longer than I had to. The tears were starting to fall.

Back in my condo, I double-bolted the door and cried.

★11★

A few hours later, I had finally calmed down, but I was still at a complete loss. *How had everything gone so wrong?* I thought as I dialed home.

"Mama?" I sniffled, barely holding it together.

"Honey? Are you all right?" Mama answered. She sounded alert, but tired.

"Did you just wake up? Did I wake you? I'm sorry—"

"No, no, I was just lyin' down, readin' my Bible. Your daddy said some great things this morning, so I'm just mullin' over a few passages. We missed you."

That broke my heart. "I miss you guys so much, Mama."

"Sweetie? What's wrong?"

Her Southern drawl was so much sweeter than I remembered. Up until that point, I thought I'd cried every last tear out of my body, but I was wrong. The floodgates reopened for round two.

"My whole life has been a sham!" I cried.

"Whaaat?"

"Everything is falling apart!"

"Honey, it can't be that bad. Shh, shh."

My mama had soothed me this way more times than I could remember, but it was different through the phone. I howled and hiccupped for a minute or two before I finally calmed down enough to speak again. That part wasn't different.

"Sweetheart, what happened?"

The lump in my throat felt as big as a softball, but I managed to croak out JoBeth's name.

"What about her?"

"She's trying to ruin my life! She tried to take the boy I like, and she said I didn't deserve a comeback."

"Well, of course, that's not true."

"I know," I agreed, hoping I wouldn't have to go any further into the whole Owen thing.

But Mama was quiet.

"Mama?"

"Yes, honey."

"Why aren't you sayin' anything?"

"Oh, it's nothin'. It's just that I've always thought JoBeth was a little too jealous of you, honey," she said meekly.

"She thinks I'm jealous of her," I sniffled.

"Well, are you?"

"Not now! She went absolutely nuts, Mom!"

"I think it's completely normal for us to want what our friends have. But JoBeth always had her own way of doing things. I think her way of controlling her insecurities was to keep you where she wanted you. She kept you popular, but never more than her. And then when you decided to leave for Nashville, I think maybe it forced her out of her comfort zone."

"Her comfort zone?"

"Mobile, high school."

"She wanted to leave Mobile more than me."

"She probably did, baby, but on her terms, not yours."

"Why didn't you tell me what you thought of her back then?"

"Well, honey, you thought she hung the moon, kind of. For a friend at least. You always thanked God for her in your prayers at night, and I thought she would grow up. I hoped she would, at least."

"I don't know if she was ever really my friend, Mama. And remember when I told you about Michael cheating on me?"

"That darn boy broke your heart. You're not still thinkin' about him are you, honey? He's bad news. Once a cheater, always a cheater."

"It was JoBeth the whole time!" I interrupted, starting to tear up again. My throat started to form another lump, and my nose stung. It was so embarrassing.

"Oh, my, I can't believe it," my mom said quietly, concerned. She was the slow-burn type, a full 180 degrees from my animated father.

"I know," I sobbed. "I feel so stupid!"

"Sweetheart, I hate to hear you hurt like this. Now I wish I'd said something earlier about how I felt about that JoBeth."

I took a deep breath and tried to calm down again.

"I wouldn't have listened."

Mama laughed, and then we were both laughing. My heart rate finally slowed down a little.

"Well, honey, she's definitely jealous, and jealousy can eat you alive if you let it. If she started that long ago and never let go of it, her heart is bound to be full of it by now. Oh, I bet she's heavy, Lily, heavy with so much negativity. That poor child."

"Her? Poor? She sabotaged not one but two of my relationships and she's gunnin' for my career!"

"Look at it this way. She's not happy. She's not like you—well, most of the time. People see right through that kind of person.

"You, on the other hand aren't carryin' around those weights on your heart. You aren't perfect, but you're free of what she's holdin' onto. And now that she's been caught, so to speak, she might not be able to keep up the charade for long."

"What do you mean, 'charade?'"

"I just wouldn't be surprised if other things spun out of control, that's all. She's like a sweater that's got a pull. Once something catches it, it starts unravelin' till there's nothin' left."

"So what do I do? I got her the job with Jake in the first place. Do I tell him?"

"Hmm . . . I don't think so. I think you *should* ask her to leave your house—"

"I already did that."

"Good. Well, as far as callin' Jake, I don't think it's necessary. Let JoBeth deal with it herself. If something were to happen, I wouldn't think you would want to be associated."

My mama was one smart woman. She was an

occupational therapist, so it made sense that she would be intelligent, but I had always just thought of her as a mom. It sounded awful, but that's who she was to me. She rarely talked about anything else besides church and family stuff.

"Mama, should I come home? Maybe this is a sign."

"I don't think you should."

"Wow, I thought you'd be all for me coming back, doing the regular thing."

"You're taking a risk, but I admire it. You always were my curious one, tryin' things. At first, your daddy and I were just blindsided by your decision . . . and a little worried it might not be the same as you remembered it bein'. But you're doin' it, baby! And it's not always easy, but you're on your way. So don't let some silly little friendship jeopardize what you've been working for. Don't let that girl destroy this for you . . . but forgive her anyway."

"How do you always know what to do?"

"Call it mother's intuition."

"I hope I get it someday."

"You will," she answered softly.

"Do you swear you're OK?"

"Yeah, I'm just tired, baby."

"That's not like you to be so tired."

"Just a long week workin'. I'll be fine! Don't you know your mama? I'm a survivor. That's how I know you'll survive this and everything there is to come."

I sighed, emotionally exhausted. "Thanks. Guess I'll just have to keep my head up and keep workin'. Otherwise, I might give it all up and come runnin' home."

"Don't do that. I believe in you, Lily. You're my shining star. Keep at it until you get your dreams to come down from the sky, ya hear?"

"You got it. Love you. Go lie down."

"All right, baby. Have a good rest of your Sunday. And try to find it in your heart to forgive JoBeth. It will be hard I know, especially today, but just try. Just like that jealousy consumed her, your anger and resentment can consume you. And that's not livin'."

"OK," I answered, wanting to be able to be that type of person. My mom was that kind of person, and she was always right about stuff like this. But I was still too hurt and shocked to let it go just yet. JoBeth hadn't even come by to pick up her stuff from the apartment.

I looked around and realized that I didn't want to be here when JoBeth *did* come back. But . . . everything I owned was sitting here in these rooms, and if JoBeth was that bat crazy, it would be no surprise if she raided the place or burnt everything in it. I would not be getting my security deposit back. That was certain.

But I was tired of this day, and so I made a decision I hoped Mama would be proud of. I grabbed a duffel bag and put my most valuable things in it, things like a piece of jewelry that had been in my family for ten generations, some street clothes, my novels, my Dictaphone, my laptop, my Folgers can of emergency cash, my journal, and my Bible. Luckily, I hadn't unpacked the suitcase my stylist Darla had sent over with my new wardrobe, so I wheeled it to my car in the garage, put it in the trunk, and went back to grab my overnight items. And at the last minute, I grabbed a few framed photographs of my family. With my belongings in hand, I walked next door to the Embassy Suites.

Everything left in the condo could be replaced—that's what money was for—especially the corkboard full of pictures of the two of us. I left those for dear ole JB to mull over, to ponder, to dispose of if she so desired.

In my room at the Embassy Suites (a positive use for a fake ID), I took a bath, ordered way too much room service, and made some in-room hot herbal tea. I toasted my family back home, my mama's wisdom, her heart, and my newfound journey.

Here's to making it happen no matter what, I vowed as I raised my paper cup in the bathtub, the lights dim, the room calm.

I spent the rest of my Sunday watching *I Love Lucy* reruns (my comfort show) on TV Land. And taking my mama's advice, I quickly and reluctantly prayed for JoBeth before I fell asleep early in the deep, plush pillows for a full ten hours of uninterrupted bliss.

The next morning, after a continental breakfast and a late checkout, I walked back to my condo with fingers crossed. The good news was that most of my things were still there and intact. The bad news? There were a couple of burnt pictures sitting in the middle of the floor, likely the work of a cigarette lighter. *Guess she didn't want them either,* I thought.

The door was unlocked, the lights all on, and it smelled like a smokestack. I opened up the balcony door to ventilate the room and picked up the iron table that had fallen on its side, and I stepped on glass. Lots of it, white and clear. And ashes stuck to everything. I bent down to see exactly what it was that she'd broken.

It was hard to make it out with all the ashes, but the smell of vodka was hard to miss. The clear glass was probably from a bottle of it. Whew, it stank. The white glass pieces looked like one of our little bowls we ate Lucky Charms out of. It had been one of my original Wal-mart purchases on my first day. A day ago, I probably would have called the bowl sentimental, but today, it was where it should be: broken on the floor.

To be honest, after my peaceful night, I didn't care to spend one second contemplating it or reliving the events from twenty-four hours before. So I cleaned up, took out the trash, lit a few candles, called Mama, and took her suggestion to call a locksmith ASAP.

I sat back on my couch and looked around. Six hundred and thirty-five square feet was definitely meant for one.

Well, my mama was right. The whole JoBeth/Jake/Owen thing took care of itself—without any intervention from me.

Apparently, Owen told his dad *half* the story, the half about how JoBeth had been using company calendars to keep tabs on me. Jake wasn't a big fan of being screwed with—big shock—especially by his own employee, so she was fired on the spot. Ha.

So with JoBeth gone and new door locks installed, I dodged one bullet, but there was still Owen. So, I did all I could do: stay away from Slaughter House as much as possible. And it wasn't as hard as I thought it might be.

"Before we get to business, are you OK?" Jake asked between bites of his cheddar omelette at Noshville Deli.

I assumed he meant JoBeth, but I didn't know which details he'd been supplied by his faithful offspring.

"I'm OK," I said.

"Well, I heard she went a little cuckoo."

I nodded, still unsure of how much to say.

"I rest my case, then. Aren't you glad you didn't entertain that duet idea?"

"Oh, yes," I said. He had no idea.

"Shame though. She was a pretty good assistant. You any good with computers?"

"I'm all right."

"OK, good. Between you and Owen, I'm gonna need some help learning the shared calendar thing she set up."

"You should probably change your passwords."

He took a long sip of his coffee. "Good thinking. OK, moving on. It's truth time, Lil. We have a showcase coming up, and we don't have enough original songs to make it through an entire set. We can't show up without new material. It's showcase suicide."

I nodded. "What do you suggest?"

"Co-writes. You ready?"

"No better time than the present, right?"

"That's the spirit! I'll call some people and get a few lined up. It'll be great. I have a good feeling about you and Clint Lagerberg. You guys will click; I know it. He's a really good dude, and he's getting tons of cuts right now."

"Set it up!"

Now that it was here, I was a tad bit nervous, but I tried to hide it from Jake (really hard to in person.). Writing was something I needed and wanted to do. But unlike singing, I wasn't as gifted at putting my thoughts on paper in verse, pre-chorus, chorus, bridge form. I could plunk around on a piano, but I wasn't good, and I could barely pick up a guitar correctly. And I didn't dream in melodies or chords like I'd heard the "true" songwriters did. But I would try. I had to. I was an artist, for goodness sake. The real money was in songwriting anyway. (Why do you think Taylor Swift writes every single song of hers?)

The next thing I knew, it was the second week in July. Co-writes gobbled up all the free time I had in my schedule, and my calendar (the calendar JoBeth no longer had access to) was booked solid.

Co-writing wasn't all that bad, and the people I wrote with were super nice. But, geez, it wasn't easy. Jake promised me it would get better, that it would get easier over time, and with practice. He went as far as to compare songwriting, in the beginning, to blind dating. You either clicked or you didn't. You would try for a second date, or you wouldn't. There was magic, chemistry, or there wasn't. And if there wasn't any, you moved on until you found someone you did click with. Jake's comparison was pretty accurate, but after a week of it, I thought it actually resembled speed dating a little more.

Every day I wrote somewhere different: at a studio, a writer room that a publisher provided, or at the writer's home studio, depending on the other writers' preferences.

It was taxing. And even though I moved around a lot, it still felt a bit like Groundhog Day; I walked in the front door around ten or eleven in the morning, usually met by my co-writer, and we went straight to the lounge/kitchen/ wherever the coffeemaker was. The writer would ask if I wanted coffee and the answer was always a passionate yes. Some of them asked if I wanted a beer or a shot, and that was always a "no, thanks, it's early." I didn't want any of them to think I was a lush . . . or find out that I was only seventeen. Plus, alcohol in the morning? Gross.

While my coffee brewed, I always unpacked my writer bag. I brought my laptop, a pocket thesaurus, a songwriter's rhyming dictionary that probably screamed "NEW WRITER!" a legal pad, a Phillips Dictaphone, and a little journal-like book I used for ideas. When the coffee was ready, we'd doctor it up in the little kitchen and then settle into our places on the couch. Next came the getting to know each other portion of the program. And as if on cue, all my co-writers all asked the same few questions, wanting to know if I was the same Lily Black from "way back then," as if it were a million years ago. That led to the next question of what had happened. I would explain the whole ordeal with radio stations not playing the song even after they promised to. And because they were all writers, emotionally invested in each one of their creations, they took it personally, usually matching my story with some horror stories of their own. That part was nice. At least I wasn't the only one who had been let down, I always thought. The third question: So, are you trying to get back into music now?

That one was always mind-boggling, and I wanted to say, "Yes: Why do you think I'm here? To observe? To audit?" But I never said anything; I just smiled and said, "Of course! I'm glad I got to lead a fairly regular life back in Mobile, but I'm ready to get back in the grind!" Whatever "the grind" was.

After all that, we finally started the process of throwing out ideas. Some days my co-writer would have already started a melody during breakfast, on a morning run, or in the shower. Other days, my co-writer's "well would be dry," and he/she'd ask me what I had . . . if I was "feelin' anything." And then there were the days when they looked like they couldn't wait to get out of there, or be on their phones, the Internet, or Facebook the whole time. Those days were the longest.

One afternoon, I called Natalie on my way home from one of those exhausting writes and made the big mistake of complaining about it.

"Are you seriously telling me that sittin' on a couch with another adult and coming up with about fifty words or less and a melody to sing 'em to—that's exhausting?"

It wasn't so much a question as a statement. And I knew what Natalie would say next. And she did. Gosh, why was it always a darn competition with her?

"Try wranglin' twenty kids with snotty noses and three-second attention spans all day, then eating a cafeteria lunch in so much noise you can't hear yourself chew ice cubes, nursing boo-boos on the playground, staying forty-five minutes after the car-rider line empties with a crying kid whose mom lost track of time . . . again. Then going home to your own family and trying to be supermom and super wife. I'll show you exhausting. Me and exhausting go way back. We're best buds."

"I know. Your life is way crazier than mine, and I'm honestly not trying to complain. It's just been really emotionally draining. You, like, put your life out there, your thoughts, and your fears. You have to! Otherwise, the songs, they mean nothing! Anyway, it's not a big deal . . . ," I trailed off.

It wasn't just Natalie. It was the combination of that and the Vanderbilt traffic that was really stressing me out.

"Wait; stop. I'm sorry. Mom told me you and JoBeth had a big falling out and everything, and I know you live in a big city alone, tryin' new things, without anyone there

to support you. I'm sorry I snapped. I'm just stressed out
today because Summer's day care lady told me that Summer's pinchin' the other kids," she said with a sigh.

"Oh, no!"

"I know. I'm so embarrassed."

"Oh, she's just a kid, Nat!"

"I know. . . . Anyway, so please continue. Tell me all
about your writing. I promise not to say a word."

I hesitated, thinking that my problems really weren't
that big of a deal, but it felt good to get to talk to someone
about it. I'd kept it in for weeks.

"Well, to be honest, I don't know how these people do
it every day."

"Do what?"

"Co-write! I'm just not inspired at ten or eleven in the
morning every morning. Sometimes I think about stuff
late at night, and I'll write it down in my little idea book.
Or, when I'm driving, I'll pull over to jot something down.
I always write it down so I can bring it into my co-write
the next morning . . . so I can bring something to the table,
contribute, you know? But by then, the idea seems stupid
or too wild, and I don't even want to bring it up!"

"Who cares what they think?"

"I do! It's very vulnerable in there. It's like I said: you
go in there, throw ideas out to an equal partner for hours,
and essentially put your heart, brain, and soul on display.
And some writers, like the one today, are simply not im-
press-able. They like nothing unless it comes from their
minds, their mouths. And the worst is when I've said the
same thing twenty minutes before, but by the time they
actually get it in their thick skulls, they think it was *their*
idea. But you can't get mad—Nashville has some serious

politics. And word gets around fast."

"I'd call 'em out on it, but you know me! No mercy!" She laughed. "And no; Mobile is small. Nashville is huge!"

"Maybe on a map. I've already heard through the grapevine—even from a couple writers—that JoBeth has a pretty bad reputation. People talk here as much as they do back home. It's just about different stuff."

"Wow, so is JoBeth movin' back home?"

"I don't know. Mom suggested I stay out of it. If I don't know anything, I can't get caught in the middle. She's called a few times, though. I didn't answer."

"That's probably for the best. Wonder if she'll still go to U of M—you know Mom and Dad still haven't told the people in administration that you're not going, but I think it's because they forgot. I haven't heard 'em talk about it in a while."

Finally.

"Speaking of Mama, how's she been?"

"She's fine. She thinks maybe it's her age that's making her tired, but I'm making her go see someone at primary care anyway. I want her to hear the doctor say she should take it easy . . . that's the only way she'll slow down."

"I bet she fought you on going."

"She doesn't know I'm taking her . . . yet."

I laughed. "That's something you'd do to Summer to get her to go."

"Works like a charm."

"Well, let me know how she takes the bait. And what does Summer have to say for herself . . . pinchin' people! Ha! Hey, I'm pulling into my garage and I'll probably lose ya. Love you, Nat. Thanks for listenin'."

"Of course. And I'm so excited to hear some new songs

when you get them done. Love you, girl. Bye."

I pulled into the garage, happy to finally have an ally in my sister. It was about time.

★ ＊ ★ ＊

"It's Friday the thirteenth . . . got any plans?" Jake joked during one of our rare office meetings. I had already seen Owen that morning, which felt like enough of a cruel trick, but I wouldn't bring that up.

"It's *July*, so, no . . . not really." I laughed from my normal spot on his office couch. "I do have a co-write, though, which you know I'll need a prayer for."

"Are they not getting any better? I feel like I've been putting you with some of the best of the best!"

"They are getting better. It's just that I literally don't know a soul in this town, and I haven't written with anyone twice yet, so it's like the first day of school every day. Are you sure I'm cut out for this writing thing?"

"Have I ever—"

"No, you've never steered me wrong . . . on purpose," I joked.

"This life, this *job*, you remember how hard it can get, right? Are you up to it?"

I nodded, but Jake didn't seem convinced. It wasn't that he didn't believe in me: I knew that he did. It was just his paternal side coming out. Jake leaned back in his leather chair, his arms stretched behind his head. He was either about to tell a story or lecture me.

"I remember those first couple of bus trips." *Thank goodness*, I thought. It wasn't a lecture. "We would meet at the Kroger in Brentwood, and you would sit in the

Chambers' minivan for as long as you could. You loved singing, but you were a kid, and kids like to be normal sometimes. When you become a public figure, you lose that normal."

"I remember. But once we got on the interstate, I was OK, right?"

"Sure, you were!" Jake laughed. "I'm sayin' all this because I want to make sure you remember all that goes into this. You gain some, you lose some. You get to travel, but that means you'll wake up in the same bus every morning underground at another arena, a venue that looks exactly like the last one. Remember you had to ask me where we were every day on that first tour? I finally got you to start lookin' at the daily call sheet in the front of the bus to figure it out for yourself. No one else on the planet gets Oklahoma City and New York City confused."

I laughed. "You thought I was crazy."

"You were a little crazy, but that's what I liked aboutcha," Jake chuckled. "Anyway, I don't want to make you rethink any of this. I think you're gonna make it. I've always thought that. And this time, no Dane Kimmel is gonna get in the way of that. Because this time, we won't just have one hit; we'll have so many, he won't be able to stand it. He'll *have* to play 'em."

Inside my head, I was doing that little doubt thing. Today's headline: "You'll never even get a record deal to find out." But Papa Jake saw right through me.

"Hey."

I looked up. "Yeah?"

"If you want to throw in the towel on writing, just say the word. You don't have to."

"No, I want to."

"Are you positive? Don't do this for me. But I have a feeling you'll click with someone soon. It's just a matter of time. When's your write with Clint? Tuesday?"

"Wednesday."

"Great."

"I might be fresh out of ideas by then," I said.

"All it takes is one."

"Haven't found that *one* yet."

"You'll know when it's right. Well, you better get going. 440 is murder this time of the morning."

I got up, walked over to the door, and turned around. "Hey, Jake? I know you know this—you know everything. But I *want* to do this, no matter the downsides. They're worth it to me."

"I know they are, kiddo. I just want you to get to make your own life choices this time around. I owe you that."

"Thanks, but I trust you."

Jake smiled and nodded. "That's what makes us a good team. And, Lily? You *will* write a hit. I have no doubt."

"Thanks, Jake."

While I was stuck in traffic on 440—as Jake had warned—I thought more about what he'd said. Back then, it hadn't been all fun and games. I had made some sacrifices.

I had to miss stuff—birthday parties and holidays including Christmas and Thanksgiving—in order to play a show or be in a parade. The money was really good during the holidays for a reason. I'd probably traded in lifelong memories for that money, though. Ah, well.

I remembered not being able to go anywhere by myself back then. My road manager always had to take me places. He'd been nice, but a total hall monitor, always warning me about stuff like safety and not attracting any unwanted attention.

That part was probably for my own good. I couldn't have walked around any city without it turning up in a magazine or on the news anyway! There had been headlines that read "TOO MUCH, TOO SOON?" and "LILY BLACK, WHAT IS SHE HIDING?" and "LILY BLACK. WILL SHE TURN OUT LIKE ALL THE OTHER CHILD STARS?"

My band, background singers, and crew got to walk around all day in every city. They brought back souvenirs, shopping bags, and newly developed photos of their sightseeing adventures. They spent all of the per diem on expensive restaurants and gift shops, and I was always so jealous. I had never even had time to spend my own per diem.

I remembered feeling particularly envious when I would see them walking down the hall toward their "Lily Black Band" dressing rooms every day. They'd always be laughing and swinging their bags around playfully, wearing their own favorite "street" clothes. But not me. I had to stay in wardrobe twenty-four hours a day. I wasn't even allowed to wear the multi-colored nail polishes all the girls back in Mobile were wearing because *everything* had to match the Lily Black brand, just like it did now, only I had no say so in what that was. Once I asked to wear some Old Navy flip-flops. You can imagine how that went over.

By the time the traffic cleared, I was sure what I'd just told Jake was the truth. No, life as an artist wasn't easy, not in the slightest. But it was all worth it, just to be on stage, to be under the lights with my microphone, looking out at the audience. So worth it.

I found myself chanting "TGIF" all day, as if I were in high school, waiting on the final bell to ring at three o'clock. Of course in songwriting, there was no bell. You never knew when school was out. If the other writer was late, slow to get started, wanted to break for coffee or lunch, you could be talkin' two to three hours on top of how long it took to write the song itself—if you even finished one at all.

But today was not one of those. It was wonderful actually. My co-writer (Claire Wyndham) was Australian and had been in Nashville with her husband for three years. I listened to her story with total understanding, and yet I felt a little silly. I had thought my own excursion to Nashville had been so monumental, but seven hours in a car was dinky in comparison to twenty hours on a plane!

Wow, I thought, *I've had it pretty good.*

After we wrote a song called "Wildcard," Claire asked me to join her and her husband for an early dinner at a nearby Mexican place. Normally, I made an excuse to go home, but because I'd shared my entire life's history during our co-write, it was quite obvious that I had absolutely nowhere to go. Plus, I was starving, and I liked their company. And their Aussie accents.

For as much as I loved the weekend, I hated how lonely they were. Without JoBeth or Owen, my days off were simple and limited: I watched TV or read a book. So yeah, I welcomed the plans and hoped we could stretch dinner out after the sun started to set so I could feel like I'd successfully done *something* other than work.

While we sat around and nursed our fourth round of chips and salsa, my phone rang. I was so popular all of a sudden! I excused myself to an empty back patio— Tennessee humidity: the moisture in the ninety-degree weather left me instantly sticky.

"Hello?"

"Lilah."

"Daddy?"

"You might want to plan a trip home soon."

"I know it's been a long time. I miss y'all too. So much—"

"No, Lilah, maybe right now."

"It's seven hours! You're crazy, Daddy!"

But he was calling me Lilah, and I sensed he wasn't joking around.

"What's wrong, Daddy?"

He hesitated.

"It's your mother."

Time stopped. My once flowy tank top clung to my body like a wet napkin. The overhead fans on the patio clicked loudly at every spin. The car horns on the road were clearer and felt like they were three feet away. I swear I heard an ambulance somewhere out there, and I was sure it was headed straight for me. My mama? I was too afraid to ask.

"Did she . . . die?" I held my breath.

"No, no, she's not dead."

My breath poured out of my lungs.

"Then, what is it?"

"Well, we went to the doctor today and . . . she . . . has cancer."

That word, that six-letter word, was so foreign to me. Cancer was something that happened to other people's families. Cancer was for women who were old, not for a fifty-five-year-old woman who had no wrinkles on her face. Not for a physically active woman who gardened and took walks daily with her granddaughter. Not for a woman who read her Bible on the back patio every morning, who never bought anything for herself, who never said a bad thing about anyone, who would do anything for others before herself.

Cancer did not happen to Sandy Northcutt Carson.

"What kind? How bad is it?"

"It's a rare bone cancer called multiple myeloma. There's no cure, of course, but they are going to start treatment next week."

His voice was so not my daddy. That alone was enough to make me want to cry.

"Is she OK?" I stuttered out.

"You know your mother. She's a rock. Once we got the diagnosis, we left the hospital, went back home, and she started making soup for a sick friend. She said she'd made a commitment, and she had 'things to do.'"

I could barely smile through my tears, but this was a true picture of Mama.

"Can I talk to her?"

"You should come on home. Don't you drive too fast, though. Your mama wants it to be peaceful. She doesn't want you to be worried."

"How can I not worry, Daddy!" I yelped.

"Don't worry unless I do."

But he was. And so, I was.

"I'll leave right now."

"I love you, sweetheart. Please drive safely, and I'll see you soon. And sorry to take you away from whatever you're doin . . . ," he trailed off.

"It's OK, Daddy," I choked. "Bye."

"Bye."

For a second, I couldn't move. My feet were cement. But then, suddenly, I sprang into action. I hustled back into the restaurant, gave my Australian mates some cash, and was on I-65 South within the next ten minutes, only stopping to get a full tank of gas.

I didn't even have it in me to go back to my condo to pack a change of clothes. Leaving Nashville this late would get me to Mobile around midnight if I was lucky, and I most certainly was not lucky. I needed every second. Time was precious.

It was the longest seven hours of my life. I yelled at God, and I cried until I couldn't cry anymore. I tried to listen to music, but it all reminded me of Mama. I couldn't tell anyone in Nashville yet, not until I knew more, knew what I was dealing with. Not until I saw her for myself. So I just sat there and tried not to think, tried not to feel.

I passed the exit for Cullman, Alabama, where my mom had grown up; passed First Baptist Gardendale with the big white cross; passed Birmingham; passed Clanton Peach Park, where Mama adored the peach pies and the peach ice cream cones; passed Priester's Pecans. My Mama loved to sit there for forever watching them make the candy at Priester's.

I passed the Dolly Parton Bridge (unofficially named after Ms. Parton because the two bridges were in the form of two large humps, and at night, there were two red lights that blinked on top.) From the bridge, you could see downtown Mobile. That's how I knew I was close to home.

Every landmark was more painful than the last, and yet, each one I passed signified that I was getting closer. Closer to my sweet, sick mama.

The clock read 11:59 p.m. when I pulled into the driveway at 1493 Carrington Road. It felt so familiar yet completely different. This sandy brown brick house with a nicely manicured lawn—even in the unbelievable Alabama humidity. This house with an oversized, white "C" hanging on the front door. This place was home, but never had it felt so black and white, so big and scary.

Cancer was in this house now, and things would never be the same.

But I had to go in sometime. I turned off my headlights so as not to wake anyone, drove beside the garage that held the rejects of our last few garage sales. So much was in there that we all had to park out in the driveway. Now, I wondered if it would ever be cleaned out. Priorities were shifting at lightning speed. I pressed the garage button until the door raised just enough so that I could duck under it and opened the door to the kitchen slowly and quietly.

Mama was sitting at the kitchen table with a chair facing the back door, reading her Bible.

"Mama? What are you doing up?" I whispered.

"Waitin' for you, honey." She looked up and smiled. "Welcome home."

Mama stood up carefully from the table. She wore her long, white linen nightgown, the one she wore when she was hot. Her body was small and delicate underneath. Mama had gone prematurely gray at sixteen, and I could see that she had stopped dying it brown recently. Maybe since I had been gone.

As if she could read my mind, my mama put a hand up to her short graying hair. "I know," she said. "I got lazy." She smiled again.

Mama pulled me into a tight hug, and all my fear and worry fell away for the moment.

For the seven hours in the car, I had tried to picture what she would look like when I got home. Maybe I figured she would look different, sickly and helpless in some way. I thought she would look like she had cancer. But she looked like Mama, like her regular self. Her regular, night-owl self.

That night, Mama and I slept upstairs in my old double bed, talking for hours in the dark about life, Nashville, JoBeth—dumb, useless stuff in comparison to her diagnosis—while we stared up at the glow-in-the-dark stars that I'd sticky tacked to the ceiling when I was thirteen. We talked and talked until I fell asleep, just like the old days.

The next morning, I woke to the smell of my daddy's famous Pancake Delight—usually reserved for the weekends. I was alone in my bed.

Did I dream all that stuff about the cancer? Am I still in high school? I wondered as I crept down the stairs toward the smell. Natalie was standing in the kitchen with an iced Starbucks coffee, no smile, no Summer, no Judd. The reality rushed back . . . and my mind filled back up with worry.

"Good mornin'," I said as nonchalantly as possible. As if the reason I had come home was for Christmas or Easter.

"De-lilah . . . ," Daddy sang, like the radio show. The one I wasn't able to keep on for five minutes last night on my way home because it reminded me of my mom. Daddy was all smiles for the moment, trying to be as cheerful as Mama was. But even I could see the worry behind his eyes.

After breakfast, the original four Carsons went into the living room. Mama sat down in her old wooden rocking chair, Natalie and I sat on the couch, and Daddy on the Lord's Chair. He spoke first.

"This isn't something we were trained to discuss as parents. Both of you know what's goin' on, but we want to tell you as much as we know and then try to answer any questions you might have."

"Are you in pain, Mama?" I asked.

"A little in my back, but it only comes in occasional waves."

"Is this why you've been so tired?"

She nodded. "It seemed to explain it. It's been hurtin' since before you left, but you know, I thought I was just gettin' older at first. I would vacuum a room or two, and then I'd feel completely wiped out for two days afterwards. Like I was payin' for it or something. Your sister and your daddy finally convinced me to get it checked out, so I went with Natalie."

"You knew back *then*?"

"No, no. They did a blood test and then called me back a week or so later. The doctor rattled off a couple different possibilities, and one of 'em was multiple myeloma, and I remembered that term from when my great-grandmother passed away. She'd had that, so I immediately thought that was the best guess."

"Is it hereditary?" I asked, suddenly very aware of my genetics.

"No, they said it's not."

"Then why did you think you had that?"

"I don't know. The name just stuck out to me for some reason. The doctor didn't even know at that point. He looked grave, but unsure. So he sent me to an oncology specialist at Mobile Infirmary to get a real diagnosis."

"When did you do that?"

"Yesterday," Daddy answered. "Your mama and I went together, and the oncologist told us the news."

"Oh, yeah, you told me that. Sorry, yesterday was a blur."

"So, what's next?" Natalie asked, finally speaking.

"Well, I start chemo treatment next week at the Infirmary, and there's a support group that meets once a week at the same church that Summer goes to daycare at. That's all I can do for now."

"What can we be doing to help, Mama?" Natalie asked.

"Prayers are good, I guess."

Natalie and I nodded fervently.

"Anything else?" I asked.

"How long do you plan to stay, honey?" my mom asked.

Reality smacked me in the face once again. I hadn't even thought about going back to Nashville.

"I'll stay for as long as you need me here," I said, thinking, *This is my mother.* I'd figure out everything else when the time came.

⋆⋆12

By Sunday night, I knew I needed to call Jake and inform him of the situation. Even though it had been seven years, Jake still knew my mama and would want to know what was going on. Plus, I had co-writes scheduled for the whole week. But before I could dial his number, Mama walked outside. I was sitting on the diving board overlooking our pool. The water was murky because of all the leaves that fell in it. But it was my favorite place to think.

"I've always hated this darn pool," she laughed as she sat on one of the patio chairs. I turned around to face her.

"I know! You begged Daddy to fill it in, but Natalie and I always begged you not to—"

"Y'all swore up and down you wanted to have your

pool parties here."

"I had one!" I said, referring to my twelfth birthday. "Well, kind of."

"Yes, you did, honey."

"Remember our koi pond?" I asked, staring at the overgrown patch of lawn behind the pool.

"Of course I do," she laughed again. "That crane ate all our fish in one fell swoop!"

"I remember seein' it the night before; it was on the roof right outside my window. I told Daddy, but neither of us knew what was gonna happen by the next day!"

She laughed a little more, but I could tell she was feeling some pain.

"Honey, I need to talk to you."

"Sure, Mama."

"I want you to go back to Nashville. You shouldn't stay here in Mobile while I get treatment. I'll just be going in every day like a regular doctor's appointment."

"But Mama, I want to be here. You'll need your family. I'm sure Jake would understand."

"I have your daddy and Natalie if I need somethin'."

"You don't want me here?" I was so confused.

"It's not that, honey. I just want you to get to follow your dreams. I won't get better if I know your life stopped in order to watch me go to and from chemo."

I couldn't get mad at her, not now, but I was. I couldn't do anything to help so I had to go back to Nashville? Maybe it wasn't meant to be harsh, but that's what I heard. If I left, I knew I'd feel guilty and worry myself sick. But if I stayed, Mama would worry about me and not herself. And I couldn't argue with her, she had cancer!

"Are you sure, Mama?"

"Positive. I know you've got your writing coming up this week. That's important. Stay tomorrow and then go back Tuesday."

I nodded reluctantly, suddenly feeling a little bit unwanted. I wondered if Natalie would be told to stay away, too. Or, if because she had local dreams, the rules didn't apply to her—as usual. I kept my mouth shut, though. I didn't want the rest of my short time to be taken over by a fight. It was the first time I wished I'd been normal since I'd gotten to Nashville, still called Lilah, headed to my first dorm at U of M. I would have been thirty minutes away from Mama. Now, I was being asked to go back to Tennessee. Gosh, I should've never said anything about my dreams being bigger or better.

Jake was sympathetic, just as I expected, and told me it would be no problem at all to cancel the Monday and Tuesday co-writes. Luckily, based on my mom's orders to leave Tuesday, I would make it back in time to write with Clint Lagerberg—the one writer who was supposed to "get me."

I wasn't feeling all that lucky, though. Everything was different. How was I supposed to focus on my music knowing that my mom's health hinged upon my success? Wondering if I would ever get to see her again. And whom in Nashville, besides Jake, would I even talk to about any of it? I had no friends, no boyfriend (which I figured was the last thing I needed). But for some reason, at this moment, I wished Owen had been different, so I could call him. If I could have, I would have told him the whole story and may have felt a little less ousted by my own mother. Anything to feel less lonely. The cold hard truth was that I couldn't tell Owen. Not even JoBeth. But Michael knew

Mama . . .

I texted him.

<Hey, just thought you should know. Mama's sick. It's cancer. Say a prayer.>

He never wrote back.

Monday was fine (considering). It consisted of the four of us, plus Judd and Summer, doing "family things": Going to eat at Cracker Barrel. Taking a ride out to the scenic town of Fairhope, where we could go to the pier. We watched Summer play on the playground for hours, while the rest of us read books and magazines under the trees at the park.

I figured we probably looked normal to everyone else, like a regular family doing things together. But we knew. We knew we were just making memories while we could. Just in case the worst possible thing happened: she never got any better.

Tuesday, in general, felt a lot like nausea: I was uncomfortable with the possibility that I could lose it at any moment. It was nothing like that day back in May when I'd packed up my car to move to Nashville. That day had been full of promise and excitement. This day sucked. Before I drove back, Daddy took everyone to Walmart for some retail therapy and a grocery run. I saw all the "Back to School" aisles (and a couple of my old classmates) and wished again and again for things to be simple. I'd had no idea how easy I had it before. I had been way too busy thinking about myself those days when Mama had been healthy as a horse.

I didn't want to say it out loud, but a terrible thought flashed through my mind over and over: *What if this is the last time I ever see my mom alive again?*

I drove away with it on repeat.

By Wednesday morning, I felt even worse than I had when I'd first gotten the news about the diagnosis, as if that was even possible. I felt alone, really alone. Where was the Nashville sparkle? When was the nightmare going to end? My mama had a rare bone cancer, and rare meant that fewer people got it, which meant that fewer people got treated for it, which meant that fewer laboratories were working on a cure for it. The odds were not in our favor.

Seriously, was this one of those dreams within a dream? Where you wake up, get awful news or find your leg chopped off and then wake up all over again? If so, I'd like to wake up for real, please.

Cancer. It changed everything, just by being there. Just weeks ago my best friend screwed me over, and now this? I could barely think of anything else as I drove to Clint's in "deep Brentwood," as Jake called it. It was out where Dolly Parton lived, which would have been cool on a regular, non-cancerous day. But remember, I wasn't that lucky.

Clint worked out of his basement studio, and we were scheduled to start right at eleven. It should have been an easy morning, but no, I just had to get off on the wrong exit.

Trying to navigate myself without looking at my Google Maps printout (like it would've helped anyway), I kept driving until I recognized something. I *had* spent a lot of time in Brentwood as a child, but it had been at a time when I hadn't had a license. I really only remembered two things: McDonald's and Kroger. And, oh, by the way, Brentwood wasn't as far as I thought. Just twenty minutes. Crazy how long it felt when I was little!

"Aha!" I yelled as I spotted that Kroger. I had a vague memory of Mr. Chambers getting a ticket right in front of it, and if I remembered correctly, the Chambers lived ahead on the right. That meant I was headed in the correct direction—I hoped. Another couple minutes later, I saw a sign for Concord Road. Clint's address was something Concord Pass, so it had to be close!

On Concord, I saw a huge church that had definitely not been there the last time I was here. It looked fairly new. The sign read Brentwood Baptist Church. It made Daddy's little Cherry Hill Baptist look like a trailer.

Seeing churches always made me miss him. And since there were churches on every corner in Tennessee, that happened a lot. But I didn't have time to dwell on family matters. I was late.

Clint's house was a ways out there. By the time I arrived, it was ten after eleven. *Great way to start a co-write you've been waiting all summer for,* I thought. But Clint came outside and told me he had been running late, so I was right on time.

Scratch that. This might be a good day after all.

"Did ya find the place OK?" he asked. "I know it's far out."

"Yeah, eventually! It's so nice out here. Kind of reminds me of home."

"Where's home?"

"Alabama. Mobile."

"Sweet. I'm from Maine, so the South was pretty much all new to me. I tried out Music Row for a couple years, but this place, this is my haven," he said, looking around his wooded backyard.

"What was wrong with Music Row?"

"You hear that?"

Silence.

"No, I don't hear anything."

"Exactly."

I laughed for the first time in weeks. It felt good. Maybe he was onto something, living away from everything. Maybe someday.

"Shall we go in?" We walked down a small stone path to the back of the house. "Don't mind the feet pattering. My kids like to run around upstairs."

"Aw! How many?"

"Two, almost three. A boy and a girl. Abby and Ely and one on the way."

"I have a niece. She's three."

"That's a fun age. My Ely's three." Clint opened two sets of doors (which provided soundproofing). "So, here's the studio."

I literally stepped into a piece of art, a studio unlike I'd ever seen. I might have just graduated from high school in Alabama, but I knew a good studio when I saw one. The equipment was standard. The computer screens butted up next to each other to give the illusion of one big computer monitor, and included the computer keyboard, the actual keyboard, and the thousands of knobs and cords called a "patch bay." The amps, the pre-amps, the microphones, and the iso-booth for vocal recording and specialty instrument solos were meticulously organized. The guitars and their cases lined the walls, and the drum set sat atop a large weathered rug in a separate room with glass so thick it looked like a pair of heavy prescription glasses. All that was typical. What took my breath away was the soul in the room. I could feel it.

It was the carefully selected furniture—a white linen couch, a skinny white wooden coffee table, and a comfy rug—that made me want to take my shoes off. It was the walls that were covered with reclaimed wood. And it wasn't like cheap wood panels in an old office from the 70s. It looked cool, country, and creative.

"This is the most beautiful basement I've ever seen," I whispered as I made my way to the couch, feeling comfortable, right at home. And we just met!

"Thanks. It's been a work in progress for a while, but this room is finally done."

"You did this?"

"Yeah, it's a hobby of mine, sort of. Gets me out of my head, you know? Writing every single day either gets boring or overwhelms me."

"I'm so glad I'm not the only one who feels that way. I kind of got the feeling from other writers that they *live* for the everyday co-write, that they never get tired of it. I thought there was something wrong with *me*."

He laughed, but it wasn't at my expense.

"No, no. Everyone is different. Some thrive on being busy and writing songs until four in the morning or writing two and three times a day. Not me. I get burnt out if I do that. Don't get me wrong, I'll work on a song every now and then until four in the morning, but I'd rather use the quality versus quantity approach."

"How often are you down here?"

"A lot, but it's all good as long as I have my window. I used to work in the garage at our old house, and I started to feel like a caveman!"

I smiled. Jake had been spot on—as usual. Even if we didn't write "the song" that day, I was just happy to have met someone who seemed to be making the dream happen without cashing in every minute of his life. I welcomed that little piece of good news with outstretched arms.

For the rest of the morning, Clint and I went through the usual co-write motions, going back and forth, talking about our respective life journeys. I focused more on the old Lily Black days—what I had of the "glory days"—instead of the present. I was wary of getting super personal and telling Clint about the whole JoBeth situation or my mama's earth-shattering diagnosis. I had heard other writers in my first couple weeks dump all their woes on the table, but for whatever reason, I didn't want to burden Clint. It didn't feel right. I didn't want him to feel compelled to say anything or do anything to try to make me feel less, well, crappy. It wasn't fair to bring that kind of thing into such a beautiful room. It trumped everything. It would change the entire day, and my good days were few and far between. I wasn't going to mess with this one, especially so soon.

Clint finally asked the question that all writers eventually asked in the co-write. The question that signified the end of the "getting to know you" time and the beginning of the "let's write a hit" time.

"Do you have anything you want to write about?" he asked.

As usual, I just wanted to scream "I DON'T KNOW WHAT I'M DOING HERE. I'M NO GOOD AT THIS! I'M JUST A GOOD SINGER! THAT'S IT!"

But instead, I picked up my idea book and started

flipping through the pages one by one, hoping and praying that just one of the words or phrases I had written down would jump off the page and inspire me. Just one!

This act of flipping through my book was my "go-to." I did it in every co-write, and it worked about 30 percent of the time. I really needed this day to be one of those rare times.

"Tell me about you," he said before I could get halfway.

"I . . . just did."

"I know about your career, but not about *you*."

Was there a difference these days?

"That's the first time anyone's asked me that," I said, taken a little off guard.

Clint laughed. "Well, then whom are you working with? 'Cause songs aren't written about careers. They are about life, real life."

"I'm only seventeen," I admitted.

"So?"

"So . . . I don't have much life to talk about . . . or write about."

"Excuse my French, but that's bullcrap."

I laughed again, a recurring theme with this guy.

"Come on, tell me something. What's your name? Let's start there. 'Lily Black' is too slick to be a given name by a true mama bear."

"You're good. It's Lilah Marie Carson."

"Now, that's a solid Southern name if I ever heard one."

"Thanks, it was my grandma's name."

"All right. Tell me something else. Something about Lilah."

I proceeded to go into my life as a preacher's daughter, my terrible awkward stages, and got all the way to day I sang the national anthem. Clint listened, just as I expected, but he stopped me.

"If I sound like a guidance counselor, please forgive me—I am a professional dad. But I'm looking for something you feel *really* passionate about. Either good or bad. In co-writes, I like to start with extremes, and then see where it takes us."

"OK," I bit the inside of my lip. "I moved here with a girl, my best friend. But she turned out to be a she-devil, for lack of a better term. I just kind of found out she never actually wanted to be my friend."

"How did you find out?"

"I found her . . . oh, gosh: this is embarrassing." I put my head in my sticky hands. Why was I so nervous?

"You don't have to tell me if you don't want to."

But I *did* want to, for some reason. I felt safe in his studio, miles away from Music Row, where that horrible day had happened. I felt like I'd known Clint for years instead of hours. I took a deep breath and rubbed off the sweat on my black pants.

"She was sleeping with my boyfriend . . . and I caught them. Well, I don't know if he was my official boyfriend— wait: she *did* sleep with my first real boyfriend, Michael, and I just found that out, too—but this other guy obviously wasn't my boyfriend if he was sleeping with her—"

"Lilah?" Clint stopped me. "Can I call you Lilah?"

I nodded, sure I'd turned red.

"I'm so sorry," he said.

"Why are you sorry?"

"That whole thing sounds like it was awful. Losing a best friend, a boyfriend, and trust, all in one day. I promise that's not how it has to be."

Clint looked up at the ceiling as we heard a roll across the floor . . . some toy.

I didn't feel judged. I didn't feel stupid. I felt listened to, sort of confident, even.

"Have you had anything like that happen?"

Clint chuckled. "No, not exactly that. That story would make a great song though. There's something there . . . So you *caught* 'em doing it? Huh, enough people could probably relate to that. . . ." He stalled, seeming to be thinking about the idea. "Anyway, yes, yes: I've had people betray me left and right. I don't know anyone who's done anything great that hasn't faced some crap like that. Think about it. What great person hasn't had someone try to screw him or her over?"

I shrugged. Clint continued.

"Greatness is envied, coveted, and there are people out there who just want to bring greatness down to their level. It's human nature, sadly, but *you* can turn it into something. You're a songwriter. You can make freakin' hit lemonade out of those lemons!"

I sat in awe. The wisdom, the honesty, the therapy I was getting was worth money. *I should be paying him for this!* I thought. Sure, I had heard these things at home, in a school discussion, definitely at church. But it seemed totally different coming from someone who was more like me. He was a successful songwriter. He had come from another state and wrangled the beast of Nashville; he knew what he was talking about because he lived it day in and day out.

It wasn't someone from back home telling me I was "gonna be a huge star." If I had a nickel for every time someone told me that . . . and the "don't forget the little people when you're big time," I would have the lottery jackpot in my piggy bank.

Clint was someone who really, actually practiced what he preached in the industry. Someone who knew how hard it could be, how dishonest, how *mean* people could be. How unglamorous it was most of the time.

"Well, while we are talking about lemons . . . I have another one. Wait, what are those really sour candies? The ones that kind of hurt they're so sour . . . ?"

"Warheads?"

"Yeah, I have a Warhead."

"But I thought you just told me—"

"My mom has cancer," I blurted.

Clint looked up from his guitar, but he sat still. Only then did I realize he had been strumming, somehow creating background music during our entire conversation. Before I realized what I should say next, Clint had put his guitar down, gotten up, walked around the coffee table, and bear-hugged me. Like a big brother would.

"Look, I don't want you to talk about anything you're not comfortable with. Just because you have events in your life that we could write songs about doesn't mean you have to tell me. I understand some things are private."

"No, it's OK." It was. Even though he was technically a stranger. I don't know, maybe that helped.

"Are you sure? We don't even have to write about it. Heck, we don't even have to write today. We can just talk."

I thought about it and smiled.

"I'm sure," I nodded. "She just got diagnosed on Friday, so it's still pretty new. It's a rare bone cancer. multiple . . . mya, crap."

"Hey, I'm just a songwriter. I don't mess with those big

medical terms," he joked.

"Let's say 'MM.'"

"Deal. So, how are *you*?"

"What do you mean? I'm not the one with cancer."

"Trust me. The actual patient can suffer less than the family. Your mom, even though I don't actually know her—if she's anything like what I see in you—she's strong. And she'll find a way to cope. She'll find a threshold for the pain and make peace with it. The family actually fears a lot more: They worry about her comfort level, and how to act around her. They also struggle with moving on with their lives, worrying if they should go on or change all their plans entirely."

"Were you a psychologist in a past life?"

"Me? No: heck, no. I didn't even go to college. I worked in a factory . . . school of hard knocks, girl!" he said. "I'm kidding—not about the factory; I did work at one—but seriously, it wasn't that hard, it was just my path. And the other stuff? I just know people who have been in your situation before, that's all."

A tear slid down my cheek without my permission. And then I couldn't stop them. They came in twos, then fours, then tens, and before I could do anything, the floodgates opened.

"I'm sorry," I cried, reaching for a tissue on the coffee table.

"Let it all out. I've got all the time in the world. This is our job, believe it or not." He patted me on the back.

"It's just that my mom is the reason I'm here and not back home in Mobile right now. She told me she wanted me to come back to Nashville and make my dreams come true."

"Is your mom the reason you're here in the first place?"

"Well, no. I moved here on my own a few months ago. But now that she's gotten diagnosed, I thought maybe I should go home and be with her. But she told me no. That I should finish what I started."

"So you feel like your dreams might be changing a little?"

"Yes," I cried harder. "Is that bad?"

"Are they changing because of her or because of you?"

"I don't know. I just feel like my timeline is all jacked up now. I'm not even eighteen yet! Like, what if she dies and I don't get to have her help me get dressed on my wedding day? Or what if she never gets to meet my kids one day?"

Clint paused.

"So, you're not actually ready to settle down, but you're worried that you should so that you can make sure she's there for it all."

"Are you sure you didn't at least go to college?" I sniffled.

He laughed and started strumming again.

falling stars

[l. black, c. lagerberg]

d.o.c.
july 18,
2007

used to stare up at the diamond lights
just like heaven through the bama pines
i wish i might...

never knew they were so far from home
till i tried to reach them on my own
i've never known
such all alone...

glitter's all but gone, be sure what you wish on

Chorus {
sometimes the sun, it shines on your face
sometimes it just burns out
it just burns out

sometimes the stars, they all fall in place
sometimes they just fall down
they just fall down
some times
}

never had my world so turned around
what always used to be my sky is now
the cold, hard ground
that's where i found

pre-chorus
chorus
↓
solo
broken down chorus

Mom

13

People say music can change you. Well, "Falling Stars" changed me. It became a mantra, an anthem, and one thing was certain: I wanted to write my songs. I was hooked, thanks to Clint.

Because we spent most of our first day talking, we barely finished writing the song at all. So all I had to listen to in the car on my way back to Jake's office was a crappy, out-of-tune work tape. But I didn't care. I think I replayed it forty times.

Jake was one of those people in Nashville who could "hear past the work tape," meaning he didn't have to have a finished product to hear how it would eventually sound on a record. Not everyone could do that, so we decided to limit the amount of people we let hear it until Clint and

I got back together to record it properly. My family was in that "do not give" column. I wanted it to be absolutely perfect when they heard it, especially Mama.

Speaking of Mama, I got updates from my daddy every day on her progress, but I hadn't talked to *her* that much since I'd left Mobile. I don't know, maybe it was the whole "be strong and don't break down" mentality that kept me from calling.

I knew Clint was probably right that she would find strength within the process of chemotherapy. But that didn't mean I should add to the worry by telling her the truth, that I'd been having nightmares. That would certainly not help her focus on getting better. That would depress her. (As if she wasn't already.)

So through Daddy, I found out most of the news: Mama had been attending that cancer support group every week, and it was a blessing, he'd said. And so far, the chemo was going well. She'd had no pain during treatments, and if she ever started to feel nauseous, all she had to do was ask for a pill. I didn't know the exact protocol for chemotherapy, but I had kind of assumed there would be a lot of pain involved, so the fact that there wasn't (at least at this point) took a load off my shoulders.

"Your mother is still out there on the patio with her Bible every mornin', God bless her," Daddy had said.

He always asked how I was coping. And I always said the same thing: "I'm doin' all right, Daddy. Just workin' hard so I can give Mama good news."

"Don't overdo it, sweetie. I know she wants you to be happy, but she also wants you to be sane," he'd say.

Even in the midst of all these curveballs, he was still able to make jokes, laugh, be somewhat normal. It was a good sign. My daddy was a bear, but the Teddy kind. And he still loved his wife like it was their first day together. We all loved Mama, but Daddy was the shining example. And every time I talked to him, it made me more determined than ever to get a record deal so I could get back home, too.

Since the diagnosis, life had a different spin, a different perspective. Stardom, fame . . . even retaliation or proof that I still had "it"; those were motives of my past. Now it was my Mama's health that drove me.

I started doing little things to remind myself of my goals. I drew "sCɴ" on the inside of my wrist (in black ink of course) every morning. It started my days off right. Of course I knew I could get a tattoo, but to me, a tattoo wouldn't be permanent enough. Let me explain: If I had to retrace it each day, I had to remember where I was, why I was there, and what I was working toward. Retracing her name rejuvenated me, gave me energy work harder than I ever had. Getting a tattoo would be too easy. Too easy to forget.

Aside from music, my goals, and my mom, I had another problem. Being with Clint for just one day, writing one measly song with him showed me what I was missing in my life: friends. I needed to find a group of girls my age. It would be hard, I knew, to trust again, but I also knew I couldn't be a hermit forever and survive.

"Dad, can I get a phone number for the Chambers?" I asked during one of my daily calls home.

"The Chambers? Let me see if it's in your mother's drawer here in the kitchen. Ah! Here it is."

"Thanks."

"You gonna see 'em? Tell ole Robert I said hello."

"How do you even know him, again? I thought he was a dentist?"

"He is, but we met through a mutual friend in college, and you know me, I make friends easily. He told me about his church back home in Tennessee, and my interest in seminary was sparked. Then, we just kept in touch on occasion, and he's kept me updated with his church. Man, that new place they built is huge, and the pastor . . . wow."

"You've been there?"

"Yeah, well, at the *old* location. That guy is legendary in the Baptist circles! I went to a service or two with Robert when I came up to visit you while you worked on your first album. Remember? I asked you to come with us!"

I guess I had forgotten more about those days than I thought.

"Not really."

"Oh, who am I kiddin'? You weren't worried about all that stuff. You were nine and livin' the dream!" He laughed at the memory.

I laughed a little, too, and thanked him for the number. Before dialing, I said a quick prayer that the Chambers would remember me fondly and *not* as a spoiled brat.

"Hello?"

"Mrs. Chambers?"

"Yes?"

"This is Lilah Carson, uhh, Lily Black?"

"Oh my gosh! Little Lilah! How are you, darlin'? It's been years! Are you coming in town? Do you need a place to stay?"

Still the nicest woman ever. How refreshing.

"No, no, I live here, now—in town, I mean. I was just

wondering how I could get in touch with Allie."

Allie was youngest Chambers daughter and the closest one to my age.

"Oh! Well, actually, she's about to start college! Belmont! Music business major, can you believe it? Of all my girls, finally one's interested in something our city's known for. I probably have you to thank for that. I'm sure she'd love to get together with you. You were her first famous friend, you know."

"Ha, well . . . ," I wanted to make a joke and tell her how fame had dropped me from its graces or something, but I stopped myself. Life was too short to keep making fun of it. I needed to live and move forward, starting now.

"I'm honored," I said instead.

Mrs. Chambers chit-chatted, asked questions about my family, and eventually gave me Allie's number. And she promised to forward the message to her husband Robert that "Ole Cole" had said hello.

"Hello?"

"Is this Allie?"

"Yeah! Who's this?"

"Lilah—Lily Black?"

"Hi! Oh my gosh! How are you? It's been, like, forever!"

Like mother like daughter.

"I'm good! I got your number from your mom; I hope that's OK! She said you were going to Belmont?"

"Yep. Freshman and everything."

"Do you live near campus?" I asked.

"I will. In the stinky dorms though. I already can't wait to get my own place."

"I don't know Nashville all that well yet, but is it by

chance close to the Bristol?"

"Yeah!" she yelled into the phone "Oops, sorry! It's right down the street I think! Why?"

"Well, I moved to Nashville and I'm leasing a place there, actually."

"No way! That's so fun! We need to get together!"

"I would love that," I sighed, grateful. "Not to sound totally lame, but it's a little hard to make friends when you didn't grow up here."

"Oh, I totally understand! Well, I don't, but I can imagine. My sister went to UT in Knoxville and said the only thing that saved her was rushing Kappa Delta. Hey, it might be too last minute, but what are you doing tonight?"

"I'm free, I think." I was totally free—no doubt about it.

"Well, if you don't want to, it's no big deal, but I started going to this Bible study at church. It's called 'Preparing for Marriage'—as if I'm even dating! Ha! But it is literally the best decision I have ever made. The girls are such wonderful new friends of mine, now. Maybe they could be yours, too!"

I laughed. "Well, I'm not exactly preparing for marriage, either, but friends sound good! I'm in."

I was thankful for plans, thankful for Allie's blind acceptance, thankful for an invitation back to church. Especially one my daddy condoned.

"That's the spirit. It's at seven. Bring your Bible and something to take lots of notes with. Our leader says so much good stuff, you'll want to write it all down!"

"OK! I'll meet you there! And hey, Allie? Thanks."

"Are you kidding me? I can't wait to see you again. It's been so long!"

I hung up and felt a rush of excitement. Nashville wasn't

so bad. I grabbed my Bible and started reading, brushing up for tonight.

"Hey, everybody!" Allie practically shouted as she led me into the Bible study room. There were about fourteen chairs in a circle, over half of them filled with all types of girls. Some blonde, some brunette, some short, some tall, some wearing Phi Mu or college-wear, some in sweats or workout clothes, and some in business attire.

"This is Lilah! She's a friend of mine from when I was younger."

All the girls gushed and stood up to give me a hug—no questions asked. On the way into Brentwood Baptist, Allie had asked me whom I wanted to be introduced as, and I had instinctively chosen my real name. Church was a place I wanted to be myself; it wasn't about music here or my career. And I'd noticed over the years that once people knew about my past, the focus always shifted . . . and I didn't want that. Not during my first time. I needed real friends, not fans.

Growing up in the South as a preacher's daughter, church hadn't been an option, a place I could discover on my own. Not that it was a bad thing, but I'd just been brought up in the same building with the same people all my life. But at Brentwood Baptist, with a little wiggle room, I was finally able to see what all the fuss was about.

And my prayers were answered, even the ones I didn't ask for. By the time Allie and I left the church two hours later, I had eight new friends, their phone numbers, and a full three pages of wisdom from our leader Diane on ways to prepare my heart for God's ultimate plan for me: marriage to a Godly man. Laugh all you want, but I needed assistance in that department. Plus, I had a new church home, somewhere else to go (besides my condo) on Sunday mornings and Tuesday nights for Kairos (a more casual service for young adults that Allie said I'd love). Honestly, I didn't care if I hated it. I had friends. And I would go anywhere they went . . . well, within reason.

★ * ★ *

Mama had been in treatment for two months, and, according to Daddy and Natalie, things were going pretty well—as well as one could hope for with multiple myeloma.

It was getting harder and harder to be away from them here in Nashville. All I wanted to do was go home and see her—*them*. I wanted to give my mama a big hug and tell her how great she was doing. But I couldn't: the showcase was tonight!

My band looked amazing in all black, my background singer Kiley sparkled in her purple sequin mini dress, and the stage was ready to go, amps and instruments all set up.

Jake had come through yet again and arranged for all the label heads to be in attendance. Through the curtains, I spotted a few I recognized, including someone from my former label. Way to go, Jake. The latest rendition of "Burning Blue" had worked after all, which meant I had to deliver the goods.

My short black dress was itching the inside of my arms from a last minute alteration Darla had made. "It needs to be tighter in the boobs," she'd said plainly. But a wardrobe issue couldn't keep me down. High heels, check. Black cross, check. Cat eyes, check. Red lips, double check. I was ready and focused. Oh, and my mama's initials were there, too; don't worry.

I was going to play a ten-song set. Normally, a new artist would cap it at four or five, but I wasn't a new artist. Jake had said, "If you're askin' people to come out on their Monday night, you need to give 'em a real show! Not a taste! Give 'em the whole Lily Black experience!"

Ten songs. It was a lot to remember. So, I did what I'd always done: I wrote a set list on a piece of paper and taped it on the stage behind my vocal monitor. That way, I could focus on the music and not worry about forgetting the order of the show. Adrenaline and nerves were not to be underestimated. Plus, it was a show I wanted to *feel*, not be graded on. This wasn't school—I could cheat all day if I wanted to!

SHOWCASE!!

1. burning blue
   → [welcome / thank you]
2. see it
3. good for goodbye
   → [call up clint]
4. always never enough
5. live love learn
6. wildcard
7. something ~~so~~ steady
8. only one
9. snake in the grass
10. FALLING STARS!

Jake and I decided to start the show with "Burning Blue." It was a bit of a departure from the norm, since shows usually started out with an upbeat, boot-stompin' song to get the energy up. But these were special circumstances. I had been here before. I'd had a bona fide number one hit. And a number one was as good as anything to get a crowd going.

The rest of the songs on my set list were ones I'd co-written in the past several months. We picked the best ones, and then I rehearsed them with the band until they were second nature. I needed to be on autopilot tonight.

Ever been to a show where the singer seemed to have a script or something? They probably did. But I needed real. I needed unforgettable. This showcase was my last shot— my only shot if I wanted to get a remotely good offer. With each attempt after tonight, fewer record executives would show up, the ones with industry clout anyway.

The house lights dimmed, and I walked out in the dark and took a deep breath. After a few whistles and whoops, I heard Brandon's signature guitar riff to the song that start- ed this whole dream. *Here we go!* And I sang "Burning Blue" like I never had before. Right when I sang the first note, I knew why I was here. I felt at home. All my wor- ry, all those years back in Mobile, Michael, JoBeth, Owen, even Mama's cancer (if just for a moment) . . . it all fell away. I was in my zone.

I walked out to the front of the small Twelfth & Porter stage to greet the audience. If I went out to the very edge, I could actually see them.

"You have no idea how grateful I am that all of you came out tonight. Before I say anything else, I want to thank you . . . All right, enough sappy stuff! Welcome! I'm Lily Black—yes, *that* Lily Black—the one you saw back in 2000 with the overly teased hair and the overly sparkly dresses," I joked.

Everyone laughed.

Jake had advised me against taking myself too serious- ly on stage tonight, to address the pseudo elephant in the room (if I was really Lily and why I was back). If I told them early on, I could get to the really important part of the show: the music, my voice.

"I bet some of you are wonderin' where I've been for the past seven years."

I saw some silhouettes nod their heads.

"Well, in a nutshell . . . I was growing up. I'm from a town called Mobile, Alabama, so I went back home, went to high school, and tried to live a normal life. But when I graduated, I realized I really missed Nashville. In the short years I spent here, it had become as much a part of me as these here freckles!"

Another laugh. I was on a roll!

"So, I skipped college—against my mama and daddy's will—and here I am! Where I belong. So sit back, relax, and enjoy some of the original songs I've been writin' with some of my new friends."

The songs were seamless, and they sounded way better live, with a band, with energy, with practice, and with that extra "Lily Black touch." I couldn't tell you exactly what that touch was, but it was there. And I wasn't questioning it.

Once I reached "Always Never Enough" on the set list, I walked back up to the front of the stage. "All right, these next ones are very dear to me. Clint, if you could come on up to the stage? Clint Lagerberg, everyone."

Applause, applause.

"If you know Clint, you know he can write like no-body's business. He can sing like nobody's business. Check the charts, they'll tell ya. But what I love about him is his heart. We wrote for the first time when I was going through some pretty hard stuff, and he basically just let me vent . . . for hours. Sorry, Clint. The song we wrote that first day is undoubtedly my all-time favorite . . . which you'll hear a little later. But right now, I'd love to show you two more we've done together. This is 'Always Never Enough' and then 'Live, Love, Learn.'"

Clint sang the lead on the two songs while I sang backgrounds. It wasn't exactly customary for someone else to sing a lead during an artist's showcase, but Jake and I had agreed that if done right, the alternative approach could actually help my chances, especially if the song was meant for a male lead. Of course, we had different motives. On the business side, Jake wanted to demonstrate that I was confident enough to step out of the spotlight for two whole songs without skipping a beat. Second, he said he wanted people to realize that I was more than just a voice, that I was songwriter as well, capable of getting cuts outside my own albums. And lastly, it was important to show that I had made some serious friends in the industry since my return to Nashville. That I wasn't too good to get my hands dirty and work for it. Hopefully, record executives would see it translating into future collaborations, tours, etc.

Jake's reasons were fine and very important, but I had my own. On the personal side, I wanted to prove that I had, in fact, grown up. That I had learned how to be an adult, done something useful with my seven years away from the spotlight. And playing my songs with Clint would undoubtedly show them another side to Lily Black, a side that had not existed when I was ten and eleven years old.

On top of strategy and proving my own personal growth, I adored Clint. He had truly become the big brother I never had. Well, besides Judd. He was my Nashville brother, and Allie was my Nashville sister (who had brought all the Bible study girls along with her tonight). They were easy to spot in the crowd with all their hootin' and hollerin'.

As more songs ended, I found myself wishing that the

show would never end. I was having too much fun. After Clint's songs, I got an idea. I noticed some of my other co-writers in the audience, so I invited them up to sing on the songs they had written. Nashville was a songwriter's town, so none of the writers declined, thankfully.

Claire Wyndham (the Australian writer I'd had been eating Mexican food with the night I found out about Mama) came up to sing the sweet, lovey-dovey "Wildcard." The amazingly talented Matt Wertz stepped up to sing our laid back "Something Steady," the super tall and soulful Adam James jumped in on "Only One," and Brandon Hood and Steven Lee Olsen partied on while we all sang my tribute to Owen and Michael, "Snake In The Grass."

The night turned into my own little Bluebird show—by accident! I could've easily stuck to the plan, worrying about hitting high notes and wowing the record execs. But they knew I could sing. What I wanted them see was my adult personality, how I worked the stage, the audience, and how I handled myself when the show took on an unexpected life of its own. They needed to see a professional up there. And a pro they got.

"All right, y'all. It's time for the last one . . . ooh, goodness, I don't wanna go. This has been the most fun I've had in seven whole years . . . that's sad, huh?"

Laughter.

"But this won't be the last of me . . . not if ole Jake Slaughter has anything to do it; right, Jake?"

"RIGHT!" Jake hollered.

More laughter. I could tell by the amount of laughter I heard that the house was still packed. No one had left early—a really good sign.

"I told y'all this before, but I wrote this one with Clint,

and it was right after I got some real bad news. My mama has cancer . . . and she's fightin' it right now back home in Mobile. So, Mama? This is for you. This is 'Falling Stars.'"

Used to stare up at the diamond lights . . .
Just like heaven through the 'Bama pines
I wish I might . . .

Standing ovation. Wild applause. It went on for much longer than I expected. And during those moments, I knew. I knew I'd done it. And if I hadn't . . . I wouldn't quit. I would hound those labels until they gave me a dang deal!

As soon as I grabbed a bottled water backstage, thanked my band and background singer (who had ended up with a very easy job) profusely, I was back out front, jumping off the stage toward my friends.

"Oh my gosh, you were so good!" Allie hugged me for the tenth time since I had gotten off stage. "We will see you tomorrow night, right?"

"Yep, Kairos! I'll be there! Hey, thanks for coming, girls!"

"Ms. Black?" a man said from behind me.

"Of course! We love you!" the other girls said, hugging me, too. But then they saw the man and quickly understood their cue to go. I turned around to the voice.

"Yes? Sorry about that," I said.

"That was one heck of a show."

"Thank you very much, sir."

"Scott Betina. Big Little Records," he said as he reached out his hand.

"Nice to meet you, Mr. Betina. And thank you for

making it out on a Monday night."

"It's worth it when you find a gem. And the Gold Miner knows how to find 'em."

I exhaled. Before I could continue the conversation, Jake walked up with an expectant smile.

"Scottie! Hey, thanks for coming, man," he said as he patted Mr. Betina on the back. "Is she fantastic, or what?"

"I was just telling her that making time for someone who is worth signing is well worth a Monday night for me. And that song you sang at the end? Big hit."

Jake's smile grew wider.

"I'll call you tomorrow morning, Jake. And Lily? It was so nice to meet you. I hope to see you in my office this week." He winked as he shook my hand again.

I was unsure of exactly what Mr. Betina meant, but a quick look from Jake told me it was a very good thing, so I smiled and simply answered with "Me too! Have a good night!"

Once Scott Betina left the room, Jake hurriedly led me behind the tower of amplifiers to talk in private.

He put his hands on my shoulders.

"I just want to tell you how proud I am. Wonderful job, Lily. Wonderful. So wonderful that you will be receiving not one, not two, but *three* record-deal offers because of tonight." Jake beamed.

I screamed, and all the stragglers in the room stopped, looked around, and then continued on with their conversations.

"Are you kidding?"

"No! Thankfully, I'm not. I spoke to two other executives before Scottie. They all loved 'Falling Stars,' Lily. All of 'em."

"It was Clint. He's the genius."

"That's not what I heard. He said you were a natural. I knew you would be."

"Really?"

Jake nodded. "Well, I'll get on the phone early tomorrow and start comparin' the offers on the table. But I think Scottie's our guy. You go on and get some sleep. I'm proud of you, kiddo. Whatever you started tapping into, it's working. And I loved what you did up there with all the writers coming up . . . great stuff."

"You didn't think it was too much?"

"No! Labels need to see the kind of gal you are. You're not just a singer; you're a writer! And you got friends in the biz! Good ones! Oh, and speakin' of good ones, Brandon had to go home before you came back out, but he told me to tell you you were 'killer.'"

"Aw, that's nice! And, Jake? Thanks for everything."

"Honey, you did all the work. But you're welcome. I'm proud to be a part of team Lily again. Did you see Owen? He told me to tell you good luck, but I forgot."

"No, I didn't see him! Well, darn! Tell him I said thanks! Bye Jake!"

I started walking backstage again. I felt a little guilty that I still hadn't mentioned anything to Jake about my former relations with Owen or my current disdain for him. I would someday, but not tonight. Tonight wasn't about backstabbing friends or slutty almost-boyfriends or exes who didn't respond to very important text messages. Tonight was about music. Tonight was about my dream.

"Mama?"

"Yes, honey?"

"I did it. I did what you asked."

"What do you mean?"

Mama sounded a little frailer each time we spoke, which was still not very often. It scared me, but I pretended not to notice so as not to draw attention to it. I didn't want her to think about cancer twenty-four hours a day.

"I got a record deal. Another one, Mama."

"Oh my, Cole! Honey!" Her voice was excited, but quiet. "Get in here. Lilah's called, tellin' me she got a record deal!"

I could hear Daddy hootin' and hollerin' in the background, and it made me smile.

"Are you happier now? I'm living my dream—for you, Mama."

She paused.

"Lilah, that's not what I meant. You don't have to do anything for me, don't you see? I don't want you to miss out on life because I got this stupid cancer."

"But, I thought you just didn't want me to come back until I—"

"I would be thrilled if you became a librarian if that's what you wanted, sweetheart."

"Really?"

"Really, honey. Is that what you've been thinking all along? Why you haven't been callin' me as much?"

I felt guilty, sad, silly, and embarrassed—all at once.

"Yes. . . ."

"I am so sorry. When I got my diagnosis, I started thinking in fast forward. I started thinkin' about you and Natalie and how much livin' you two have left to do. You living in Tennessee is a dream come true for me because I know that deep down, it's where you want to be. You want to be up on those stages singing to those people. Your voice is so beautiful, like an angel, Lilah. But if you don't want to do it, don't do it. Do you hear me?"

She was crying softly now, and the wrench in my stomach twisted further. All I wanted at that moment was to be sitting at the foot of her rocking chair, listening to her read out of the book of Psalms. But instead, I was in the shared parking garage of my building, sitting in my hot car after meeting with Jake, gripping the steering wheel with all my might.

"Mama, please don't cry. It was my fault. I misunderstood. I don't want you to be upset."

She sniffled a little and cleared her throat.

"Lilah . . . Lily . . . don't worry about me. I'm not going to break. I'm not made of glass. I'm steel, ya hear? And cryin's not always a bad thing. This cancer isn't gonna break my spirit. The Lord has me safe in His hands. And just because I have cancer, it does *not* mean I quit bein' your mama."

"Mmm-hmm," I sniffled.

"I love you, and I want you to be happy and do what you want to do."

"What if I wanna come home and see you?"

I heard rustling, the sound of my mama's hand covering the phone while she talked to Daddy. A moment later, I heard a click. I was on speaker.

"Hey, darlin," Daddy said. "Mama said you might want to come home?"

"Yeah, is that not OK?"

"Well, we are actually in the process of deciding on

whether your mom should stay here in Mobile or go to a hospital in Arkansas."

"Arkansas? What's in Arkansas! Couldn't you just come to Nashville—to Vanderbilt? I live right down the street!"

My mind was spinning. Where was this conversation leading? One minute ago, it sounded like things were good and steady, but now, I wasn't so sure.

"A couple of women in your mother's support group have multiple myeloma, and they've been encouragin' her to check this place out. It's world renowned, Lily. Even treated Sam Walton of Walmart."

"But she'll be too far away! She won't have family."

"Her sisters are gonna take turns and stay if she ends up going, so she won't be totally alone. And I'll visit as much as I can. The doctors here are wonderful, but they don't do stem cell transplants, and that's what your mother needs right now. If she had a more common cancer, it would be fine to stay here. But her type needs a particular regimen of care—care she can only get in Arkansas."

"Mom? Are you OK with this?"

"Your father doesn't want me to wonder later what would've happened if I had gone to Little Rock, and I agree with him. We'll find a way to make it work."

"Sounds like you already made up your mind."

"I think so. The women in my support group, especially the leader, Ann Lampley, rave about the facility and the nurses and doctors and stuff. And all the homework your daddy and I have done points us in that direction."

I took a breath.

"OK, so what's next?"

"Your mother and I go up there to check it out. Then, if we think it's a fit, we'll have to find an apartment, and then we move her up there to start treatment."

"And all that has to happen now? It's almost Christmas! Can't it wait till after?"

"The sooner the better, honey," Daddy said. "The sooner the better."

"OK." I sighed, taking it all in. "Well, if you need me, I'll be there in a second. I can take a flight."

"That's a waste of money," he said. "We'll call you with all the details and once she gets all settled, we'll all meet in Little Rock. You can come down here to Mobile for Christmas with Natalie and Judd. They have an extra room." Dad paused. "Look, Lily, I know this isn't ideal, and I know Christmas will be different this year. If we could change it, we would. It's your mother's favorite holiday. But we need to think about what's best for her in the long run."

What could I do but comply? He was right. Mama was going to get the best care in the country. Christmas-as-usual could wait.

"I agree, Daddy. Get her the best doctor out there."

"We love you, child." Mama piped in.

"I love you, too. Both of you."

After that conversation, I fell off a cliff. I lost my appetite. And not just for food. But also for music, for Nashville. For anything besides my mom. Knowing she wasn't going to be in Mobile, in her own house, sleeping in her bed, with her patio and her filled-in koi pond, with her husband and her neighbors—it made me sick with worry. It was already hard to live that far away from her. But what would happen when she didn't have anyone? No comforts of home?

I Googled Little Rock, and . . . I wasn't exactly blown away. It wasn't terrible, but it definitely did not scream "Best Place for Your Mom to Possibly Live Out the Rest of Her Days." The doctor's track record was pretty amazing, but his portrait on the website looked like he had the bed-side manner of Nurse Ratchet. The facility looked squeaky clean and brand new, but who knew how old the pictures were?

It wasn't that bad, I guessed, but it wasn't home. It wasn't familiar, and I, quite frankly, wasn't sold yet. Not that it made any difference what I thought anyway, since it clearly wasn't my decision. But I still had my doubts.

"Sometimes I wonder if my mom got cancer because I moved here. She didn't have it until I left, until I decided that Mobile wasn't good enough for my dreams," I admitted to my Bible study through a steady stream of tears.

"Lilah, your mom already had the cancer, she just didn't know it yet," our leader Diane said in her calm voice.

"But what if it's God's way of showing me I'm not supposed to be here? If her cancer shows up the minute I leave?"

"I'm not sure that's why she got cancer. And I wouldn't make any sudden conclusions. Remember what we talked about? Try to sift through your head and your heart, and really listen to your gut." She gestured to her lower abdomen.

I nodded, my guilt and anxiety temporarily subsiding. The other girls nodded, too.

"We women tend to listen to our emotions first and

our logic, second. We knee-jerk. We think if we 'feel' it enough or 'think' it enough, it's the right thought or the right feeling, but I've found that it's down here where the wisdom lives. Take some time to really listen to it, and I think you'll find your answer, Lilah."

I nodded again, eager to listen . . . eager to find answers.

After Bible study let out, I walked to the car, the early signs of winter nipping at my ears and nose. Once I got in, and cranked up the heat, I checked my voicemail:

Hey, Lily-Lou, it's C-c-c-c-c-cole Carson! I would like to formally invite you to a party for the one and only Sandy-Sue before she makes her way to Arkansas!

(His voice changed out of bad DJ mode and back into his regular voice.)

But seriously, we are having a little get-together at Natalie's house this weekend, if you're available. I know I told you not to waste your time on comin' home, but maybe I jumped the gun. Your mother wants to say goodbye to everyone before she goes away for a while. It's going to be a happy party, not a sad one. She wants to go ahead and celebrate Christmas early, so we are going to put up our tree and sing carols around the fire. I hope you can make it, sweet pea, but I understand I didn't give you much notice. Love you, Lily-Lou-Who.

I immediately called Jake's office, and Owen answered, so I hung up. Nope. Nope. Nope. My parade was not going to be rained on, not even sprinkled on. Instead I sent Jake a quick text telling him I would be gone for a few days to see Mama, and that I'd be back ASAP.

Jake responded, <Roger that.> Then he mentioned that

Scott Betina had sent the recording contract back over to my lawyer, Seth, so it was a great time for a break. "The calm before the storm," he called it. He could say that again.

Next, I texted Allie that I was leaving and rushed back to my condo to pack the few items I wished I'd had the last time I went to Alabama. For one, my Chi. It was worth driving twenty minutes in the opposite direction. Trust me.

I knew driving all night wasn't safe, but honestly, I didn't care. Life was too short to follow all the rules. Mama's party was in two days, so I didn't have to go right then, but I wanted to surprise her and have as much time with her as I could. A Christmas party. How perfect. Christmas in October was better than no Christmas with Mama and Daddy at all. And I knew what I wanted for Christmas. For every Christmas after. Time. Nine lives. How come cats got them? They didn't even like people half of the time!

Three forty-five in the morning was a quiet hour. The last time I'd been up this late, besides going out, I was cramming for an English final, trying to finish *Paradise Lost* before the sun came up. That night had sucked, but I would have gladly read and reread that thing ten times in one sitting if it could erase Mama's cancer. I would have started high school all over again.

But when I finally walked in the door and saw my mama sitting at the table with her Bible again, I was so happy to have what I had, even if it wasn't perfect.

"Mom! What are you doing? You should be in bed, I mean, shouldn't you?"

Mama looked a tad bit skinnier this time, but mostly,

she looked the same. I guess I figured she would have at least lost some of her hair by then. Guess not.

"Your daddy could never keep a secret. He let it slip that he called you tonight. I had a feeling you'd come tonight, and I have a hard time sleepin' when one of my babies is out on the road. Come here, give me a hug."

"I'm sorry I drove this late," I said as she squeezed me gently. "I just got so excited when I heard Dad's voicemail, and I wanted to surprise you."

"Oh, honey, I'm so glad to see you. This house needs you in it, sometimes. It's way too quiet."

I smiled and started to feel that lump in my throat.

"Let's go on and get you to bed. I cleaned your shower and pulled back your covers."

"Mom. . . ."

"Hush, I'm fine. I'm still your mother."

The words had never sounded so good, and I savored the normality of my mama's light reprimands.

"OK, Mama. I love you," I whispered as I scaled the carpeted stairs to my bedroom.

★ * ★ *

The next morning, I woke up to the sound of Daddy laughing down in the kitchen. The clock said 10:30 a.m., which meant Mama told him to let me sleep in. I could picture their conversation at the foot of the stairs.

Daddy: *I'm going to get our girl.*

Mama: *Let her sleep, honey.*

Daddy: *But she'll miss my Pancake Delight.*

Mama: *She won't be any good to us if she's a zombie!*

Then he would wrap his arms a couple times around

her small little shoulders and tell her how beautiful she was. And she would get on her tiptoes and kiss his nose.

How did I know? I had witnessed the same exact transaction a million times before. But this time it hit me a little harder. Lately, I had been so busy thinking about how awful my own life would be without Mama that I'd plum forgotten to think about how anyone else would cope.

How would my daddy survive without his queen? They had been married for over thirty-five years: one piece, inseparable. Daddy had all the big ideas, and Mama brought reason and reality to the table. They needed each other. I would be fine . . . I hadn't found my soul mate yet. But what about my sweet, lovable Teddy bear daddy? Would he be the same without his? Could any of us be the same?

I heard him laugh again and tried to commit it to memory right then and there, just in case.

"Hey, y'all," I said as I came down, tying my robe and yawning.

"It's Lily-Lou-Who!" Daddy yelled, reprising his fake DJ voice.

"Hey honey, you sleep all right?" Mama asked quietly.

"Yeah, like a rock. I haven't slept like that in a long time."

My mama smiled.

"Party's not till tomorrow night, ma'am. You'll have to check into a hotel or work in the kitchen. Your choice," he laughed.

"I'll check into a hotel."

He bear hugged me until it hurt. "Daddy! Owww!"

"Cole! You're killin' her!" She swatted him.

"Yeah, Daddy, listen to her!" I laughed.

He let go. "You guys are no fun. After breakfast, Lil, you want to help us back? It'll be thrilling!" he sang as he did a little embarrassing dad jig.

"Umm, yeah. I'll be right there."

Mama pulled her dancing bear back to the bedroom while I helped myself to a few pancakes.

Buzz. It was coming from my robe pocket.

It was probably Allie checking in to see if I made it, so I pulled the phone out to answer it quickly. But it wasn't Allie at all.

<Sorry it took me so long to get back. I hate to hear that about Sandy Bear. She was always my favorite.>

Michael. He was texting me back now. Now, of all days.

I shoved the phone back into my pocket. How dare he, I thought, regretting that I'd texted him in the first place. If I'd still been with Owen—and if Owen hadn't been a male slut—the text would have had the opposite effect. I would have felt empowered, not depressed or pissed. Even wanted, maybe. But it was bad timing, as usual.

After breakfast, I caught up with my parents in their bedroom to pack as much as we could of Mama's world to take to Little Rock.

"How long will you be there, Mama?" I asked as she rolled night gowns and "comfy" clothes into tiny little balls and placed them into the old fabric suitcase that had surely come from the eighties, if not earlier.

"I don't know yet, but I do know it will be for a while. I have to go through a couple rounds of stronger chemo and each one takes time. All in all, it depends on how my body responds, I guess."

I said nothing because I wasn't about to say what I was

thinking out loud. It was too selfish. *What about my album release party?* See? Not coming out.

I guess Daddy sensed that something else was the reason for my silence. "She'll be fine. It will pass so quickly, and we will be so glad she got the best care. This is just a blip on the radar. A scary blip, but just a blip. And, in a few years, we'll all sit around and laugh about how worried we were."

If I hadn't known my daddy like the back of my hand, I would have missed it. But at the end of his "it's all good" speech, I heard his voice snag on the word "years." He was worried, too—real worried—but he would forever put on his brave face for his women. It was here and now that I decided to try my best to make it easier on him and be strong too. I owed him that much.

"I can't wait for that day . . . and your party tomorrow. Who's all comin'?" I perked up.

"Oh, a little bit of everybody. Some church staff, my sisters, some of our neighbors, Judd's family, my cancer support group ladies. You know, people like that. It's a potluck, so I'm not entirely sure how it's all going to turn out," Mama said.

"I'm sure it will be amazing, Mama. And Natalie will make sure of it—she'll quadruple check it!"

The thought of Natalie standing in the doorjamb ready to intercept potluck dishes and put them in their designated places got everyone laughing. But it wasn't a joke—it was pure reality.

For the rest of the day, I almost forgot about

everything—all the drama in my life, the good and the bad: JoBeth, cancer, my new record deal, Owen, Michael, Nashville, Allie. I was home with my parents, eating the best pancakes on the planet (sorry, Pancake Pantry), watching Christmas movies, hanging ornaments, and singing carols. It was a white December in the Carson household, not a fairly warm October.

The only time I had to think was when Daddy took Mama for one of her last chemo sessions before they left. And that idle time was dangerous for me. I tried to figure out what exactly to text back to Michael. "Too little, too late?" "Sorry, wrong number?" Either way, I wanted him to know I had seen his response and purposely hadn't bothered to text back in a timely fashion. Otherwise, I would have just ignored it.

I came up with something short and unsweet:

<It's fine.>

I didn't know if it was my best comeback ever (clearly not), but there was no "undo" button on text messages. So I waited like an idiot for another text back, putting the phone on silent, then taking it off silent; putting it in my pocket and then on the table in front of me.

My failed strategies for "not caring" if he wrote back didn't matter in the end. He texted back.

<Are you in town?>

Why would he ask that? And why was he so available on a Thursday afternoon? Didn't he have class?

<Yes.>

Why was I responding to this idiot?

<Can I see you?>

It had to be a joke, right? A mean joke. JoBeth had probably moved back to Mobile, moved right into his dorm (even though she wasn't allowed by RA rules), and they were just sitting there screwing with me from his bed.

<I don't think so. Tell JoBeth I said hi.>

<?>

<I know she's with you.>

<?>

<No, it's actually perfect. You deserve each other.>

<What are you talking about, Lilah?>

I sat there, my head exploding with questions. What did he mean "what was I talking about"? I didn't have much time to think about it, though, because my phone started ringing, startling me so much I screamed. I didn't recognize the Mobile number, but I thought it might be Mama and Daddy at the Mobile Infirmary. Maybe something happened?

"Hello?"

"Li, hey. Sorry, my phone's about to die. I called from my dorm phone. Do you have a second?"

"Umm, yeah, I have a second."

The world just kept turning cartwheels.

"Great. So how is she? Your mom, I mean. And your dad, I bet he's acting like everything's just fine."

"Michael, I would love to talk to you about my mom and dad, but why are you calling?"

Michael cleared his throat, and I could hear someone else coming in the room, probably his jock roommate, Teddy. I used to think he was nice. But I bet he knew the whole time and didn't even think to fill me in. Guy code sucked.

"Hey Mike! Big party tonight at Pat's. You coming?"

"Naah, I'm gonna stay in tonight. You go, though; sounds fun."

"Mike, someday you're gonna have to get over that chick. Move on already. Some girls are just bad news, man. She's not worth it, bro."

"Thanks, Ted. Hey, I'm on the phone. Could you give me a minute?"

"Sure thing. Hope that's a date in the making! Peace."

"Sorry about that."

"Was that Teddy?"

"Yeah."

"Who's the girl—the one he was going on about?"

"Ohhh . . . " he trailed off.

"JoBeth dumped you, huh?"

"What? No."

"Then who is she? Someone else from Cherry Hill? Amy or Lauren, perhaps?"

I knew I was being a brat, but I didn't care. He kind of deserved to feel like the idiot he was.

"Lilah?"

"Yeah?"

"It's you he's talking about."

What?

"Is this a sick joke? I'm honestly going through way too much to deal with this kind of thing. Please don't call back. I have to go."

I was about to hang up when I heard him say, "Wait, please." Only because I had spent a year and a half attached at the hip to the boy, had all my firsts with him—he was my first love—I gave him the benefit of the doubt just this once.

"What . . . ," I snapped.

"Look, I don't know what's going on, either."

"What's going on is that you cheated on me with my

ashlyne huff revelette

best friend . . . my ex best friend."

"JoBeth? Heck, no. That chick is crazy."

"You didn't cheat on me with her? Then, whom?"

"No one! You cheated on me! At least that's what . . ."

"What? Who told you that?"

"JoBeth. Oh my gosh, I'm an idiot."

"So, she told both of us the other cheated?"

"And she succeeded. That's why I never called. I was pissed at first, and then I was just depressed. You just didn't seem like the kind of girl who would do that."

This was actually happening. Really happening. Michael didn't cheat . . . he wasn't a total frog. But JoBeth was one of those piranhas lurking in the waters and willing to bite anything and anyone to get what she wanted. If Michael hadn't still been on the phone, I would have raced over to the Miller's house and punched ole JoBeth right in the freakin' face. She'd cost us, both of us, at least ten months of happiness, not to mention my failed rebound attempt with Owen.

Michael had been wallowing, turning down parties, waiting for me. Michael was still my Michael. What in the world?

"Lilah?"

"Yeah, sorry."

"Are you OK?"

"Just wrapping my head around this."

"You and me both. Hey, what are you doing?"

"Right now?"

"No, I mean *tonight*. You probably have plans with your mom and dad."

"Yeah, I think we are doing a little Chinese food take-out."

"Well, what about after that?"

"They'll probably go to bed. . . ."

"Well, would you want to go with me to that party at Pat's?"

I thought about it for like half a second. "YES. I'd love to."

Michael laughed. "Well, that didn't take long. OK, awesome. I'll pick you up around ten?"

"See you then. Oh, and hey, Mike? Normally under healthier circumstances, I would tell you to come to the door and come in and stuff, but tonight might not be the night. I have a lot of explaining to do before they will understand this whole deal, and I don't really want to put one more thing on my mama's plate once she gets home from chemo. I hope you understand."

"Oh, totally. I'll text you when I pull up."

"Thanks. I will tell them though . . . clear your name," I said, smiling into the phone. "Bye, Michael."

I closed my Razr and threw myself back onto the couch . . . my cheeks ached from smiling for far too long.

All through dinner, I checked the time on the microwave: seven o'clock . . . seven fifteen . . . seven sixteen. . . . And just as we opened our fortune cookies to read them aloud (mine was "Luck is just around the corner"— duh), I told my parents I was meeting some of my friends from U of M.

"Is that OK with you guys?" I asked.

"Sure, just don't be out till 4:00 a.m." Daddy winked. "What do you think, Sandy?"

"Our girl is smart, and she works hard . . . so I say yes. Everyone deserves a little fun. Plus, if you were at U of M, we wouldn't even be havin' this little conversation. This would be a regular night for you!"

"You're gonna get your fun tomorrow night! I can't wait!" I said, squeezing my mama's hand.

"It's gonna be great to see everyone."

Mama's weak smile couldn't fool anyone at the table, but neither Daddy nor I were going to be seen breaking down, so he changed the subject to something everyone could laugh at: Summer.

Ten o'clock on the dot. I got a text from Michael.

<Here.>

My heart skipped a beat.

I tiptoed into my parents' room to whisper goodbye, and then I was out the door. There it was. His black Jeep Wrangler. Michael had gotten out and stood in front of the driver's side door, leaning back against it with his arms crossed. Looking like the man I wanted to marry. Looking faithful and caring . . . looking like the love of my life. Tall, dark, handsome, sage-green eyes. Yep, it was still my Michael.

"Hey, you."

"Hey there back," I said as I rolled my ankle nervously, standing a healthy but excruciating three feet away, trying not to jump in his arms and kiss him like old times.

"Come here," he said softly.

I obeyed.

He grabbed my waist, pulled me into his body, and kissed me. It was something out of an Oscar-winning movie, only we weren't acting. His lips were exactly as I

236

remembered. Exactly . . . soft and gentle . . . and then passionate . . . and then back to gentle. If there had ever been a class for how to reunite with a girlfriend, Michael Kimsky was a straight A student.

"Holy cow," I cooed once we parted lips.

"I missed that."

I melted, agreeing with my entire heart.

"Ready to go? Teddy is dying to see you."

"He doesn't still hate me?"

"Naahh . . . he put the picture with all the dart holes away."

"Just away?"

"Yeah, he said he needed to see you for himself."

I laughed, and we were off to Pat's.

I had a boyfriend . . . well, in theory. It wasn't something we'd talked about (probably the only thing we hadn't discussed at length), but what exactly was the protocol in our situation? Boy meets girl, boy dates girl, boy and girl break up when a psychopath tells both of them the other cheated. Boy and girl reunite and make out until 2:30 a.m. in boy's Jeep after a college party. Would the boy really find the time to utter the words "Would you re-be my girlfriend?" Probably not.

Either way, I was ecstatic. I'd told Michael everything: about Jake, about my record deal, about writing "Falling Stars," about my showcase. Well, almost everything. I decided not to go into the whole Owen/JoBeth saga just yet. It was a lot to take in for one night. And a night that neither JoBeth nor Owen could take away from me.

While I sat at the breakfast table the next morning, sipping coffee and trying to read the latest Emily Giffin novel, I kept reliving our first kiss from the night before. It was so good, I actually felt sorry that JoBeth never got to experience it for real. Just kidding.

"Late night?" Mama asked as she washed dishes—something she had insisted on doing to keep things as normal as possible.

"Yeah," I sighed dreamily.

"What's his name?"

"Umm, it's kind of complicated."

"I could use someone else's version of complicated for a change."

"OK," I said, and I told her the latest development in the soap opera of my life. At first she looked concerned, but she smiled by the end, giving me her full support.

"Do you want him to come tonight?" Mama asked.

"Yeah, but I don't know if he can stay the whole time."

"That's all right. It's a come-and-go sort of thing anyway. I'd love for him to stop by if he could."

"Oh my gosh, yes! And thank you! You're the coolest mom ever," I squealed as I ran and hugged her, gently, gently.

"It's your world, Lily Black. And we're all just livin' in it."

"Now you sound like Natalie. Speaking of, what time are we going over there? Should I go early to help set up?"

"Natalie won't get home from teachin' until around 4:30 or 5:00 p.m. anyway, so I think we could shoot for sixish?"

"I'll make sure to be ready. What are we doin' till then?"

"I'll just be packin' a little more. Might go be with your

daddy at church while he writes the sermon for this week. We're leavin' for Little Rock right after the service."

"Could I come?"

"Of course, honey."

When I walked into Natalie's, Summer met me at the door in a mint green and pink flowery dress. She got the rest of the world's memo: it was October—Halloween—not December. And before I could tell anyone else I was home, I was ushered (more like pulled and dragged) into Summer's bedroom. I remembered when Natalie and Judd had first brought her home from the hospital to her girly palace. Now there was a big girl bed in place of the delicate crib. Her closet used to be filled with the tiniest little hangers with onesies and smocked dresses with Summer's name or initials embroidered on them, but now there was also an elaborate organization system for all her toys, which she pointed out one by one before grabbing a bubblegum pink dress out of the dress-up chest and putting up her hands.

"Will you help me?" she squeaked.

It was a costume change, one of many I would witness over the course of the night.

"Can I wear your heel highs, Aunt Wiwah?"

I looked down at my "high heels" and laughed. "You might fall, Summer Sault!"

"Will you wead to me?"

"Maybe I—"

"OH MY GOSH!" Natalie burst in. "Sum! Honey, you were supposed to tell me when Aunt Lilah got here, not hide her!"

Summmer giggled and put a cardboard book on top of her head.

"Hey, Nat," I laughed.

"Sorry . . . I specifically told my child to bring you to the kitchen. . . ."

"She's three."

"I know, but we're tryin' to train her early."

I rolled my eyes. "How can I help?"

"The strawberry pretzel salad could use a chef if you remember the recipe."

"Couldn't forget it if I tried. All right, Summer: Aunt Lilah has to go help your mama in the kitchen. Can you keep readin' on your own for a little while?"

Summer bowed her head to give the slightest pout before Natalie snapped her fingers. She then said, "Yes, ma'am," in a soft baby voice.

"Crack the whip, dontcha?" I said as we left Summer's room. I was secretly grateful Natalie wasn't my mom—she was strict. Yikes!

The party was a success by West Mobile standards. People from all parts of Mama's life came in, spent time with her, prayed with her, and brought mighty delicious dishes. Natalie had surprised us and decorated for Christmas as well, but it had confused poor Summer, who kept asking people if they brought her a present to go under the tree.

Michael arrived around seven, only able to stay for about an hour at best because he had a study group that *had* to meet that night on campus to do a project that was due the following Monday.

"We procrastinated big time," Michael said as we sat down on the couch in Natalie's living room. We weren't alone at all, but you coulda fooled me. I only had eyes for one person.

"You think? Who's in your group?"

"It's all guys except for one girl."

"How does this girl feel about y'all meeting on a Friday night?"

"She's pissed," he said, laughing.

"I think I would be fine . . . ," I whispered in his ear. "But only if you wouldn't mind seeing to it that I made it home."

"Oh, I would make sure you got all tucked in and everything." Michael put his arms around me and kissed my neck.

"Michael!"

"Sorry, baby, I'm just making up for lost time."

How could I be mad? He was just so adorable.

"Then tell me more about that 'tucked in and everything . . . ,'" I teased.

"Well, hey there, Mikey!" my daddy bellowed as he came in from the kitchen, and I snapped up. "We're headed out to do another round of burgers and dogs in a half hour. Sure wouldn't mind your help!"

"I wish I could, Mr. C., but I have to go back to campus. For a project . . . don't ask. I'm just as mad."

"Aww, man. Well, at least come and see the guest of honor before you go."

"Oh, I already have, but I'll come see her again. Can never have too much Mrs. C!"

"You got that right!"

"Mital, catch me!" Summer yelled running toward

him in her fifth costume change of the night: a Christmas nightgown. It was a game of Catch & Twirl she'd started when Michael had first come in, but luckily, Michael didn't mind. I felt all warm and fuzzy when I watched them, thinking about our on-again future together. Kids, a house in Nashville, and Mobile. Private school, for sure.

"Weee!" Summer screamed in delight. "Go 'gin, go 'gin!"

"I think it's time for a break, Sum," Judd interrupted, saving Michael's back. "Pop needs help in the kitchen."

"Don't you go nowhere!" Summer said over Judd's shoulder, cheesing for all she was worth.

Flirty little thing.

"Sorry about that. It looks like I may have a little competition," I sank back down into the couch."

"She's too short for me," Michael smiled and then turned serious. "I hate to say this, but I have to scoot."

I pouted, just like my niece had, but worse.

"Can I see you tomorrow?" he asked.

I perked up instantly. How old was I?

"Of course!"

"When do you go back to Nashville?"

Pout.

"Sunday."

"Dang."

The reality of our rekindled relationship set in. I didn't live thirty minutes away from his dorm. I didn't live on the same campus. I wasn't in high school or college—I worked in the real world, and there were no junior or senior labels, no statuses, no semesters to put a spring or summer break between.

My original plan for the future would have to be

tweaked, but it was doable, assuming Michael was OK with making a few trips to Nashville and possibly tagging along on some bus tours. I was sure that wouldn't be a problem.

I walked him out to his car as another was parking on the street. Unsure if it was another church elder or, heaven forbid, someone from my old high school, I opted for the safe hug. Being a preacher's daughter was something I would never graduate from—not in Mobile, at least.

"I miss you already," I said from the sidewalk.

"Tomorrow," he said as he got into his Jeep.

"Yes," I sighed. "The whole day?"

"If Sandy says so."

"Come over to our house."

"All right. See you in the morning."

I walked back up toward the house in my own little dreamland, my concentration only stolen away when my Razr buzzed in my back pocket.

<I love you.>

There it was. What I'd been waiting for. Now I could really enjoy the rest of the party.

Back in the house, it seemed like a whole new group of people had materialized from nowhere. *Where did these people come from?*

"Hey." Natalie cornered me. Her smile was either creepy or fun . . . but I was at a loss for which.

"Someone's here," she said, her eyes getting wide.

"No . . . is it JoBeth? Seriously, she is a stalker! I bet

she's watching Michael's and my every move on some spy device."

"Oh my gosh, Lilah, I swear! Like I'd even let that girl in my house!"

"True. Is she back?"

"I haven't heard much about her, to be honest, but that's probably a good thing. She might need to stay away from the Carson clan for a while . . . if ya know what I mean."

"You mean stay away from *you*," I said.

Natalie laughed. That was a yes.

"So, if it's not her, who *is* here?"

"It's that lady Ann, you know Mama's friend? She brought her son with her and ooh, if I wasn't married!" she fanned herself.

"Oh, Nat. I'm *off* the market. You saw Michael."

"Well, you just might want to check your options. He is fine."

"Well, I'll be *fine* without him."

"Suit yourself . . . I give you ten seconds before you want to jump his bones!" she said with a giggle.

"I wanna jump bones, Mommy! Watch me!" Summer did a gyration that she could only have seen on a Beyonce music video.

"Summer!" I gasped.

"Oh, girl. This is nothin'. Judd taped her Sunday school performance. Good Lord, my child is headed for a life as a freakin' stripper."

"Yep! Swipper! That's me!"

Summer kept going with her moves, and I took it as my cue to exit. I absolutely did not envy my sister at that moment. I wandered into the kitchen and found the lady of the evening, Mama, chatting like it was her birthday party. Or like it was a going away party before she went on a cruise or something—not Little Rock, Arkansas, for intense chemotherapy. But, hey, that was Mama.

"Hey, Mama. Need a refill on your tea?" I asked.

"Lilah . . . I mean . . . oh, whatever. Honey, I'd like you to meet Ann Lampley. Ann, this is my youngest daughter."

Ann was in remission, and she looked strong and healthy, a picture of the future, I hoped.

"Pleased to meet you, Mrs. Lampley. I've heard a lot about you. Thanks for takin' my mama under your wing with all this Arkansas business."

"Oh, darling, your mother is a saint! A saint! She has been such a wonderful example for all of us!"

"And look, honey, Ann just gave me this," Mama said, holding up a small green and yellow quilt with long pieces of thread hanging off and small handwriting on the edges. "Ann's quite the seamstress! See these verses? They're my favorites! And these strings represent different prayers."

"That's amazing." I beamed, happy to see her happy.

"And if you're wonderin' why it's so tiny, it's because it's a heck of a lot easier to take in while you're gettin' chemo," Ann chuckled. "Someone gave me one that was twice that size, and I felt like I was luggin' a whole bed set around!"

Everyone laughed.

Daddy opened the back door, letting a burst of cool air inside. "Y'all ready for some heart-cloggers?" he said holding up a tray of hamburgers, cheeseburgers, and hot dogs.

"Hey, Daddy," I kissed the chef and went to close the door behind him.

And *that's* when I saw him. Judd poked at the second round of burgers and dogs on the grill while he talked to him. He was tall and athletic looking, and he leaned against the carport wall seemingly unaware of how windy it had gotten all of a sudden.

Eight . . . nine . . . ten . . . darn. Natalie was right.

He looked up and caught my eye right as I was inspecting the rest of his body, and I slammed the door—obviously not thinking at all.

"Well, *honey*?" Mama chirped. "Don't break the door!"

I saw Natalie smirking from behind the sink. "Has Lilah met Vance yet?"

Clearly, here at a home, I was still Lilah. And clearly, here in Mobile, I was back to being the younger sister. I rolled my eyes and tried to change the subject by taking the tray of meat from my dad and walking it to the counter, where the rest of dinner was set up buffet-style.

"No, I don't think so," Ann, Vance's mother, answered. "Cole, could you get him?"

"Sure can, Ann," he winked.

I shot Natalie a look, one I hoped would stop this whole thing it its tracks. Before I could Jedi-mind cuss her out any further, the back door opened, and Judd and Vance came into the kitchen.

"Vance, honey, this is Sandy and Cole's other daughter, Lilah."

"Hi, Lilah. Nice to meet you." He walked up and stuck out his hand. *Well, he's a gentleman,* I thought.

"Hi, Vance. You, too." I nodded as our hands continued to shake.

★ ✦ ★ ✦

"Ok, you're gonna have to start over and slow down, little miss," Allie said on the phone a little while later after

I had gotten back to my parents' house.

"I can't. This is all so . . . what's the word . . . confusing and wonderful all at the same time!"

"OK, then, I'll ask the questions. You answer."

"OK," I said breathing heavily, calming down, and climbing into my bed.

"All right. First, Michael. So you're telling me he's *not* a total scuzzbucket. He didn't cheat on you, and he's been pining for you ever since because he thought *you* cheated on him?"

"Correct. One point," I joked.

"Second, this new guy. What's his name?"

"Vance . . . Lampley," I whispered back, just in case my parents were anywhere near my bedroom.

"Sounds like a cowboy to me!" Allie gushed.

"Girl, he's something. Maybe not a cowboy, but mmm, mmm."

"K, so I still don't see the problem."

"Seriously, you don't see the problem here?"

"No, you have *two* hotties. When has that ever been a problem in the history of womankind?"

"Normally, I would see your point, but it's just . . . there are two. And I can only have one, right?"

"Give one to me. I'll help your little problem disappear."

"They both live in Mobile."

"No big deal. See, I have this really awesome friend who grew up there . . . I bet she'd let me ride home with her all the time."

"Funny. Al, this is serious!"

"Who's kidding?"

When I said nothing, Allie backtracked.

"OK, OK, OK, let's try another strategy. Pros and cons.

ashlyne huff rovolette

Pros for Michael. Go."

"Well, he was my first everything. And we were together for a year and a half. It wouldn't have even ended at all if it hadn't been for JoBeth's psychotic need to have me all to herself."

"Then I think it's settled. You have to give this thing with Michael a chance. Unfinished business."

"Plus, we already picked our kids' names."

"Oh, well, in *that* case," Allie teased, but I knew she wasn't actually making fun.

"Why am I even talking about this?" I smashed my pillow on my face.

"Oh, you drama queen. Hey, how's your mom?"

"Oh, gosh, see? This is the problem . . . right here. I am totally distracted! My mother is downstairs with a rare bone cancer, and she's about to leave for who knows how long for intense treatment, and I'm up here complaining about two hot boys."

"Don't beat yourself up, Lily. You're allowed to live. And I bet if you asked your mom, she'd say the same. No one expects you to be a shut-in while you're mom's gone."

"I know, but still . . . I could at least wait until she leaves."

"Maybe, but don't you need to talk to Michael before *you* leave? You know, about how all of this would work for you two?"

"The relationship? Yeah, I've been trying to figure it out all night. I have to figure out something before I see him tomorrow."

"See? You already made up your mind about Michael. Just one question; why did you even consider Vance anyway?"

I sighed.

"I've been a little boy crazy these days. Trust me: I'm not exactly proud of it. Just gets me into trouble."

"Well, you've had a lot going on; your wires are bound to cross. Your decision is made, boom, done. Plus, you don't even know . . . what's his name. Vance. You don't even know Vance. He could be one of those guys with a great first impression but sucks underneath. I've met a few of those in my day. A few too many for as young as I am."

"You're right. Michael *is* my soul mate. I don't even know what I was thinking."

"Perfect, now give me Vance's number."

"Seriously?"

"No . . . I'm not good with long distance relationships. I get really depressed."

"Well, thanks!" I laughed.

"No! No, I didn't mean it couldn't be done! I'm sure you and Michael will be totally fine," Allie said, eating her words. "Plus! You already know each other. You have a history."

Couple points back.

"Thin ice, Al. Haha!"

"Oh, no. I'm sorry, I seriously didn't mean. . . ."

"Don't worry, I won't hold it against you. I can't wait until you get to meet him. You'll just love him. Ooh, and talk up Belmont, would ya? Maybe he could transfer!"

"On it."

"OK, I'm headed to sleep. Night, Al. Love you."

"Love you. So happy you found your man. See you Tuesday night!"

I texted Michael and fell asleep dreaming about my future as Mrs. Kimsky: locking arms with him on the red carpet at the Grammys, us on the front of *OK!* magazine debuting our first bundle of joy, running from the paps in the LAX terminal, shooting our own version of *Newlyweds* for MTV, and becoming the new Nick and Jessica. Being famous would be so much better with a husband.

Scott Betina at Big Little Records was no joke. He was intense, way more involved than my last label head. Big Little Records was small, according to past industry standards, but it was "the way it had to be if labels want to stay relevant" Jake explained. Back in the golden age of music (the 80s and the 90s), there were departments for every aspect of the label. Departments *for* departments! Each label had a massive building with hundreds of people flowing in and out, first class tickets, huge CMA parties, and basic unlimited-ness.

But with the advent of the Internet, Napster, and digital downloads in general (illegal or paid for), CDs had become more and more obsolete. Sam Goody, Tower Records, Virgin Megastore, and FYE were starting to see the future, or maybe, the lack thereof. It hadn't happened yet, but everyone already knew that the tried and true method of buying and selling music would never be the same. So, Scott Betina decided to change things up a bit and keep things small (physically speaking). The label was in a tiny, discreet house on Music Row, and he only hired a few select staff. It was a little place with big ideas (hence the name of the label).

At Big Little Records, there were no bad ideas. Any I had were taken seriously, me being "of the generation" of the digital age. Ideas for a YouTube channel and a daily

"On the Road" video diary were praised. Facebook and Myspace friends . . . not fans. Fans really could be friends with social media; they had access to their favorite stars' daily lives. Gone were the old fan clubs run by one of those non-existent departments. The power (and the work) was in my hands.

Jake had kept me super busy pre-record deal with the vocal lessons, shopping trips with Darla, co-writing sessions (which I was finally getting the hang of), and early mornings with my trainer. But according to Scott Betina, the work had only begun: now I had an album to record. All this would have been a total drag if I didn't like my job, but I *loved* it. Music didn't even feel like work, even though it was way more involved than my job at Club Sun during high school. Twelve hours in the studio with no sunlight couldn't even touch one shift at a tanning salon.

And the best part about the long hours? It helped me keep my mind off the fact that my mom was sick.

Michael was just as I remembered, pretty much amazing. The distance was hard for me some nights—well, most nights—but I finally had someone to call when I got back to my condo after working all day. Gone were the days of boredom! I had a long lost love to catch up on.

We talked for hours and hours, just leaving our phones on speaker so we could pretend to be with each other for real. And after my first six-hundred-dollar cell phone bill, I switched to an unlimited plan, while Michael primarily called from his dorm. I'm not *made* of money.

"When are you coming back to Mobile?" he asked . . .

again. He asked the same question every night, and I always had to give him the same answer.

"I don't know, babe. I asked Jake . . . I even asked Mr. Betina today when he came to the studio, but I think I need to stop asking."

"Why do you say that?"

"Because Mr. Betina asked me if I was really serious about being a star or if I was just one foot out the door."

"Who does he think he is? He works for you!" Michael got all macho.

"Actually, I work for him right now. He's funding my record and getting my career off the ground . . . again. He's taking a chance on me with all this, and I know it seems like everything's all in the bag, but there are no guarantees it will work. The music business is just one big gamble, especially nowadays."

"Whatever, I just feel like you don't make time for us. I thought what we had was important to you." He was pretty awesome, but sometimes, he got pretty pouty.

"It's been a few weeks, Michael, not months! And I told you it was even a fluke I got to go back to see my mom. The lawyers just happened to be going back and forth. But now, I've signed the contract, and I have a strict schedule. The album isn't going to record itself!"

Surely, he could understand that.

"Yeah, but why do you have to be at the studio like every second. You've already sung your stuff; don't they have people to do the rest?"

I breathed in, ready to repeat myself once again. Long distance, Michael was great, but sometimes he could be a broken record.

"It's *my* album, babe. I don't clock in and out. I wrote

these songs, and yes, I have an amazing producer, but I want to be there. I love to see the song come to life in the speakers. You know I have the best musicians in all of Nashville playing on the record? Do you know how awesome that is? I mean, it's a dream come true! They all play on the biggest albums."

Michael never really geeked out quite like I did, but I guess I could understand why. He was taking tests, going to class, dealing with advisors and class schedules for next semester . . . and he was still "undeclared" as a sophomore. I was totally declared, but I remembered how it felt when I wasn't as sure. He would figure it out, though, and it was only a matter of time before things would go back to the way they were. He just needed to toughen up a little and hold on until the next time we were sure we got to see each other. And it wasn't that far away! We'd already made plans!

During his Christmas break, Michael was going fly up to Nashville and stay with me for the week before Christmas (I'd already bought him the ticket and everything), and I told him I'd take him to a show at the Ryman, shop at the Green Hills Mall, check out Broadway (every bar besides Wanna B's), and maybe even go out to the Grand Ole Opry. It was going to be great. I was finally going to get to show Michael a peek into my world and have him meet my friends (Allie had memorized the Belmont brochure). The plan was fool proof; he'd be a cute Tennessean. If only I could get him to be patient.

And after his magical week in Nashville, we were going to drive back to Mobile in my Pathfinder for Christmas at home. Mama and Daddy wouldn't be there, but it was the best I could do.

★ ✶ ★ ✦

"Hello?"

"Lily?"

"Nat! Hey! How are you?"

Natalie grew quiet, and it scared me to death. A hundred possibilities ran through my head. Did they lose Mama's spot? Did she decide to quit? Had she taken a turn for the worse all of a sudden? Had the cancer spread unexpectedly? Was it even treatable now? Oh, my goodness, I feared, did she *die*?

"NATALIE!" I screamed in a panic. "What's wrong?"

"I'm pregnant."

Natalie was weeping.

I had never been pregnant—thankfully—but I understood what made my sister cry (besides the hormones). Our mom was *sick*. She might not get to come home for a long time . . . or ever. Natalie had Judd, Lily, Summer, and Daddy, but there was something extra special about sharing those kinds of moments with a mother during a pregnancy. And now she wouldn't get to. I understood because I had that same fear. Natalie was sad—and scared.

I knew scared. I knew it very well.

"How far along are you?" It was all I could say. I didn't want Natalie to break down.

"Four weeks. I missed my period, but I thought it was just the stress from thinkin' about Mama. But—"

"Shh, shh . . . it's OK! I'm gonna be an aunt again!" I tried to sound more excited, because I really was happy! Just emotionally drained.

"I know," Natalie cried. "I'm thrilled. Judd and I were

tryin' for a second one until we found out about Mama. But I guess God had other plans! I just don't want it to make her change her mind about staying in Little Rock."

"You *wanted* her to go?"

"Of course. They have the best doctors and the best track record, Lily. I don't want her to get anything less than the best. She deserves a fair fight."

Click. Somehow, some way, it clicked. I got it. I understood. It wasn't exactly the same as me moving to Nashville, but it had similarities. I moved so I could go for my dream, so I could be where the people lived and worked with dreams like mine every day. I moved to rub shoulders with the experts, the ones who had the goods, the clout to get me where I wanted to be. Mama was just doing the same thing.

"Are you going to tell Mama yet?" I asked.

"Yeah, I'm gonna call her later tonight. Wish you were here."

"Me, too."

"Well, I've gotta get dinner started. . . ."

I was overwhelmed with homesickness. I wished I could be there to help set the table for dinner, help Summer do the dishes (or rather do them while *Summer* pretended to help), and be there to tell Natalie in person that she was already just like our mama: amazing.

"I love you, Lilah—I mean, Lily."

"Love you too, Natasha—I mean, Natalie." I laughed. "Tell Judd and Summer Sault I love them and congratulations! Ooooh, wait: how did Summer react?"

"Oh, gosh. She can't wait. And she's already 100 percent positive it's gonna be a girl, so I've been instructed to buy her a baby doll with a pink dress so she can practice."

Natalie had snapped back into her old self. She was a true mom; she lived for her kids.

"Such a little diva! Let's hope it's a girl, then!"

"Lord help us all if it's a boy!"

My new album, aptly named *Falling Stars,* would be released the following summer, but I was booked solid until then. Radio tours to support the release of the first single, "Falling Stars" (which would debut months before the album), would take weeks and undoubtedly be the worst part. Mostly because I would be shuffled from city to city in cars during the coldest months of the year, catching naps when I could in the backseat in between the schmoozing, the awkward acoustic performances, and the dinners. The other part I dreaded was the prospect of facing the ever-honest Dane Kimmel. Yuck.

I had photo shoots for promotional shots, website artwork, autograph prints, and early press for the "Return of Lily Black" campaign. And, of course, my album recording process was in full swing.

Daddy called with a weekly update on Mama's progress at the University of Arkansas for Medical Sciences. Her apartment was "fine," my aunts were "stepping up big time," the doctor was "nice, German, different," and her APNs (Advanced Practical Nurses) were "top notch."

Mama had learned to text so that she could send messages to our family throughout the day. I loved getting them, especially the shorthand messages with LOLs and TTYLs in them. They made me smile.

<Hey gurl. I miss u and ur sister. Place is nice but Id

rather b home. How is singin?>

or

<LOL, thats funny. G2G, TTYL. chemo time :)) ILY.>

At least I knew what my mama would be like at age fourteen in 2007.

It was a few weeks into her treatment that I received the first letter. It was so unexpected that I stared at it for a minute before opening the envelope ...

Dear Lilah,

I'm calling you by your real name because right now, that's who you are. You're not a superstar, although you shine brighter than any star I've ever seen. You're Lilah Marie Carson, weighing a whopping eight pounds, crying louder than anyone else in the delivery room, making your presence known right from the get-go. You were a lot like Summer is now, actually, always dancing and singing for everyone, staying up lots later than Natalie, and falling asleep on the couch with all the adults. You might be a singer to a lot of people, but you're much more than that to me.

One day when you have children, you'll understand why I hesitated when you wanted to move to Nashville and then changed my mind again and urged you to stay there after my diagnosis. I've been thinking about it a lot. About how confusing it probably was for you. Maybe it still is.

As a mother, you want to protect your children from everything you can. All I could think about when you first told me you were moving was how devastated you were when Jake called all those years ago and told you that the label was dropping you and you would have to come home. You were so heart-broken, you didn't smile for weeks. And I just couldn't stand the thought of you being let down by anyone else in that town again.

But then, your daddy reminded me that I couldn't protect you any more in Alabama than I could in the big city. You were meant to be in Nashville, sweetie, just like Natalie was meant to stay in Mobile. You can turn that industry around and be a light to those who have lost their focus. God is going to use your good heart and angel voice to do wonderful things. I pray for you every morning and every night, any chance I get. And I can't wait to hear your new music. Your dad's been saying you're writing your own songs these days. And I know I'll love it, just like everything about you. Do you understand why I wanted you to stay in Nashville now?

The facility here is as good as I hoped. Right when I got here, they ran a bunch of tests. Some of them I had already had in Mobile. But most of them were new and way more extensive than back home. They put me into a category called "Total Therapy 6," which they figured up from my type of myeloma and the fact that I was treated somewhere else before I came up here. Ideally, they want you to be treated here from the first day, but when I was first diagnosed, you know, I wasn't ready to jump off to several states away.

Your daddy told me not to tell you this, but I'm going say it anyway. He said you weren't too keen on me being here in Little Rock. I want you to know that it's not all bad. I've never spent the night at the hospital, and I probably would have if I had stayed in Mobile.

Knowing how you feel now, I do appreciate you being a good sport at my going away party. It was better than any birthday party I ever had. And it was good to see Michael there, too. I noticed that little spark in your step that you've been missing for months, and I'm so happy you found out the truth about that whole thing. See, honey? Things are most definitely not always what they seem. But I still encourage you to pray for JoBeth. You probably don't know her whole story either.

O.K, back to the boring stuff! They want us to be "outpatient" so we can stay away from germs and stuff, but mostly they want us to be in an environment where we are most likely to get to eat the things we like, go outside when we want, and feel like we are kind of getting to go home at the end of the day.

My treatment isn't too bad, either. I come every day (even Sunday) for it. I come around two o'clock in the afternoon, and sometimes it's an hour and a half, sometimes up to four hours. It all depends on what my blood counts are. If they are off, and I need blood, it takes longer because I have to get what's called a cross match from the blood bank. Then it's a whole 'nother hour from then to the get the new blood in me. Those days are long, but once I get that blood in me, I sure feel better.

I'll write you again soon! P.S. I Love You.
Mama

Hearing from Mama in a real letter (a paper one with her handwriting) was exactly what I needed. I needed a piece of her to hold in my hands. And it couldn't have come at a better time.

I had just gotten off another frustrating call with Michael. He just couldn't understand why I couldn't come to Mobile for his birthday weekend. It was literally one week from the day he was coming up to Nashville. First of all, it didn't make sense to make an extra trip, but I couldn't have even if I had found a way to justify the traveling back and forth. It was the most critical part of recording right now, right when we were deciding the whole vibe of the record, deciding which songs to keep and which to cut (only "Falling Stars" was safe from the chopping block).

I pictured the process as kind of a mini *American Idol* or a *So You Think You Can Dance,* each song standing up nervously in front of the judges waiting to be told whether it would make it to the next round of competition. Brutal but necessary.

But Michael just wasn't getting it. He was so "hurt" that I wouldn't even try to make it happen. I'd tried to tell him that a birthday was just an arbitrary date on the calendar, that it was all about when you celebrated it, but that didn't go over well. And he definitely hadn't liked when I mentioned that turning nineteen was an "in-between" year. Instead of trying to see my point, he'd just whined.

Either way, I couldn't go, so it helped to have Mama's letter to redirect my feelings toward something more positive. I bet Michael would be a lot less worried about something as silly as his birthday if he had a mom in Arkansas.

Her cancer was doing that a lot: changing the situations that had once seemed so life-altering into inconsequential ones. Gosh, why couldn't Michael see the bigger picture here?

My phone rang. Surely, it was Michael calling back with

an apology the size of Texas. But I didn't recognize the number. It was definitely from Mobile; maybe it was another dorm number . . . maybe Michael was calling from a friend's room.

"Hello?"

"Is this Lily?"

"Yeah? Who's this?"

"I apologize for calling so late, but I just wanted to check in. This is Vance Lampley, Ann's son. I met you at your mom's party?"

"Hi, Vance. Yeah, I remember. How are you?" My voice sounded steady (I hope), but my eyes were bugging out. Why in the heck was he calling? And "checking in"? What did that even mean?

He said nothing. Awkward.

"Oh! Sorry, I was pulling out of the school into traffic, and I'm not all that great at multi-tasking with cars. No, me first. How are you?"

It was so nice that it crossed over into annoying. It would've have been rude to hang up right?

"I'm good," I said, rolling my eyes. "Just finished reading a letter my mama wrote me, so that made my day a little better."

"Hard day?"

Should I go into it? I didn't know him *that* well. Nah.

"Just a lot in the studio. Crunch time, you know," I said as if Vance would know anything about the music industry in Nashville.

"Ah, well, I'm definitely lost when it comes to that stuff, but I'd love to hear about it sometime. Sounds real interesting."

"It is . . . ," I mumbled, trying to figure out how I could

get off the phone with him. But all I could think of was that he had been a lot cuter when we were just shaking hands.

"Well, hey, my mom just got a call from yours, and she mentioned that things were going pretty well in Little Rock. I remember when my mom left . . . it was pretty lonely and scary. So I was just callin' to let you know that if you ever have any questions or just want to vent, give me a call. This is my number."

"Thanks."

"Ok, well, have a great night, Lily. And for the record, I'm a fan of Lilah, too."

I closed my eyes, embarrassed for Vance. If this was flirting, there was no wonder why he was still single. Poor guy.

I sighed, but not loud enough for him to hear.

"Thanks, yeah, my grandma would probably agree with you. And I'll give you a call if I need anything. Thanks, Vance. That's so nice of you," I said while shaking my head.

"Great, well, have a great night."

"You, too."

Click.

I wasn't going to call him. Desperate much?

<HAPPY BIRTHDAY! I LOVE YOU! SEE YOU IN T-MINUS 7 DAYS!>

It was the third text after the fourth voicemail I'd left that day. If Michael was trying to make me feel seven hours away, it was working.

But I had a job to do. It was listening day in the studio.

Scott Betina, Jake, Owen (don't even start), Brandon Hood, Clint Lagerberg, my producer Dann Huff (the same one who had let me sing at Faith Hill's session all those years ago), and engineer Justin Niebank all sat around the console with their heads down, slightly swaying to the rise and fall of "Wildcard." They were listening to each note, each strum of the guitar, each shake of the shaker while Mr. Niebank turned knobs all over the console, adjusting the sound.

It was supposed to be a day I'd never forget, a day I could finally appreciate now that I was over the age of ten. But I was irritated instead. Irritated that Michael was being childish, that he had let an entire day go by without so much as responding. Actually, it had almost been two days; he'd started his no answering crap last night. Birthday eve? You get one day, buddy; it's not Christmas. I was also irritated that he couldn't find a way to be happy for me. That he couldn't grow up and see that seven days wasn't going to make that much of a difference in the grand scheme of life. We had already been apart for so long!

Didn't he realize it was only going to get worse when the album released and the radio, press, and world tours started? What about when I had a tour date in Cleveland until 10:00 p.m. only to get on a red eye for a 4:00 a.m. sound check for *Good Morning America*? This, these weeks, they were child's play. Kid stuff. Did Faith Hill or Martina McBride have the option to meet their husbands whenever they wanted to? Not at the beginning of their careers, they didn't! It was the price you paid to play the game! Until you made it big, the job was to be available pretty much every minute of every day.

Whatever, I shrugged (literally). I wasn't going to be

able to change anything now, so I might as well listen and enjoy the moment.

"What do you think about the string section during the last part of the bridge?" Mr. Huff asked.

I felt awful. I hadn't even heard it because of all the stupid voices in my head. But luckily, he wasn't asking me.

"They feel too close, don't they? Yeah, I'll bring 'em back a little. Everyone else OK with that?"

Everyone nodded, and Mr. Niebank turned a couple tiny knobs slightly left and then tapped the space bar on the computer to replay the section. I would never understand how they knew where everything was. It was crazy. And the funniest thing was that no one else in the room seemed to be impressed. Like it was normal . . . and maybe it was.

While they tweaked the rest of the string section, some background vocal parts, and some guitar solo stuff, my thoughts drifted back to the letter my mom had written.

I could call her, but the letter had been much more meaningful. I'd probably read it ten times since I got it, reminding myself constantly that she was in good hands and not begging to be brought home.

I wanted to write a letter, one that would really show her how much I loved her, how much she meant to the family. I was a songwriter, so how hard could it be? But after a few tries, all I had to show for my headache were a few bad starts.

Dear Mama,
  You mean everything.

Dear Mama,
    I'll never be able to tell you how much you mean
to me on paper.

Dear Mama, I can't believe we are going to have
Christmas without you and Daddy. It will be the 1st
time & hopefully the last.

Dear Mama,
    I'm sorry.

Dear Mama,
    What do I do? I'm scared you're going to die.

Dear Mama,
    How would I make it without you? Get married
without you? Go through a pregnancy without getting
to ask you all the questions Natalie got to ask?

"Lily, you still with us?" Jake asked while we were on a fifteen-minute break.

"Yeah, why?" I answered, but I was lying. My head was a mess.

"You just seem to be somewhere else. Are the songs what you were hoping?"

"Yes, oh my gosh, yes. They are so good. As far as I'm concerned, all keepers so far."

Jake looked like he half believed me. "I agree, but tell me what's eatin' you. Come on, Lil, don't make me beg."

"It's really not important, Jake."

"Look at me. It's all those guys' jobs to make you sound phenomenal. And they're doing a heck of a job of it. It's my job to take care of you, whatever that means."

I nodded, seeing Owen out of the corner of my eye. *Don't roll your eyes,* I thought. *It's not the time or the place.*

"I'm serious, kiddo."

"I know you are, Jake. It's just more . . . personal, I guess."

"Your mama?"

"Yeah, I just miss her." Well, it was half true.

Jake was satisfied with that answer, and he thankfully moved on, giving me a quick hug and a promise to tend to any need I had. Clint Lagerberg, however, wasn't buying it. He sat down on the edge of the couch next to me and gave me the I-overheard-you-and-you're-full-of-crap look. Busted.

"Spill it."

"What do you mean? I am worried about my mom. She's—"

"I know what she's going through, but I also know Lilah."

"Lily," I corrected.

"You're Lilah to me," he said. "And I know you. You never look up from your phone on a normal day. But I've seen you frown more at it tonight than ever. Does your mom text you?"

"Actually, she does. Not well, but she does." I giggled.

"But . . . ," Clint said knowingly.

I sighed. "No, it's not her. It's my boyfriend."

"What's his name . . . Mitchell?"

"Michael . . . and it's his birthday."

"And you're here. I'm sorry."

"No, it's really OK with me. It's what I signed up for, right?"

"I guess, but you're still seventeen."

"He's not very happy that I'm here."

"Hasn't texted you back, huh?"

I shook my head and bit into my lower lip.

"Can I do the big brother thing?"

Clint did that "thing" a lot, but to date, he'd never said anything I was sorry for later, even if I didn't like to hear it at the time.

"Could I stop you if I said no?" I joked.

"Mmm, no. But I thought it was polite to ask, wasn't it?"

"Ha, go ahead 'Ye Olde Wise Non-College Grad.'"

"Hey now, we're alike in that way."

"I'm not old yet, though."

"Touché." Clint turned toward me, all dad-like. I bet he was a good dad to his kids.

"I've seen this before, and I should warn you to warn him."

"Warn him what?" I asked.

"When you get big and famous, things change, relationships especially. You already know that, but does he?"

I immediately thought yes, but then I changed my mind. Michael knew me as Lilah Marie Carson, cheerleader, preacher's daughter. He knew the version of me who refused to talk about music or speak the name "Lily" or "Black" in the same sentence. Had I properly warned him? When would I have?

"I don't think so, but surely he's not completely in the dark—I mean he's seen as many tabloids and MTV specials as anyone."

"Those shows and mags show extremes. They show the very best moments of those people's days and then the very worst, just for drama. It's not real. I mean, I heard that one time, one of those shows used a scene where a woman was crying to illustrate the moment she had found out about an affair. But she had just been chopping an onion!"

"An onion?" I gave him a look.

"Look, the point is, they don't show the moments that are actually the hardest, the ones I'm sure you got to experience when you were younger. The goodbyes, the long drives, the lonely nights."

I started to frown. It sounded awful. Clint noticed.

"Not that it's all bad, just the price of the gig. I've never toured like as an artist, but I've gone on the road with a few for writing trips, and I always have a tough time. But I think my wife has it worse."

"Because of the kids?"

"Well, yeah, I mean I'm sure she could use the help, but it's more about the fact that I'm gone when she's at home."

Was he speaking in tongues or just in between the

lines?

"Clint, I'm seventeen. Speak clearly."

He laughed and continued. "It's funny. Sometimes you seem more like thirty-five. OK, broken-down version: My wife has no idea that all I do when I'm not writing is think about her and the little ones. She has no idea what I'm doing all day. All she knows is that I'm out "livin' the dream" and that it must be fantastic."

"Sooo . . . your point?"

"There's that teenager," he said with a smile. "My point is you should tell Michael that you're going to be leaving all the time, but that you'll always come back. And when you can, you'll always try to bring him with you."

"That's all it takes?"

"Well, no. But it's all you can do about it, right? You signed a contract."

"Yep, all but signing away the rights of my future children, according to my lawyer."

Clint laughed again and patted me on the head, the way a big brother would.

"Thanks for the pep talk."

"Hey, anytime. I got your back. Oh, and let me know what Mitchell says," he teased.

I swatted him and hurried to grab a quick cup of black coffee before we started up on another song.

I wanted to tell Michael. And I really wished I'd recorded what Clint said so I could say it the exact same way because I had a feeling I was going to say it all wrong. That whatever I said, it would somehow make him break up with me or make it sound way worse than it was. It couldn't be that bad right? Faith, Martina, Reba—they all had husbands and kids. We could do it.

I decided I would have the conversation in person. And before that, I would butter him up with a killer birthday. There was a tattoo parlor on Music Row (aptly named Music City Tattoo), another little bitty house transformed. I had never been in there—my parents would kill me—and plus, I wasn't even eighteen yet, and I cut my fake ID in half. But Michael was. Bingo.

Arriving at the airport, I pictured his reaction to the night I had planned. He was going to be so stoked. Tattoo and dinner at this sports grill the Chambers had raved about: Jonathan's Grille. Michael loved sports.

"Hi!" I waved frantically when I spotted him coming down the escalator.

Michael smiled and waved. He was carrying his BHS basketball duffel and wearing huge headphones around his neck. He was also sporting his Auburn hat—one of the few things we disagreed on, on principle alone.

"Hey, baby," he said *in person.*

I was ready to suck it all in, go in for a first-day-back-to-gether kiss right there in the middle of the baggage claim, when my stupid phone rang. Unable to take my eyes of Michael, I answered without looking to see who it was.

"Hello?" I beamed at Michael.

"Hey, Lilah." My smile faded.

"Hey, Vance, how are you?" I said grimacing and trying to tell Michael it would just take a minute.

I'm sorry, I mouthed to him as he walked over to the baggage claim in a huff. I wanted to tell him that Vance was just a geek, a guy whose mom also had cancer, so I had to be nice. Oh, and I could add that he had the worst timing ever.

"I'm great," Vance answered. "Just talked to my mom and she mentioned that your dad was going up to see your mom again in the next couple days."

And? I thought, *Why do you care?*

Michael was giving me dirty looks from across the room, but I knew I couldn't hang up just yet. It would surely get back to my parents, and they just didn't need that kind of aggravation right now. But, wait: was Michael mad at me or Vance?

I shook it off and focused on finishing the conversation both swiftly and cordially.

"Yes, Mama is so excited to see him again. She texted me like four times yesterday, which is a new thing in the first place. It was mainly exclamation points and LOLs . . . she is definitely one of the cool kids."

Vance laughed, a sweet, hearty sound, and I felt bad that he was being so genuine while I faked it. Geez, why did he have to call now? There had been plenty of times when I could have used a good phone friend when I'd been JoBeth-less and Owen-less. Michael-less.

"Well, I know it must make you feel a little bit better knowing he'll be there during Christmas time, even if he won't be with you. And I remember the worst was when I felt like any stress or bad news I had would change the course of my mom's progress. Talk about pins and nee-dles."

"I know what you mean," I answered. "That's kind of

how I feel right now. I tried to write my mom like five letters but everything I wrote seemed too. . . ."

"Insignificant?"

"YES!" I said a little too loudly. Michael obviously heard it, because he darted over and gave me the are-you-effing-serious look.

Vance was talking about how he he'd called his mom with a complaint about his little sister (he'd only been a freshman in high school) stealing his new cleats and putting rhinestones all over them. Apparently, his dad sat him down and told him the seriousness of his mother's illness, which he hadn't fully grasped yet or whatever. It was a great story, but Michael looked like he was about to blow a gasket.

"Heeeeeey, Vance?"

"Yeah!" He was still so nice.

"I'm picking someone up from the airport and uh . . . he just got there; I mean, here. . . ."

"Oh my goodness, why didn'tcha say something! I am so sorry. Please don't worry about tellin' me to shut up the next time I call you while you're in the middle of some-thin.'"

"No, no—it's no big deal. I'll talk to you later?"

"Sounds great. Tell Mr. Michael I said hello."

"How did you—"

"Oh, I took a shot in the dark. I went to BHS, too. One year older than ole Michael. I saw him at your mom's par-ty."

"You went to BHS, too?" I basically whispered. Michael was almost to me, and I didn't want to fight. We had a tat-too parlor to get to.

"Yep. OK, I promised not to keep you. Have a great

night, Lilah."

"You, too. Bye." I shut my Razr right as Michael got to me.

"Sorry, babe. Vance just wanted to tell me about his mom."

"I know what he's doin'. He's tryin' to weasel his way in with my girl. Vance Lampley is bad news. You should be careful, Lily."

Vance? No way, I thought. But I had no reason *not* to believe my own boyfriend.

"OK," I said timidly. "Are you ready for your birthday surprise?"

"Sure. OK."

Michael had always taken a little while to get out of a funk. Before (back in high school), it hadn't really mattered all that much to me. I only saw him during lunch and study hall. But now, things were a little bit weirder without school periods to buffer our time together. But, hey, we had a fifteen minute drive to Music Row. Hopefully, that would be enough.

"Where's your luggage? Didn't it come through the carousel?" I said, noticing there was only a pink bag left on the conveyer belt.

"Oh, I didn't have anything. I just couldn't stand hearing you talk to Vance, so I left."

Seems mature, I thought as we walked to my car in short-term parking, the thirty-degree weather biting the back of my neck on the way. I tried to breathe in deeply to relieve my stress level, but the freezing air dang near made it impossible to breathe in at all!

Tattoos never sounded so easy.

We rolled into the parlor's driveway. Michael looked over from the passenger seat and grunted, "What's this?"

"Your birthday surprise! Well, the first part!" I cheered.

"You're getting me a tattoo?"

"If I remember correctly, you wanted a cross like this." I pulled out a crinkled up piece of paper and unfolded it. It was our original drawing from high school.

"Wow, you kept that?"

"Pretty impressive, huh?"

"It looks like it was thrown away."

"Well, I started to when JoBeth told me . . . never mind; the point is I kept it. I had faith."

Michael looked up, and . . . well, I couldn't tell. Was he mad at me or just really surprised?

"Michael, what's wrong?" I asked after a few awkward seconds.

"I just . . . don't want it anymore."

"The tattoo? I thought we were gonna put our babies' names. . . ."

"I don't want the tattoo. I don't like those names anymore anyway. I mean, we were in high school."

"And what's so wrong with that?" I said, thinking I had just graduated.

"Nothing!" he yelled. "I just changed!"

I was so confused. Were we fighting about a tattoo? About babies? About being different? What was going on?

"Let's just go to your place, OK? Do you live close?"

"But I made dinner reservations at this sports grill."

"I'm not hungry," he snapped.

"Uh . . . OK," I said, dumbfounded.

I was at a loss, but I put the car in reverse after texting Allie to tell my Bible study girls and their dates to enjoy the food, cake, and balloons without us.

<He's not feeling well.>

<Oh, no. Plane sick?>

<Something like that.>

<Sorry girl. See you Tuesday?>

<I'll get back to you on that one.>

When we got to my door, Michael waited semi patiently for me to get the key. But once we got inside, he slammed me against the wall and kissed me like he used to. My heart dropped like an elevator with its cables cut. I wanted to ask him why he was so being so confusing, but I couldn't. I wanted to tell him that his tantrum resulted in sixteen people eating cake without us, but I was preoccupied.

"I think I've just been . . . frustrated," he grunted as he started undressing both of us at the same time. One pull down on his shirt, one pull up of mine. It wasn't graceful, but I didn't care. This was our first time to make love since we had gotten back together—we hadn't had anywhere to go back in Mobile on such short notice. Teddy had reserved the dorm room in advance. I'd been waiting for this day, this actual moment, for an entire year. Last year at this time, Michael was on a ski trip with his grandmother, and she had had a strict no-cell-phone policy. That's when JoBeth had told me about the cheating. Why I had blindly believed her, I would never know, but now I was suddenly curious about that whole trip. Had Michael talked to JoBeth? Is that why he never called me? I had to know right now, and I pulled away just as I realized he was "ready to go." But it was too late.

"Did JoBeth text you while you were on that ski trip?"

"What?" His face looked like a scared/angry cartoon.

"In Utah, last year, how did you find out that I was

'cheating'? Did she call you?"

Michael fell back onto my bed, barely dressed and breathing heavily. "You can't be serious. You miss my birthday for your stupid career and now you're turning me down? Unbelievable. I haven't had sex in two freakin' months!" he yelled.

My stupid career? I got up as quickly as I could and looked at him, eyes wide. "I told you I had to work. Last year you always told me you had to do 'college stuff.' You made me feel stupid for not understanding, so I backed off. How is my *actual* job any different?"

"It keeps you away from me."

"Not on purpose! It's my job, for goodness sake, Michael! And I live in Nashville now . . . maybe you could transfer to Belmont or Lipscomb or something?"

Michael stared, mouth open, like I'd just asked him to join a monastery and be celibate for the rest of his life.

"You're seriously asking me to follow *you*?"

"The schools are really similar. My friend Allie goes there and she said—"

"I don't *care* about your friend or her stupid opinion. I still can't believe what I'm hearing. The woman is supposed to follow the man, not the other way around! Do you honestly want everyone in the world to think I'm a loser? Is that what you want? For you and me to be in a magazine with the caption 'Mr. Lily Black? Who wears the pants in that relationship?'"

"You're a jerk, Michael."

"You're a jerk, Michael," he mimicked.

"Get out," I said, calmly somehow.

"You can't be freaking ser—"

"I'm serious, Michael," I growled, turning red. "I've

never been more *freaking* serious. I tried so hard to make up for missing your birthday by treating you to a new tattoo and dinner with all my friends—whom *I* was sure you'd love. I tried to make you feel comfortable here so you just might see what I see in Tennessee, and I don't know . . . give it a chance. Because I can't come back to Mobile, but you *could* come here."

"What's so wrong with Mobile? Not good enough for the Lily Black?"

Had he talked to Natalie? Surely, not.

"Mobile is great! But music is in Nashville. And I'm music!"

"That's the problem."

"What's the problem? That I'm a singer?"

"I liked you better when you were just a cheerleader."

"Cheering for *you*? Like I should be continually serving you and your wants and needs only?"

"Says so in the Bible."

My Bible study had just gone over that particular verse controversy, so I was ready to go.

"Ephesians 5:22-24 says wives should submit to their husbands like the church submits to Christ. So there are two holes in this little argument of yours."

Michael looked dumbfounded, so I kept going.

"First, you are not my husband. And as much as I've always tried to pretend that you are, it's not true." (At the last second I opted not to tack on the word "yet.") "And second, the whole reason a wife should submit to her husband is because the husband is worthy, like Christ is worthy of the church. And I don't have to tell you how worthy the Lord is. So, if you were my husband, would this situation right here beg me to be submissive? And, oh, by the way, being submissive isn't the same as being a doormat."

Boom.

Michael started to answer but instead looked as if he was going to throw up. If he did, I would have probably laughed at that point. The truth *can* make you nauseous.

"Who are you?" he asked. He wasn't really asking, though: he was accusing.

"I'm the same girl!" I answered, thinking *Backatcha*!

"No, you couldn't be further from the girl I used to love. Nashville has changed you."

That one really hurt, but maybe he was right. No time for silver linings . . . ouch.

"You should probably go," I whispered.

"Where? I don't even know where I am in this stupid big freaking city."

"You could go up to 503. I'm sure Owen would be glad to harbor an idiot for a night. Like minds take care of their own," I said under my breath. Or so I thought.

"Who's Owen?"

"Oh, just the last guy I slept with," I said nonchalantly.

"My point exactly. You weren't supposed to sleep with anyone else until we got married. You're—"

"You know what? I'm actually *not* proud of myself. I unfortunately thought we weren't going to *get* married! And you said it'd been two months since you had had sex, right?"

"I never said that."

Deny, deny, deny.

"No, no: I was listening. You *yelled* that it had been two months."

Undeny.

"Well, I am a guy, Lily. You can't expect a man to not have sex. It's like . . . illegal."

"But, because I did, I'm a what?"

He looked like he wanted to say it.

"Go on, I dare you."

This was it, if he called me a—

"Slut."

Slut. It was over.

"Yep, you're out of here."

I got up, put on my robe, threw his clothes on him, and marched over to his BHS duffel. I threw it out the door into the hall.

"Oh, come on, Lily. Lilah! I was just joking! You're my one and only. Remember Mikey Jr. and Anna Kay!" he pleaded.

I shook my head, holding the door wide open.

"Please don't throw me out. I have nowhere to go."

He looked sorry. Really sorry, but I couldn't back down—I couldn't be a doormat after all that. Michael looked like he'd gotten whiplash, but before he could change my mind, I closed the door and slid down the other side, releasing my breath for the first time in probably ten minutes.

At first, it was easier for me to crawl than to get up, so I did, breaking out into a full-on sob as I climbed onto the futon.

I let it all out—like *all* out—crying about all the plans I'd made, all the different scenarios I'd dreamt up for our reunion, none of which ended up like this. I couldn't have seen this coming—I wouldn't have believed it even if someone spelled it out for me.

But a few deep breaths later, I thought about what my

mama would say. Of course, she wouldn't like me to be called names, but she would tell me to look beyond that for a night. I could hear her now:

Lilah, he has nowhere to go in the cold weather. That's no way to treat someone. Forgive.

"Forgive," I said out loud.

Forgive what he did. *It's not necessarily who he* is.

I knew my mama so well, I could practically feel her pushing me toward the door. I wiped my eyes before opening it.

"Michael?" I said into the hallway, wondering how far he had gotten.

Michael was sitting with his back to the wall right outside my door. I wondered how many more boys I was going to see in these hallways. Did any other girl have that problem? Michael's eyes were red and puffy. He was crying! Holy crap: it truly was a night for firsts.

"Come on," I said in surrender. "You can sleep on the futon."

He didn't argue, and I was grateful. One inner-Mama pep talk was all I could handle for one night.

★ ★ ★ ★

The next morning, I stared at Michael on my bed. Part of his body hung off and his mouth was wide open. If there had been a fly on a mission in the room, I knew where to look. (Although I had never actually searched for a fly before.)

He wasn't as cute today. It was the first time I'd woken up next to him. It should have been a great day, a magical morning, but it just wasn't.

Tiptoeing into the bathroom to check my phone and pee, I noticed I had missed a lot. Three text messages and one call with a voicemail. Allie accounted for two of the texts and the missed call, but the other text was from Vance. It wasn't a creepy one, thank goodness, but the fact that he had texted me at seven o'clock on a Saturday morning fell into some kind of "I Was Unpopular In School" category, right?

Allie's texts:
<Are you OK? Call me if you need!>
<Btw, I kept the cake for you. It's in my dinky freezer on campus. Better come save it before the Wright Hall girls devour!>

Her voicemail was pretty much the same—just another attempt to get in touch.

Vance's text:
<It's a beautiful morning in Arkansas. I checked the weather. I hope you have a wonderful day. V.>

Groan. Why couldn't he just be normal? I heard another groan . . . like Vance had groaned back . . . and then a thud.

"Ughhhlll."

I ran out of the bathroom, my underwear still at my ankles from when I'd gotten ready to pee. It was Michael. He had rolled off the bed onto the floor, completely naked. I silently laughed until I lost my balance and had to hold onto the wall as I made my way back to the bathroom.

"Lily?" Michael groan-yelled.

"Yeah?" I tried to act normal as I walked back into the

room, panties up, PJs intact. He wasn't a huge fan of being laughed at. "Hey," I said with a sigh, trying to act happy to see him.

"C'mere," he motioned me back to bed, where he had lain back down. He lifted the cover, revealing a space for me and much, *much* more than I wanted to see at that hour.

Unsure of what to do, I went over and lay down with him, taking short, quick breaths.

"Last night was fun," he said as he put his lips on my bare shoulder. I held back a shiver, and I didn't know why. He wasn't revolting or anything . . . but something had definitely shifted.

"Do you want to do it again?" he purred as he blew hot air in my ear. Then he bit it, and I squealed.

After Michael had come back into my apartment last night, everything had been completely normal. We had gotten in our separate beds, turned off the light, and for about twenty minutes, all I could hear were the sounds of Music City.

But just as I was falling asleep, I felt Michael climbing in bed with me. In retrospect, it was crystal clear: I should have said, "No, I don't have sex with boys who call me a slut." But in the pitch black, in a bed I'd slept alone in for months, I'd caved. Everything was so much clearer in hindsight.

We had . . . sex. It was that and that alone for me. Not intimate like it had been the times I remembered—not that that I was an expert or anything. But now I definitely knew what people meant when they separated plain ole "sex" from "making love'" and actually feeling connected with the other person. They were totally opposite, and last night had been the first time I experienced the difference.

I felt even worse than I had after the Owen/JoBeth truth had hit the fan. Probably because I'd only had time to fantasize about my future with Owen, not actually fall for him like I had Michael. But looking at him now, I was sure it was way worse. I saw the other side of the coin. He wasn't this shiny, invincible, popular guy from BHS anymore. He was someone I'd simply outgrown. And it made me sick to my stomach that I'd slept with him. Like it would have fixed anything.

But that's kind of what you grow up thinking, don't you? Good sex (or lovemaking) is the ultimate Band-aid. Makeup sex is the best—don't they say that? Maybe . . . for like two seconds. But afterward, you want a do-over . . . or maybe more like a do-never. Sex complicates things when your heart's done trying—and now I had to find a way to undo it in the harsh morning light. *Let him down easy*, I thought.

"Hey, Michael?" I said quietly.

Six days later.

"Hey, Allie," I said on speakerphone in the car. I was on my way back to the condo from another last minute vocal tweak for "Falling Stars."

"You sound like you're about to go down the drain. Don't tell me. . . ."

I would've dropped my head down in shame had I not been bumper to bumper on Sixteenth Avenue.

"Yes." I gritted my teeth in embarrassment. "He's still here."

"Lily!"

"I know: I'm a chicken. A big fat . . . no: *little*. I'm a little chicken . . . no, I'm the chicken's poop! I can't tell him, Al! He's so happy, and he's been so nice! Look, if I—"

"You're going to drive back to Mobile with him, aren't you?"

"Yes," I said meekly. "But—"

"That's almost eight hours of awkward."

"I'm getting really good at acting, though. I could probably go out for a part on a show or something."

"But you shouldn't have to act! He's not going to change."

"And I don't want him to! I just plan on letting him down on his own . . . turf. Mobile."

"Over Christmas? That's awful. Bite the bullet. Cut the cord. Rip off the Ban—"

"OK, OK, OK—someone else sounds like she's been taking drama lessons, too."

"You're wasting your time . . . and his! If you're not worried about yourself, then think about his time—even though I think that's crazy. Just . . . stop the whole thing soon, or I'm going to have a heart attack."

"I will. I just don't want to do it until I'm on Alabama soil."

"Fair enough, Just . . . never mind."

"No, what?"

"You deserve someone great. That's all."

"Thanks, Allie; so do you."

"I think my guy's pretty good, don't you?"

She had a new boyfriend.

"Yep. He's a little dorky, but I think it's cute. And he adores you."

"See? You need someone like that!"

I pressed my lips together and nodded as I whipped into my parking garage.

Lilah Marie,

The apartment bed isn't even close to my bed at home, but I am thankful it's not a hospital bed, either. The chemo has been fine, I guess, but lately it's been a lot stronger. Your daddy came this last week, and I've been spending every second I can with him when I'm not here getting my infusions. It is so wonderful to see him, if nothing else but to remind me of what God has blessed me with back home.

When he got here, my hair started falling out. Great timing, huh? I told him he was stressing me out so bad I lost my hair . . . he didn't like that joke too much. :)

I decided way before I started chemo that when my hair started falling out, I'd just get rid of it. It fell out in clumps, and I felt like a cat! And you know how I feel about cats! No, sir: no thank you.

Anyway, I had your daddy take me to a nearby salon, and this nice girl shaved it all off for me. I just didn't want to be one of those people who hung onto my hair. It was depressing! I felt bad for the hairdresser, though, because she started crying for me. Apparently, I was her first cancer patient. I didn't cry— I really haven't since early on in the process— and it surprised me a little bit. I guess I always figured I'd be a crier if I got something as serious as cancer. But now that I'm here, it just doesn't seem to help.

The good Lord is with me. And if I don't trust Him now, what has my whole life been about? My faith?

I know we're leaving you guys to do Christmas alone this year, and I hate that. I really do. But just think of it this way: if I'm here now, maybe I'll get to be home next year. Take care of each other; love on each other. And tell Michael I said Merry Christmas.

I love you, sweet girl. And I miss you to pieces.
Mama Bear

The car ride was actually less painful than I anticipated. Michael slept almost the entire way, so I didn't have to talk to him at all. And after a couple minutes of him snoring, I untangled my hand from his limp fingers.

It was dangerous, but I put my headphones on so I could listen to the new mixes of the album. It was another Scott Betina strategy to have the record ready before I went out to any radio stations. "Locked and loaded," he called it, and "ready for Lily Black to take over the world."

I listened to the album over and over again. The songs kept me alive—and awake—and from slipping back into the past week. My plan was simple: right when we got past the Dolly Parton Bridge, I would tell him I needed some time at home with my family. He would freak out and I would say, "That's it! We're over!"

Bada-bing, bada-boom.

Buzz. Buzz. Two texts. I pulled over to the side of the road to read them, braking as smoothly as possible so as

286

not to wake Sleeping Beauty.

<Drive home safely!>

<I'm not a stalker. My mom was talking to Natalie and she said you were driving home.>

I rolled my eyes and got back on the road. I was in break-up mode. Not nerdy mode. Seriously, though, did Vance really not have any friends, or was he just *that* bored?

It was dark when we drove over the Dolly Parton Bridge, and Michael was still sleeping. He hadn't moved an inch during the three bathroom breaks I'd taken or the stop at Clanton's Peach Park for some peach pie. Any member of my family would have smelled it from miles away, much less two feet away in the enclosed vehicle.

But my plan! I had to start the break up now for it to work.

"Michael?" I said softly.

Nada.

"Michael?" I said a little less softly.

Nope.

I skipped to plan C and turned the radio all the way up.

"CRAP!" Michael jumped out of his skin. "Why'd you do that?" he yelled, holding his ears like a little kid.

Good, I thought. *This is going to be easy.*

I turned the music back down a little.

"I need to talk to you," I said firmly, eyes on the road.

"OK, talk." He wasn't being as rude as I hoped, but my plan wasn't to sever ties right then anyway. I had to start out by annoying him, talking and talking and talking until we got near his actual house. Otherwise, it would be super awkward. And I'd had about as much as I could take of that feeling.

So, I talked about how cold it had gotten in Mobile, how I would never get a Christmas break again (or a spring break), how I would start my radio tours on January first and be gone for weeks and weeks and weeks. Basically, anything that I could think of that would turn him off of the idea of remaining my boyfriend. Or anything that challenged his manhood—either were welcomed.

". . . so yeah, this is going to be bittersweet . . . my *last* time back home for a *long* time. . . ."

But he wasn't taking the bait. He was just staring out the window. I panicked as I drove into his neighborhood, then on his street, rambling on and on . . . and then we were in his driveway.

"All right, we're here," I grumbled, confused, angry, exhausted. And my butt was numb.

He was still, what? Thinking? About to explode? Maybe—hopefully.

"Michael? Are you all right?"

I nudged him and clicked on the dome light.

HE WAS SLEEPING!

"How long have you been asleep?" I roared.

"Huh?" was all I got.

Just as soon as I wiped his kiss off, I immediately texted Allie about the whole thing. I wanted to get out in front of the "I can't believe you didn't do it already" conversation.

Then, I raced over to Natalie and Judd's house, mostly to get out of Michael's neighborhood. One week with him had felt like six months. A pregnant Natalie met me at the door, and we tiptoed into the kitchen to make a quick snack.

I debated on telling Natalie about the whole Michael thing or not. But was a long story, and Natalie was known to go either way, so I decided to let it wait and go to sleep.

★ * ★ *

I dreamed I was being strapped down against my will to be betrothed to Michael in some far away land—my punishment for not telling him the truth.

But when I opened my eyes, I saw the "straps" that were holding me down: Summer jumping on me.

"Summer Sault! I'm not a jungle gym," I whined sleepily.

"Aunt Wiwah, let's go get pancakes. Mommy made them for you . . . and me!"

"What time is it?"

"Seven thiwwty! It's so late! Come on!"

I moved slowly, but I did smell pancakes. Natalie got up too early, I decided. And for the first time ever, I looked at Summer as something other than my niece: birth control.

Breakfast turned into the "Summer Christmas Special," with Summer showing everyone her latest Sunday school program choreography and somehow making it look more like Britney Spears on a pole. It was sheer entertainment for Judd and me, but Natalie was less than thrilled this time around.

"Ugh," Natalie groaned as she leaned over to put another syrupy plate into the dishwasher. "I was hoping she'd grown out of that."

"It's not so bad." I tried to assuage the situation.

"It's awful! I mean it's a Christmas program at Daddy's

ashlyne huff rovelette

church! And this time, he won't be there to laugh, either!"

"How does that make it any better?"

"When everyone sees him crack up, they laugh and don't think one thing about it. I just don't know if it will be . . . different . . . this time or if people will think *I tell her* to be that way or something. It's just hard, this whole thing."

She started tearing up. I didn't know if it was the pregnancy hormones, but I doubted it—because I felt it, too (that lump), all the time—and I most certainly was not pregnant. Change was hard enough as a teenager. Or as a mother (in Nat's case). But to have your world collapse without warning . . . when your rock threatens to crumble, how are you not supposed to crumble with it?

Today, I was a little stronger, so I tried comedy. "Well, look at it this way: maybe this little one will be a girl, and they can dance together!" I said as I patted Natalie's growing belly.

"Oh, shut up. I hope it's a boy."

But Summer heard, and she threw a fit.

"NO! NO! I want a sisser. No boy!"

At first, I took Summer's little tantrum as a way to escape, but when I looked back, Natalie looked exhausted, so I went back to help her finish the dishes.

★ ✦ ★ ✦

I figured I would be getting a call or text from Michael soon about me coming over. I used to love to see the Kimsky family, but things were different now. When I opened my Razr, I had a message, and it wasn't from Michael.

<Hope you got back safely. Merry almost Christmas!

V.>

Vance. For the hundredth time, was there actually something wrong with him? Was he challenged in some way? I shut my phone in disgust. Nice had never felt so pathetic. The bright side was that it wasn't Michael . . . *buzzzz.*

I spoke too soon.

I dodged Michael's first official invitation by simply avoiding the text altogether. He had asked me to come by his parents' house for lunch, but I pretended not to get it until after the proposed window of time. Not wanting to lie completely, I danced around the truth:

<Sorry, just getting back to you! Left my phone in my room on silent.>

Which I had—on purpose. My room at Natalie's house was actually Judd's office with a pull-out couch. The room was full of mounted heads, and when I had tried to sleep the night before, I felt like I had an audience. One that didn't blink. No wonder I had bad dreams.

I fell like a tree onto the pull-out—bad idea, not a thick mattress—and I tried to remember when things had been simpler. That's what I wanted for Christmas (other than time with Mama): simple. If being single and lonely and bored meant my life was simple, I'd take it in a heartbeat. Anything but this. How had everything gotten so crappy and complicated?

"Hey, girl, you wanna go shopping?" Natalie said as she popped her head in.

I was kind of afraid to ask whether Summer was tagging along, but Natalie added "just us" at the last second, as if she was reading my mind. "I need some bras."

"Did you get new ones when you were pregnant with Sum?" I asked as we moseyed around the mall in Malbis. We had to go across the bay to get there, but it was worth the drive.

"I'm gonna need more this time. I'm already as big as a whale."

"Did you get sick this time?"

Natalie gave me a look that said yes.

"At least six times a day."

I shivered. One more double dose of birth control rushed through my veins. I hated throwing up more than anything else.

"Yeah, don't get pregnant before you have to."

"Wasn't plannin' on it." I laughed.

"Speaking of. . . ."

No, I thought. Please, no.

"Where's Michael? Normally, you two are connected at the crotch!"

"NATALIE!" I swatted her with a shopping bag.

"Don't hit a pregnant woman!" she fake whined. "But seriously, where is he?"

"At home," I said flatly.

"Are you OK? You're totally two-wording me right now. That usually means . . . oh, did something happen?"

I couldn't avoid it any more than I already had, and chances were that our mall visit would be the last of the alone time I got with Natalie. I spilled—all of it.

Six shopping bags later, Natalie and I walked out of the mall. The sun was just going down (and in December, that meant it was only five o'clock.)

"What are our dinner plans tonight?" I asked, hoping I wasn't saying anything that might cause another breakdown. But Nat was all smiles.

"Day before Christmas Eve? Thought we'd keep it low key."

"You? Low-key?" Natalie was the entertaining queen, so there was no way that was right. "Tell me."

Natalie could barely contain her excitement. "Ann Lampley is coming over for dinner."

"Just her?"

"And her husband."

"And?"

Natalie batted her eyelashes a little . . . pretending to be clueless as to where this was going.

"*And?*" I asked again.

"Ann briefly mentioned that maybe . . . probably . . . her son might join us."

"Vance?"

Natalie shrugged. "Ann just said a son; maybe she was talking about another one."

"Vance is the only boy. He has two sisters."

Natalie turned around, her shopping bags hitting one of the parked cars. I wanted to yell *Wide Load*! but my thoughts were a little preoccupied.

"So . . . someone knows Vance's sibling situation, huh?" she teased.

"Shut up! He called me," I said. "He wanted to talk to me about Mom—that's all!"

Natalie wasn't convinced.

"He's a total geek, Nat. No way."

"But he's so cute!"

"Yeah, I thought so, too, until he started calling me at the absolute worst times ever. And he's so sweet. Like, too sweet, ya know?"

Natalie shut the back of her minivan—the one she swore she'd never have—and we got in.

"No, I don't know. Sweet is something hard to find. And it only gets harder as you grow up. All the sweet ones get snatched up, I swear."

"What if I don't want dorky and sweet? Not everyone wants what you have."

As soon as I said it, I wanted to take it back. Judd was amazing.

"Fine, Lily. You don't have to want my life. But my husband is awesome. I can count on him to be the same man every morning and every night. I don't have to worry that he's going to be unfaithful to me or get tired of me or that he'll call me any names other than "honey" or "baby." I know I am getting Judd Bennett Baylor every day, and that's something you'll want. You'll find out that this whole drama-magnet crap only makes you feel special for a little while. Like Michael. And at the end of the day, you won't want to worry about that stuff."

I pretended to be put out by the whole speech, and crossed my arms in protest. I almost said, "You're not my mother," but made the wise decision not to make things worse. I was seventeen—not an idiot. We rode the rest of the way home (about thirty minutes) in silence.

When we got there, Natalie stomped off, and I decided to take a little nap on the couch while Summer watched *Thumbelina.* . . .

I woke up to the sound of the doorbell. Summer was gone, and I had drool running down my chin. My phone said it was 7:45 p.m.—the Lampleys had obviously arrived—and I sprinted into my makeshift bedroom to de-drool. Natalie hadn't woken me up. Well played.

I heard Ann's voice, and then Mr. Lampley's, and then my nightmare materialized. Vance had definitely shown up and brought his personality in full force. I could hear him cutting up with Judd, something about some sport.

I considered staying in Judd's office for the whole night. A little hiding never killed anybody. So, I lay back down on the lumpy pull-out and tried to focus my ears on something other than the houseguests. Everything was going fine until I heard Natalie knocking on the door.

"Lily?"

I pretended to be asleep.

"Lily? I saw you in the living room five minutes ago. I know you're awake."

I didn't take the bait.

Natalie burst in the door, and I sprang up, fumbling for my headphones or something to help me look less guilty. No such luck.

"Look, I know you're mad at me for not waking you up, and I'm not proud of it, but will you just please come out? You're being asked for."

"By Vance?" *Please say no; please say no.*

"By *everyone*. Ann's daughters are here, too, and they want to meet you. Come on, Lily. This doesn't have to be weird. You can *choose*."

I conceded (but not without a million "buts" in my own head), changed into something unwrinkled, smoothed my hair, and refreshed my makeup before joining everyone else in the dining room.

There they were, all of them, looking at me. Everyone was smiling, especially Natalie, who had saved me a seat across from none other than Vance. Yippee. But I sat down anyway. Mr. Lampley said grace, and everyone enjoyed a delicious home-cooked pot roast dinner. Everyone including me.

★ ⭑ ★ ⭑

"'Bout time I heard from you."

"I'm *sorry*, Al. I was busy with family stuff."

"Did you do it?"

"Do what?"

"Break up with that fool!"

"I haven't had a chance."

"How is that even possible?"

"I've been preoccupied."

"Oh, don't tell me. . . ."

"What shouldn't I tell you, exactly?"

"The other guy, what's his name?"

"You mean Vance?"

"Yes! Him! Are you already moving on?"

I sighed. "I don't know."

"But the last time you talked about him, you said he was too safe. Did I hear you wrong?"

"No . . . err . . . I don't know."

"Then what *do* you know?"

"Maybe safe . . . isn't that bad."

Allie giggled like a sixth grader, and it gave me the confidence to keep talking about my surprisingly magical night.

"Nothing happened, really."

"Well, something did. Tell me everything."

"Vance came over for dinner with his family, and at first, I wasn't really into it. But then my pushy sister got involved."

"I like your sister. She sounds like both of mine."

"Anyway, his family is really great. I really liked his sisters and his dad, and all of them seem really easy going. They were constantly telling old stories about funny moments they'd had. And I don't know when it happened, but I saw Vance differently. And don't make fun of me, but by the end of dinner, it was like he was glowing. He was cuter than I remembered, and all his geeky stuff about missing his mom and graduating from U of M and becoming a baseball coach . . . it was actually kinda hot."

"I totally think geeks are hot."

"Maybe I do too, now."

"So when are you going to see him again?"

"Tomorrow. Morning."

"So soon? It's Christmas Eve."

"I offered to do some last minute shopping."

"That early?"

"Umm, yeah, we're getting breakfast first at Cracker Barrel."

"You are in love. I can't get you up early for the life of me."

"Well, I want to see him as much as I can before I leave in five days. See if it's even worth a shot."

"Wait, does he know you like, *like* him?"

"Well, I think so. After dinner, we went out back by the basketball goal and talked until his family left."

"What did you talk about?"

"I told him about the Michael stuff, the drama, and how exhausted I was. He told me about an old girlfriend he had recently broken up with for the same reason. He wanted someone with ambition and a future other than ashlyne huff revelette

wanting to marry a rich guy."

"Is Vance rich?"

"No! But that's what I like. He wants to coach. To help kids, you know?

"So, did you tell him you were going to break up with Michael?"

"In so many words. But he knows . . . In fact, we almost kissed," I blurted.

"No way! Why almost?"

"He said he wouldn't want to cross that line until all my loose ends were tied up."

"Huh?"

"I have to break up with Michael first, basically. He said if we really want to start off right, we don't need a shady memory like that clouding it. Oh, and listen to what he said . . . 'What would we tell our kids when they ask us how we met?'"

"He did *not*!"

"Yep!"

"Sounds very ungeeky."

"I know . . . I was a little hard on him, I guess. But I think my favorite part of tonight was just talking to him. He wanted to know about my music, about how it felt to be on stage—things Michael never dreamed of asking for fear it would mean I would add an extra leg onto a tour!"

Allie laughed. "Is Vance OK with your schedule and everything?"

"He said he can't wait to turn on the TV and tell everyone around he knows me."

"As a lover."

"Hush. Hey, I have to go, but I wanted to tell you one more thing."

"Yeah?"

"Remember when I told you about that time I sang the national anthem back in the spring—the anthem that made me want to sing again and move and change my life forever?"

"Dramatic much—but yeah, why?"

"Vance was there. He said he'd been thinking about me ever since."

Allie squealed, and I could picture my new best friend rolling around on her bed at her parents' house, trying not to be too loud—just like I was doing in Judd's office.

"Wait, where are you going this late?" Allie asked, a little out of breath.

"Oh, I'm not going anywhere. I have to call Michael. And I have a kiss to receive at the crack of dawn!"

Christmas was spectacular, even if it was different. I couldn't have dreamed a better alternate. And the best part was pretty obvious: Vance Lampley. He had kissed me on Christmas Eve in the Cracker Barrel parking lot, once he got confirmation that I was Michael-free. He'd even brought some real mistletoe and hot chocolate with him for the occasion. A day prior, I would have run for the hills, but being with Vance showed me that I'd really never been properly swept off my feet.

Watching a host of Disney classics with Summer made it clear: Princes don't make you wonder or beg. They don't play games or sleep with your best friend. They see you as a human being capable of mistakes, and they love you for making them. They don't want you to feel bad about yourself. They want to make you feel whole and hug you forever.

They stay with you until midnight, wait until you grow legs or get your voice back, and kiss you until you wake up. And they act like gentlemen, not beasts. Oh, and a real prince isn't worried about getting you naked the first chance he gets. He knows there's time if the relationship is going anywhere real.

It took me seventeen years to understand a Disney movie. Sweet.

Christmas Eve, Christmas Day, the day after Christmas, and the day after that were all full of one thing: Vance. Vance. Vance.

Once I got back to Nashville, I was going to be in full "radio mode" for two months straight. It was the only part of my career I actually dreaded, but could you blame me? Dane Kimmel had been right about one thing: radio was strictly business, and I wasn't looking forward to going through all that nonsense again. But now I had Vance, and that changed everything. And even if all the Dane Kimmels of the world were all business, it didn't mean I had to be. I was proud of my songs and who I'd become as an artist—someone who'd finally found something to say. Someone who'd lived through enough drama in one year to last a lifetime. Someone who had discovered true love. Someone who'd realized that true love was more important than any station playing a song. Radio wouldn't be that bad, I decided. Not with Vance's heart in my pocket.

★ ★ ★ ★

While I was on the road, in freezing cold Minneapolis,

a letter slid under my hotel room door. I figured Vance had sent me some sort of card—he was always doing things like that.

Recently, he had surprised me at an actual radio station out in the middle of nowhere. He had warned me that he would be out of pocket for most of the day because he had to study for a huge test, so I shouldn't call. In reality, he was on a flight.

So when I rolled out of the rented car driven by my radio rep, I saw him in the reflection of the car, holding two dozen white lilies. He said he couldn't wait for two more weeks. He really had a test, though—one he really failed.

It made sense that Vance would send another little surprise. But I was wrong. The postmark was from Little Rock.

Lilah,

Today, it's a longer one because my counts are off target, so I decided to write my darling miracle baby. Did you know you were a miracle? Probably not. Well, I guess now is as good a time as any. I got pregnant in between you and Natalie, and everything was going smooth until the end of my second trimester. I started having cramps that made me think I was going into labor. I made your daddy take me to the emergency room every other day, it felt like. But they always sent me home with some explanation. I had indigestion or my hormones were just out of whack.

And then I woke up in the middle of one night and rushed to the bathroom. I had a miscarriage right there. For a long time I was depressed. I thought it was a sign that God didn't want us to have any more babies. But then you came along out of the blue. We weren't even trying! And I knew we were just waiting on little Lilah to come into the world. It's funny how God fixes things without you even asking for them. These days, I want to pray for my health, but when I think about it, I only pray for His will. Cause whatever He wants for me is best for me. And that mindset sets me free. It sets my heart at ease, and I am able to sit around all day and think about how much I love the gifts I've been given. You, Cole, and Nat are so important to me, so important to so many people.

Anyway . . . I normally sit in my chemo pod and read my Bible or magazines. They have little televisions here, too, so sometimes I watch a show. And I've gotten better at texting, haven't I? I wanted to write to you a letter today, though, because I've been noticing how many people are in this hospital. You wouldn't believe how many nationalities are represented here . . . in Little Rock! Of all the places in the world, people come here for treatment. That should make you feel good, honey. I'm in good hands.

I really can't brag enough on this place. And the nursing staff! Right now, while I'm waiting on Tenika to come back and take my vitals, I hear this beautiful music coming from a pianist in the waiting room. The way the building is designed, the stairwell is open all the way down to the first floor, so the music just floats up all the way to the Infusion floor that I'm on. It would be even better if you were here to sing along, but I'll take what I can get.

When I think about what could have been, I honestly can't imagine staying in Mobile for this portion of my treatment. I mean, if I had stayed, I would have never known that I was "high risk." It sounds scarier than it is, but it means that they watch me very closely. Here in Little Rock (not in Mobile), they do what's called a gene array where they take a sample of the bone biopsy and put it in a machine that lets them look even deeper to see where the abnormalities are in my genes. My gene array is called IgG kappa—I remember that because Natalie's a Kappa Delta. :)

Can you believe I'm going be a grandma again? I know Nat is hiding her worry from me, but I keep telling her that this baby is a gift (a miracle like you were). I think He's using it to motivate me even more, to show me what wonderful things He has in store—because on my bad days, I find myself thinking, Hey, I'm going have another grandbaby.

I think Natalie's working it out to where I might get to come to the appointment when she finds out if it's going be a boy or girl. It wouldn't be this time coming up, but the next time.

I am so excited to see you next week! I know everything hasn't worked out like we said initially. I had hoped we could get together sooner, but once I got up here, I realized I needed to get through one round of the chemo before so I knew what to expect.

I have so many things to talk to you about, Lilah. I hope these letters don't bore you to death. I find that it's easier for me to write while I'm here than to talk on the phone. I don't know why, but writing is more therapeutic.

One more thing. I want you to know what else motivates me: your music. I cannot wait to hear your *next album. I listen to your first album on my way to treatment every single day, and it gives me strength when I hear your voice. It always has.*

Oh, and I heard all about you and Vance. I approve, I approve! But what ever happened to poor Michael? You can fill me in when I see you soon! Hallelujah!

Mama

★ ★ ★

My mom was back in Mobile for a week. And Jake had convinced Scott Betina to let me fly back to Mobile for a few days after I finished the last leg of radio stations. Jake, the saint. Plus, anything to see my man again.

Natalie was hosting yet another dinner with the entire Lampley family, insisting it be at her house so Mama wouldn't have a mess to clean up.

It was a dream come true to see my mom in person. She was definitely skinnier, wearing a silk Crimson Tide scarf around her head, but other than that, she was still Mama. She still laughed and carried on with Daddy, just like they used to.

Vance had really helped me cope with some of the changes that had come with having a mom with cancer, and I loved watching my mom light up around him. He was a natural. He was a geek—a sweet, adorable, caring geek. And I couldn't remember living my life without him.

After dinner, Vance drove me back to my parents' house, where we made out like middle schoolers in his truck until it got too late—and we ran out of saliva. I kissed him one last time and scooted in the back door.

On my way up the stairs, I checked the clock on my new fancy iPhone, a Christmas gift I'd gotten myself. I had a new email. It was from Jake.

Hey, Lily!

I hope you are having a great time back home. I just got this final mix of "Falling Stars" from the label. Thought I'd share, knowing your mom might want to hear some of what you've been working on. No need to write back. Just listen and I'll see you when you come back to Nash. (Song is attached.)

JS

Jake Slaughter

Slaughter House Productions

I turned around and went back down the stairs toward my parents' room, and I crawled into the bed. Their bed was nowhere big enough for three grown adults. But it didn't matter. What mattered was that I was home for a few days. That Mama was home, if even for a few weeks, that she was alive. That I was loved and cared for. That there were good parents out there, like mine. That the JoBeths, the Michaels, the Owens, and even the Dane Kimmels existed, and you just had to weed them out. And you had to hold on for dear life when you found the good ones.

"Mama?" I whispered, hoping I wouldn't wake up Daddy.

"Yes, honey?" she answered immediately. She was still a night owl, even with cancer, even with chemo.

"Do you want to hear a new song?"

"Of course. Let's go to the kitchen."

⋆ EPILOGUE ⋆

(Five years later)

The makeup table was always the same. The rows of eye shadows, the blushes, the brushes, the foundations, the fake eyelashes, the lip glosses. The hair accessories were lined up as if ready for a possible natural disaster. Straighteners, curlers, crimpers, dryers, teasing brushes, paddle brushes, ionized brushes, hairsprays of every strength. It was enough for an army.

Knock. Knock. Knock.

"Come in?"

"Ma'am? We will come get you in a few minutes," a woman with a walkie-talkie and a clipboard said as she poked her head in the door.

"Thanks."

My mind still wandered, even now—some things would never change. Taking a sip of water and a few deep breaths, I stared at myself in the mirror.

"They're ready for you."

And less than three minutes later, I was mic'd up, sitting comfortably in really nice studio lighting, and ready . . . ready to go.

"Hi, and welcome to a special edition of *Dateline*. I'm Matt Turner and tonight is a real treat. We are sitting down with a legend in the making: Mrs. Lilah Carson, welcome."

"Thank you, Matt. I'm glad to be here."

"Let's get right to it. We don't hear or see a lot of you unless it's on stage or at an award show. You seem to be a very private person."

"I guess I am. I mean, living in the public eye gives me no option of being totally anonymous. It's like being demoted in your job when people don't know you or follow you anymore. But I do try to separate my life into two categories. Me on stage and in public, and me at home with my friends and family."

"Do you find it to be something you can separate easily?"

"Well, living in Nashville helps. There are very little paparazzi there, if any. And country folks are pretty protective of their own. And when I am in LA or New York—or anywhere else—I don't do anything interesting enough to help *sell* a magazine. All they could say is that I went to the grocery store and bought too much Greek yogurt. Sounds pretty dull, right?"

"Even *I* go to the grocery!"

"See?" I laughed.

"Was there ever a time in your career when you *weren't* a sweet Southern Belle?"

"Oh, Matt. I'm no angel. Ask anyone! Ha! I had the same problems that every kid had growin' up . . . friends, boys, etc., even in work! I have been in situations that I don't wish on my worst enemy."

"Any of those recent?"

"Not in my personal life, no. But I did have to see a certain someone who . . . kind of lied to me when I was young. I won't say who it is because it's not important, but he was kind of instrumental in my career ending back then."

"Wow, what was that like?"

"It was better than I expected. But I wouldn't say I call

him for advice," I laughed.

"But you do you speak?"

"We're cordial. There's no point in not being nice to someone. But what it really forces me to do is lower my expectations. Not everybody in music has my back like I do. Not everybody in the industry is honest—as I'm sure it is in every other industry out there—and I am learning not to be so sensitive and to stop taking everything so dad gum personally. When you—as an artist—*are* the product, you can get pretty beat down by the pressure to please everyone. And you just can't please everyone. It's impossible. I am so lucky to have a manager and a record label that really look out for me. Not everyone's that lucky."

"That sounds like good advice. Maybe I should take it!" he said with a laugh. "Well, even though you haven't been all over the trash mags, you haven't been sitting on your bum for the last couple years. That's for sure. You have topped not only the country charts but the pop charts as well, making you a music sensation around the world. You've won two Grammys, four Country Music Awards, and three Billboard Music Awards, just to name a few. And I think you got married?"

"Yes, I did. We got hitched a little over a year ago. We kept it private and small and kind of a secret until the last day so that those helicopters wouldn't find us. Kind of distracting while you're tryin' to say your vows, don't you think?"

"I'd say you're right. You're lucky they didn't find you."

"Oh, I didn't say that! They did! But once they did, we were already well into the reception!"

"Well, that's lucky. So, are you going to change your name? I know there's a whole history of your name in the first place. You were Lily Black, now you're Lilah Carson. And then you add marriage to the mix. What are your plans?"

"Ah, names. I have had a decade-long battle with my name, my identity. Let's start at the beginning. I was born Lilah Carson . . . switched to Lily Black when I had my first record deal back in 2000, went *back* to Lilah after my career died during the rest of high school, tried to return to my former glory as Lily Black *again* in 2007 . . . and at that time, half the people in my life called me Lilah and the other half called me Lily and sometimes they flipped back and forth during a conversation—it was a very confusing time in my life, Matt. And then I met my husband. We met in Alabama, where I'm from, and it happened to be right around the time when I was finishing up my album called *Falling Stars*.

"When I met him—well, once I gave him the time of day—my whole life perspective changed. Up until that point, I thought that Lilah Carson was an old-sounding name, that Lily Black was somehow better. But once we met, *in* Alabama, I realized I was all wrong. Lilah Carson was doing all the work, and Lily was taking all the credit.

"So, right before the album came out, I basically begged my record label to put out a press release to everyone that I was changing my stage name to Lilah Carson."

"Were they OK with it?"

"Umm . . . no, not at first. Changing my name meant a lot of extra work had to be done, and they were on strict enough timetables already."

"So, how did you convince them?"

"I don't really know. I sat down with the head of my label, Scott Betina, and my longtime manager Jake Slaughter, who incidentally invented my Lily Black persona back in 2000. I told them I wanted to *be* the woman I'd been raised to be, with the name I'd done all my growing up in, and somehow marry the Lily Black persona with it."

"OK, so forgive me, but what was the point of Lily in the first place then?"

"You mean back when I was young?"

"No, no. I mean, why did you even entertain becoming Lily Black all over again when you moved to Nashville a couple years ago . . . if it wasn't who you wanted to be?"

"Oh! Well, when I first moved back, I just wanted to be a star again, and I was willing to do whatever—be whomever—to get there. Going with Lily, an established brand, was the most logical choice at the time because I knew who Lily was."

"So then. . . ."

"So, while it was much easier to be Lily—glossy, successful, skinny, clear-skinned, confident, it wasn't real. By marrying Lily with Lilah, I got to mix Lilah's heart and life experiences with Lily's stage presence and fire. And I don't know if you've noticed, Matt, but I have become quite the fashionista, thanks to Lily," I teased.

"You are fashionable," Matt teased back. "OK, so I get it now."

"Did I confuse you?"

"A little, but I'm sure you were way more confused when you were going through it!"

I laughed. He had no idea.

"OK, let's talk about someone *less* confusing, shall we?"

"Please!"

"OK, what about your husband?"

"What about him?"

"Well, let's start with the basics. What's his name? Again, you're so private!"

"Vance Lampley. And yes, it's easier when one of you isn't in the public eye."

"True. So you won't become Lilah Lampley?"

"My Tennessee driver's license says I am."

"But I thought . . . I'm confused again."

"Like I said earlier, I met Vance before I got 'big' and released that album, so to speak, but I married him after. So we sat down and decided that Lilah Carson should remain my stage name. Like Faith Hill or Reba McEntire or Carrie Underwood."

"But isn't that two identities all over again?"

"Yes, but it's different this time because I own both names. Before, Lily Black was a fictionalized persona, with no roots in the ground. But I know Lilah Carson; she has baby pictures and yearbooks. Lilah Carson comes from Mobile, Alabama, and she stands for something. And Lilah Lampley is my next chapter . . . my future. As Mrs. L, I am just a normal wife with a hot husband. We like to take long walks at Radnor Lake in Nashville, and I go watch him coach baseball for Brentwood High School. This go 'round, my two names actually help me separate my life . . . I don't know if that makes sense to anyone else but me, but I get it."

"That does make sense, actually. I'm officially unconfused. So, what would you say has been the most monumental moment in your career?"

"Wow, I have to narrow it down?"

"Well, OK, name a few."

"Ok . . . ," I sat back into the comfy blue velvet chair. "Well, I always wanted to win a Grammy . . . but winning it for 'Song of the Year' was a whole step further, because I *wrote* the song."

"That was 'Falling Stars?'"

I nodded.

"How old were you when you wrote it?"

"I was seventeen then; I'm almost twenty-three now—"

"Wow! I didn't realize you were *that* young. You were a baby!"

"What, am I aging?" I joked as I touched the skin around my eyes where I would, in fact, have wrinkles one day. I planned on aging gracefully.

"Oh, no, of course not! You're still young. It's just that you're so mature for your age. Most twenty-three-year-olds are just out of college and trying to forget the fact that they are adults or that they have officially entered the workforce. But you seem like a bit of an old soul."

"I think you're right, but I also had to grow up pretty quickly. It's weird because I was in the spotlight, rushed out of it, resumed as much of a normal adolescence as I could, and then went back into the spotlight before I turned twenty. And then my mom got cancer, and if that kind of news doesn't press fast forward, I don't know what will."

"Is that something you want to talk about?"

"Oh, yeah! She's still alive and doing quite well! Right now, she's in the highest remission possible. We've definitely had some times in the past couple years when we thought it was going to rear its ugly head again, but for the most part, we've been very blessed."

"Is she still in Mobile?"

"Actually, as of last month, she and my dad became residents of Smith Lake in Alabama. It's right outside of

Cullman, Alabama, where she grew up."

"I know you're a preacher's daughter. Was that transition hard on your dad? To leave a whole congregation?"

"In the end, no. When someone you love gets a diagnosis like cancer, you realize that while your life can't stop, you do have to change your perspective a little. At least I did. And Smith Lake is perfect for them. Plus, it's closer to Nashville."

"That's great. Well, I hate to pry, but I think America would like to learn more about Vance. When was your first date?"

"Ooh, we're getting personal now . . . ," I said, laughing.

"Inquiring minds want to know something more juicy than your Greek yogurt buying habits."

"Well, I don't know about juicy, but maybe romantic?"

Matt shrugged. "I guess we'll take what we can get."

"OK, let's see. I met Vance when I went back home for a party for my mom before she started chemo in another state. Her fellow multiple myeloma patient-friend came and brought her son, Vance."

"Do you think it was a setup?"

"I don't know. I suspect maybe a little. I asked Ann, my mother-in-law, once before she passed if it was a setup, and she smiled . . . neither denying nor confirming it."

"When did she pass?"

"About seven months ago."

"I'm sorry."

"It's OK. Of course, you never want to lose someone you love—especially someone who was so amazing like her. But she is up there, cancer-free, pain-free, and smiling down on us today. She had the cancer for eight years, so in my opinion, Ann Lampley is a success story.

"How's your husband?"

"Well, our mothers' conditions are what we first had in common, so I think he shares the same joy for his mom as I do. We will be OK knowing she's finally home."

"That's a wonderful way to look at it. See, there's that old soul again."

"Ha!"

"What was it like dating long distance?"

"It was hard; I won't lie. I would drive down to Alabama every so often, and he came up to Nashville when he could. But when you live far away, it's so temporary. It's all at once for two days and then nothing for weeks on end. Every time I saw him I was ecstatic, but I wouldn't say we had a so-called date for a while. He was accompanying me to everything, doing his grad school homework in the front of the bus while I did phone interviews in the back—that was our life for a little bit."

"Any memorable dates you can think of?"

"I can think of one. . . ."

"You're not gonna stop there, are you? Geez, you should be in television!"

"Oh, Matt, Vance will kill me!"

"What if I could promise you he won't?"

"I'm not following."

"Vance? Come on out, man."

I was stunned. How long had he known this and not told me? *Such a Vance move,* I thought.

"Hey, baby," Vance said as he sat down beside me.

"I want to say I'm surprised, but I'm not," I said looking at my husband.

"Vance, does your wife have permission to tell the story of your first date?"

"Anything for you, Matt." He smiled and reached for my hand.

"That's what I like to hear. Why can't more people be as agreeable as you?"

"I don't know. See, honey? I'm agreeable."

"Oh, don't get him started, Matt," I said.

"All right, let's just get to this date then. Lilah, you're on."

"OK. So he drove me to one of my favorite spots down in Alabama called Fairhope. It looks like a Nicholas Sparks novel down there with the little quaint downtown and the Spanish moss and the beach and stuff. We had lunch at a little bistro called Thyme, walked up and down the pier—and we almost got stuck in a swarm of hungry seagulls that were after a piece of bread. Then he took me to the legendary hotel called the Grand a little ways down the road in Point Clear, Alabama . . . what?"

"Hotel, huh?"

"Oh my gosh!" I blushed when I looked at Vance, who was smiling. "No! No! No! No! I'm a Southern girl! Tell him, Vance!"

Vance threw up his hands. "I can't lie on TV, babe."

"Ugh! Vance, I swear!"

"OK, OK. Matt, she's a perfect Southern belle," Vance mocked playfully.

"Thank you." I situated myself. "We had *dinner* by the pool *with clothes on,* and then he took me down to the boardwalk where he had another little table set up. On the table was a green book with a white rose on top."

"What was the book?"

"It had 'A Grand Occasion' in gold letters written on it, so I thought it was yet another menu from the hotel

. . . and I was stuffed from all that food we'd just had. But I opened it anyway, and it wasn't a menu at all. It was a poem that that told the story of our relationship, illustrated by my sister-in-law. And at the end, there was a drawing of a diamond ring, the same one he had in his palm."

"That sounds like one memorable date. You're making the rest of us look bad, Vance."

Vance piped up. "Well, my sister'll kill me if I don't give her credit for the idea. I just supplied the details . . . and the ring. And I didn't have many chances to take Lilah on a real date, so I had to really make it count! You learn quick that when you date—or marry—a girl in music, you have to take on that lifestyle. You don't get the luxury of planned trips to the movie theater or reservations at restaurants. You live your life around tours and appearances and meet n' greets because she has to. But music's worth it to her, and she's worth it to me."

I couldn't help it. I was extremely emotional these days.

"Honey? I didn't mean to make you cry!" Vance said, startled.

"It's OK. I love you."

He kissed me on the forehead.

"Well, my next question probably just answered itself, but I'll ask it anyway. Do the Carsons approve?"

"Of Vance?" I wiped my eyes, careful not to mess up my eyeliner.

Matt nodded.

"Oh my gosh, yes. They loved him even before I knew I did."

"That's good, especially for you, Vance."

"You're tellin' me, man."

"Do you want any kids soon?"

ashlyne huff revolette

I looked at Vance.

"Yeah, we think so. I mean we have the best time with my niece and nephew Summer and Parker Bennett, and I think mommyhood is definitely in the future."

"Do you think it would be smarter to have them sooner or later? I imagine it wouldn't be the easiest pregnancy if you had to be on the bus."

"I think my fans and those who work with me would understand that I am a family woman, and that if I needed to take some time to be pregnant and have a little Lampley, I would probably do it. Just think of it as maternity leave, Matt." I giggled.

"What's so funny?" Matt asked.

"Nothing." I looked at Vance, who nodded.

"Well, I didn't agree to do this interview to do *this*, but I guess I should tell you that I will be taking that leave of absence in a couple months," I said as I placed my hand on my still-flat tummy.

"You're already pregnant?"

I beamed at Vance again. "Yes, three months along."

"Wow, OK! Congratulations are in order, I guess! Any hopes for what it will be?"

"Healthy," Vance said.

"Yes, definitely healthy," I agreed. "And, obviously, we will be thrilled with any baby, but if it's a girl, we'd name her Sandy Ann, after our two courageous mothers."

Want to hear "Falling Stars" and "Burning Blue"?

Go to Ashlyne.co or find them on iTunes!

Also on iTunes:

Ashlyne.co for music, news, and updates!

@ashlynehuffrevelette   @ashlynehuff

Ashlyne: facebook.com/ashlynehuffrevelette
Falling Stars: facebook.com/fallingstarsnovel

FallingStarsBook.com

What About JoBeth?

Go to Ashlyne.co for the first chapter of
the sequel *Broken Pieces*, and see what
JoBeth has to say for herself.

ACKNOWLEDGEMENTS

"FS", as I've come to call it, has been one of the most exciting projects I have ever been a part of, and I could *not* have done it without a lot of help and support.

First, to my **God** above, thank You for Your grace, for Your patience, and the love You shower me with every day. Writing is a lonely game, but I was never alone, was I?

To **Mase**. You have believed in this since I Scotch-taped my goal to be a published author on the wall of our apartment in West Hollywood. Do you remember that? Thank you for not giving up on me—and for supporting my ink pen, sushi, and coffee habits. To **Charlie**. You probably witnessed the most of this process while you sat at my feet (like you're doing right now). I love my boys.

To my families (**Huffs, Andersons,** and **Revelettes**) for letting me sneak away time and time again to work in the most inopportune times. I'm sure that got old.

To **Dad** for all my hands-on music business training, official and unofficial, for writing my first song with me—I'm pretty sure that started this whole thing—and for giving me my love for reading. To **Mom** for the Nantucket memories and for the hours upon hours we talk about life. Your wisdom shows up in here. To **Maddie** for reading and giving me feedback—and for giving me the perfect sister dynamic for my scenes. To **Ell** for thinking it's "cool" that I wrote a book.

To **Grandma Donna** & **Grandpa Ronn**. See what you get for being my neighbor? Thank you for showing me where I get my writing gene, for proofing, encouraging, and being honest. And now I can't live without our Tuesday Coffees.

To **Lindsey**—my "crazy writer friend from PA". Talking to you (much to the chagrin of our husbands) about "people who don't exist" for hours on a daily basis made this book what it is. And anyway, they **do** exist.

To my wonderful **friends** who read and encouraged me as I reinvented myself.

To **Clint** and **Brandon** for letting me put words in your mouths and for writing such wonderful songs with me to go along with this book. Let's do it again for the next one.

To **Nashville** and everyone in it. I cannot imagine living anywhere else. You are my home.

To **Donnel Milam** for stopping me in the hall in 11th grade and giving me two options: 1. Learn how *you* wanted me to write my formal English papers and get high A's. 2. Continue my creative approach and get low A's, high B's. I asked your opinion, and your answer changed my writing life: "Let's face it, Ashlyne. You're probably not going to be a scholar. But you have a unique way of writing, so I say if you're ok with lower grades, keep that up."

Best advice ever. Oh, and thanks to my **mom** and **dad** for being ok with those lower grades. She wasn't kidding!

To **Tammy Kling** and **The Writer's Group**. I've said it since the day I started working with you: It's such an honor. As an editor and brand manager, you're unbelievable, but as a person, you really shine. I am so thrilled to have met you. It has made this ride ridiculously fun. **Sharon Lynch**, I feel like I've known you my whole life. Better late than never, I suppose?

To **Larry Carpenter** and **Clovercroft Publishing** for taking the time to guide me through this process. I wouldn't have wanted it any other way!

To **Suzanne Lawing, Gail Fallen**, and **Ingram** for all your integral talents in getting this book to the final stages and out there!

To **Sarah Passick**. Your dedication to championing my work and taking a chance on me will not soon be forgotten. Thank you for the hours, the chats, the edits, and the friendship we built over those two years. To **Michele Eniclerico** for bringing JoBeth down to size. To **Alison, Judy, Emmanuelle**, and **Ellen** at Stonesong for your unparalleled wisdom and for taking me seriously.

And finally, to the **McCarson** family (aka the Carsons):

Meredith (Lilah/Lily). Meeting you at our Bible Study, hearing your story, listening to your beautiful voice…it was just the beginning. Thank you for inviting me into your life, our road trip to Mobile, and believing in this.

Mrs. Cindy McCarson (Sandy). I am so grateful for the honesty about your journey with multiple myeloma. Highest remission possible? I'll take it.

Mr. Ronnie McCarson (Cole). Probably one of the best hosts in the state of Alabama. And I still love those pickles.

Natalie (Natalie), **Brian** (Judd), **Carson Lilly** (Summer), and **Parker Bennett Grimes**. You never once questioned the random girl in your house talking about writing a book. You treated me like family, and I'll never forget it. Oh, and the Grand Occasion proposal? Well done, Brian. I hope you don't mind I stole it!

There are people I have forgotten to name personally, I just know it. So I'll wrap up with one big THANK YOU. I hope you enjoyed it, and God bless.